I0638513

For
Money
or
Mayhem

Other Titles
by Nathan Everett

City Limits

GEE EVARS WANDERED into Rosebud Falls on Independence Day just in time to rescue a toddler from the rushing torrent of the Rose River. And to lose his memory. In an attempt to make Rosebud Falls his home, Gee becomes a local hero and inadvertently leads a revolt that changes the balance of power in the town. But will he ever know who he really is?

For Blood or Money

COMPUTER FORENSICS DETECTIVES Dag Hamar and Deb Riley discover secret files and hidden code can be as dangerous as dark alleys and flying bullets as they track a missing man and the billion-dollar fortune that went with him. Fourteen years after *For Money or Mayhem*.

The Gutenberg Rubric

TWO RARE BOOK librarians race across three continents to find and preserve a legendary book printed by Johannes Gutenberg. Behind them, a trail of bombed libraries draws Homeland Security to launch a worldwide search for biblio-terrorists. Keith and Maddie find love along the way, but will they survive to enjoy it?

The Volunteer

JOURNEY INSIDE THE head of a chronically homeless man. In a less politically correct time, he might have been called a hobo. But what keeps him wandering, hitching rides, and eating handouts? Piece together the story through his memories to find what made him volunteer.

Read Excerpts at http://www.NathanEverett.com

Copyright ©2012 2018 by Nathan Everett

All rights reserved. No part of this publication may be reproduced or transmitted
in any form or by any means, electronic or mechanical,
including photocopy, recording, or any information storage and retrieval system,
without permission in writing from the publisher.

Cover Art licensed from Shutterstock.com

Requests for permission to make copies of any part of the work should be submitted via
e-mail to ElderRoadBooks@outlook.com.

Second Print Edition

ISBN 978-1-939275-50-9

For Money or Mayhem

Nathan Everett

ELDER ROAD BOOKS
BELLEVUE WA

{Contents}

{1}
Just a Game

IT'S JUST A game, I reminded myself. *Just a game.* But my hands were shaking and sweat dripped from my pits. I pulled my Dick Tracy hat down lower as I locked my eyes on the screen. *All virtual. No reality.*

Lines of code flew by. This was the tipping point. I nearly had her.

Just a game. I had to remind myself often because I wouldn't be chasing a fifteen-year-old girl down a darkened alley in real life. Hell, I wouldn't even be in a darkened alley. I spend my time behind a desk with a computer screen in front of me. It's what I do. I don't chase criminals through the streets. *Not real streets, anyway.*

There was a blinding flash and ozone stung my nose. My eyes hadn't recovered from the lightning before I was deafened by the thunder. *That was close.* Lights flickered and went out, but my uninterruptable power supply and a surge protector stood between the failing power grid and my computers. The flow of information on my screen was steady. The cellular modem I used kept me connected, but my office was suddenly deathly quiet as everything but the cooling fans in my computers fell silent.

Lightning in Seattle is rare. I was waiting for another clap, but the blast had come at the trailing edge of the storm. As quickly as the lightning bolt hit, the storm had stopped. A few more drops of rain splashed in the standing water on the sidewalks.

I turned away from the window and plunged back into the alternate reality on the screen in front of me.

In the silence of my mind, I could hear her footsteps. I could almost see her, a shadow turning the corner ahead of me. But when I reached that intersection, she was gone.

I waited.

She'd been leaving tracks a noob could follow. It was almost as though she finally wanted to be caught—wanted it to be over. That happened sometimes. They just get tired of running.

There. I snatched a new receipt out of the cyberspace, looking for clues to where she was headed. But she was already gone.

Her fresh tracks led places no ordinary fifteen-year-old would go. In a space of thirty seconds, she bought automatically-renewing memberships in over a dozen different so-called dating sites—known money launderers. She'd been there before and was probably taking a commission on every sale. I was taking names and covering my tracks as fast as my fingers could move. I had user names and passwords as quickly as she created them. Jordan would have a field day with this, and in all likelihood his Federal counterparts would be sitting at his desk by morning.

Just a game. Except that this time, there were real police following my lead to an apartment building in the International District.

I was getting tired. I hadn't slept in two days. I thought back to college days when pulling all-nighters to write code or party was normal and grimaced. It was a lot easier twenty years ago. Now I fueled my drive with caffeine instead of alcohol. So far I'd managed to stay off the power drinks, but two days on a steady drip of espresso was beginning to wear on me.

I knew she was out there, but I couldn't get my eyes on her. She knew all the tricks and she was too practiced for a kid her supposed age to be. She jumped from place to place with no apparent connection, but I was beginning to see a pattern.

I rubbed my eyes and almost missed her. *Damn!* She'd just bought more merchandise at a trendy shop downtown than I figured the shop sold in a normal month. Thousands worth of designer clothes that would never be shipped.

I was exhausted and ready to put an end to this little cat-and-mouse game. Then she changed. I almost didn't recognize her when she headed straight for the casino. She was disguised as a little old man about to lose his Social Security check playing on-line poker. I had a positive ID now.

This was territory I knew and had charted before I started closing in on her. Online gambling is illegal in the State of Washington.

Casinos, in general, are high on security and they are quick to block exits if they believe they are being ripped off. They also hire guys like me to troubleshoot their systems. Of course, they weren't likely to do anything drastic as long as she was dropping cash at the rate she was. I collected the account information about the guy she was playing against and sent it into the holding tank of info for Jordan. I reported the activity to the casino and they blocked her best avenue of escape with a quick maneuver. I had her cornered. Suddenly, she was a frightened underage girl and the casino ejected her. She had an escape plan and headed for the virtual rooftops of cyberspace. *Bingo*. As soon as she moved there, I had her physical address and signaled Jordan that it was time to move in.

When an animal is stalked there comes a point when it knows it has become prey. I've watched enough nature television in my life to recognize the moment when the prey understands its fate. Its eyes go wide and there is a last panicked search for refuge before the eyes lose their depth. The gaze becomes flat. No matter how it maneuvers, it knows all actions are futile—just a delay of the inevitable.

I sometimes play darts with a local team. They talk about being 'in the zone' when they play. It's a moment when the bullseye seems to expand in front of them and there is no way they can miss it. It's like throwing a peanut through a basketball hoop. Time slowed as I crept closer to her. My target was going to be hard to miss.

By now she could tell something wasn't right. She knew the moment was near. I had a lock on her.

"Funny, but from here you don't look like a fifteen-year-old girl," I muttered. "More like a middle-aged cross-dresser with a two-day beard." I was delaying. Everything had to be perfect. There was no room for error. I needed her in exactly the right position. I watched her typing in the codes that would wipe her computer.

The rest of the team was in place. I raised my hand.

It was only a game, but this was when the game turned to reality—when somebody goes down. The red haze a gamer sees when victory is imminent settled across my eyes. She heard the knock at the door.

I took a deep breath.

And pulled the trigger.

SHE COULD HAVE been a fifteen-year-old girl partying with her parent's credit cards, I suppose. Stupid, but essentially innocent. In reality, the perp was a thirty-year-old identity thief whose latest victim was still in high school and had no idea her credit had just been trashed. He was a thief.

I hate thieves. And I'm a badass in cyberspace.

When the police pounded on his door he started the sequence to format his hard drive. Before he could execute the command I pulled the trigger and blue-screened the machine. I could practically hear him scream. Who gets a blue screen these days?

The truth is that if he had executed the command, he'd have succeeded in wiping the drive. I breathed a sigh of relief when Jordan called.

"CyberTalon, we have the perp in custody," he said. I wished I was there to see it unfolding, but Jordan was the only person on his team who knew my identity. Legally speaking, I didn't exist.

Police can't tamper with the evidence, so I didn't touch the drive. While we were playing our game of cat and mouse I took control of his monitor in the background. When the perp tried to erase the disk, I uploaded a blue screen image. The first key he hit was "ESC." That served to cancel his format command. It was beautiful. As soon as Jordan told me a cybercop and witness were in place, I released the screen and the computer mysteriously cured itself. They had immediate access to a fully logged-in computer. It only took a few minutes, with a warrant in hand, to back up the entire drive to an unencrypted device, and then change the password so they could maintain full access.

It was a nice, coordinated operation.

Detective Jordan Grant, who got me into this business in the first place, put together the strategy with me as a class exercise in our Criminal Justice course. Everything worked flawlessly.

Jordan and I have been studying together under Lars Anderson at Olympic University pretty much since the day Jordan arrested me a little over a year ago. That was the day I found out my boss had gutted the employee-owned company and stolen every dime out of our stock and retirement plans. *The son-of-a-bitch!* After he'd already taken my girlfriend, Hope… I hate thieves.

Jordan led the cybercrimes unit that came in to seize the evidence. They were going about it all wrong and all their surprise raid was going to net was more time for our precious CEO to cover his tracks. As Director of Information Technology and an employee who had just had my life savings ripped off, I offered my services to the police. The arrest was to get me out of the building without spooking the CEO before a warrant could be issued for his arrest. I was released in the parking garage.

I decrypted the entire office system backup files and nailed my boss's ass to a wall. There were still appeals to come, of course, and right now he was sitting in a luxury condo under house arrest with an ankle bracelet. But I'm not done with him yet.

Jordan and I have been working together ever since. He took me to class with him one day, where my former Navy C.O. walked into the class to stand at the front. Lars Anderson took one look at me and said, "I've been waiting for you, Hamar."

I'm not going into police work like Jordan, though. I have my own business and it's no way related to the Police Department. Sometimes they hire me to do forensic analysis of a computer. Occasionally, after hours, I'm happy to assist with a tricky sting. *Pro bono.* No official capacity. No paper trail. Usually legal. Mostly.

⌐◒‸⏃⎔⎔⊠⎍⎎⎏⎐⎑⎒⎓

I SLEPT MOST of the day on Friday. I'd been working on cracking that guy's computer for two days and wanted nothing more than a hot shower and sleep. Afterward, I'd think about eating something other than cold pizza. That opportunity would be my usual Friday night meet-up at the faculty lounge. I showered and put on a clean pair of jeans and a fresh t-shirt then set off for the Blue Bastion on Capitol Hill.

For several years before pulling the plug on my former employer, I'd taught a couple of classes at the Community College. There was a big push a few years ago to get professionals in a field to teach certain classes instead of academicians. I had one of those late Friday afternoon Computer Theory classes that only the desperate and determined ever took. It was easy to tell one from the other. After one grueling class trying to explain why the latest, trendy scripting language was not the same as writing real computer code, I stumbled out of the classroom and practically collided with an attractive young English professor.

"You look dragged down and beaten up," she quipped. "Tough class?"

"Not the easiest class. These kids know absolutely nothing."

"Why else do you think they're in your class?" she asked.

That brought me up short. Of course, they expected to learn something they didn't know. My job was to teach them, right? Wow! So simple.

"Dag Hamar," I said, offering her my hand.

"Andi Marx. It looks like you could use adult company. A bunch of us meet on Friday after class as a sort of faculty lounge. Why don't you join us?" I looked at her with a fair amount of astonishment. Was she asking me out? I was flattered, of course, but actually I was in a relationship. She could see I was hesitating and started to laugh. "It's a faculty group, not a date." She rolled her eyes and I glanced down to see a wedding ring on her hand. There were times when I was such a typical man. Well… I guess I am a typical man.

I've seldom missed a faculty lounge night since. There is a tacit agreement among those who are regulars that the goal is diversity, not departmentalism. I hadn't been teaching this year, but I was still welcome. We meet at the Blue Bastion because, even though there are dozens of fine restaurants on Capitol Hill, the majority of us are hardcore meat-eaters and wouldn't set foot inside one of the vegetarian restaurants, no matter what the nationality of their cuisine.

Jan Garrick was in line ahead of me and greeted me warmly as I walked in. "You look tired, Dag. Everything all right?"

"Thanks, Jan. Surprisingly enough, teaching isn't the only tiring profession."

Jan ordered his meal and waited while I ordered mine. Then we walked to the big table where the faculty lounge was convening. He's a full professor in physics at the U, but is one of the most down-to-earth guys I've ever met. Most of us at the lounge are community college instructors and many are part-time. It's nice to see somebody who has made tenure.

As we approached the table, I saw Andi and smiled. She immediately scooted over on the bench and I slid in beside her. She gave me a good once-over and shook her head exaggeratedly.

"When are you going to get adult clothes and quit playing teenager?"

"Hey! If I worked in a big office I might consider dressing up, but I work out of my little one-room up on 15th and don't see anyone but a barista or pizza delivery guy all day. Why choke myself with a tie?"

"Even us baristas still have to look at your mug each day," Dick Wagner said as he and his wife Paula pulled up chairs at the table.

"How many student interns are managing your coffee shops this year?" I asked. The guy was great at getting low-cost help from his business class.

"Just four, and every one of them dresses better than you do."

Well, just because he liked to serve an upscale clientele didn't mean I was going to shave anytime soon.

"You might all get your wish sooner rather than later," came the gruff voice of Lars Anderson from behind me. He hadn't gone through the food line, so I didn't see him come up to the table. It was unusual for Lars to come to the faculty lounge, but not unheard of. I'd introduced him to the group a few months earlier—Professor of Criminal Justice at SCU.

I had a strange relationship with the man. He'd been my superior officer in the Navy while I was working in the Intelligence Center in the Gulf. He'd given me a lot of instruction then, but I'd been more interested in serving my time and getting out with money for college. It was a real shock to me to find out he was in Seattle and teaching in the criminal justice program at Seattle Cascades University. But it went deeper than that. He was my mentor and still my superior officer. In the State of Washington, you can't get an investigative agency license unless you can show at least three years' practical experience investigating or pass a licensing exam from the State. I was still two months from taking my agency exam. You can, however, get an Unarmed Investigator License if you are employed by a licensed investigative agency. Lars, having been in the business for years, employed me in his agency and held my license. For all practical purposes, I functioned on my own, but any kind of work that required me to be licensed and bonded had to be funneled through him.

Before I could welcome him to the table, Jordan strode up with two beers and handed one to Lars.

"I hope you will forgive Jordan and me for inserting a different agenda into the faculty meeting this evening," Lars said, "but we'd like to toast our investigator for assisting in the capture this morning of one of the area's most prolific cyber-criminals." The folks at the table turned to me. Most of them, knowing me as a computer nerd and general support guru, were surprised when they heard about the collapse of my former employer, a year ago and the role I played in it. Now they were beginning to look at me as though I actually had some street cred.

"What's the story, Dag?" Lisa asked. "Can we get an action pose for class?" Lisa McIntyre is an art teacher at Pacific College of the Arts and Design, PCAD. We joke a lot about the fact that she sees more naked men and women each week than most people see in a lifetime. She'd kept suggesting that I come in to model for her class.

"Sorry, Lisa," I said. "All the action takes place with my fingers on a keyboard. Not an interesting subject." It wasn't so much that I'm shy about my body as that I didn't think I could hold still long enough for someone to draw me.

"Computers. They're the death of art and writing." I noted Andi didn't disagree with her.

"So what happened?" Jan asked.

"It wasn't much," I said. "I just tracked the location and then distracted the perp long enough for Jordan's gang to break in and arrest him."

"That distraction meant that we got his entire hard drive as specified in the warrant without having to go through the process of decrypting the security on it," Jordan said. "Dag's an unsung hero for Seattle."

There was a lot of general conversation about what happened and a ton of questions—most of which none of us could answer because of due process. Jordan jumped in with a tidbit that piqued all of our interest.

"Darnedest thing is, though, we don't know who the guy is."

It turned out that the perp had been stealing and adopting identities for so long that he'd pretty much erased all evidence of who he was. His fingerprints had been sent to the IAFIS division of the FBI. But even though the FBI averages only about 27 minutes to identify a fingerprint, they'd come up with a blank on our John Doe. DNA scanning was possible but was costly and time-consuming. There was still a question as to whether the DA would even want to proceed with prosecuting the case. So far, five different identities had all proven false.

An intense conversation rose up at the table regarding the need to protect and defend vs. basic privacy. Should the individual be allowed to be completely anonymous as far as the government was concerned? It was a tough call and the police department often found themselves caught between the need to enforce the law and an individual's personal rights.

Eventually, it was Andi that brought the conversation back to Lars original statement.

"Lars, why will we get our wish to see our resident geek cleaned up?"

"I've got a request for an investigator at a large financial firm downtown," Lars said. "It seems I have an expert at identifying and tracing nearly invisible signs of computer tampering on my staff, so I'm contemplating sending him in on the mission."

"I've got a couple of cases I'm working on," I said. "And you know how I feel about big corporations."

"Don't worry. This has a remarkably flexible work schedule," Lars said. "And I think you'll like the challenge."

Lars promised to send me the details by email and told me to look presentable by Monday morning. He took off fairly early, but Jordan was hanging around to see if there was any action going on later. He'd been flirting on and off with both Lisa and Andi, but I think he was hoping I'd set something up. That's when Andi started picking up her things and said she needed to get home and feed the teen.

Since she introduced me to the group seven years ago, we'd become friends, then neighbors, then best friends. She'd made it clear that she was interested in nothing more than friendship, even though her wedding ring proved to be from her deceased husband. She was a single mom and needed no men to complicate things. With that as the ground rule, we'd become close friends, especially after my disastrous breakup with Hope.

"Can I offer to walk you home?" I asked, standing from the table. Home was only a few blocks, but up on the hill, nobody drove anyplace if they could help it. I'd moved into the apartment complex next door to her duplex, so walking to school or home from the lounge together was comfortable and almost expected.

"I'd feel hurt if you didn't." She smiled at me and I shook my head. It was my turn to roll my eyes. We'd both adopted the expression from her daughter and it always made us laugh.

"I have no idea what kind of clothes to wear. I don't have anything but jeans and t-shirts anymore. I'll probably have to get Eric to go shopping with me," I said as we walked down the hill.

"Or you could use the resident fashion expert living next door to you," she laughed.

"I didn't know you were a sartorial maven," I said.

"Not me. Cali."

"I don't know," I said. "Being dressed by a teen? I'll just go down to Penney's…"

"You will not! Come on. It will be fun," Andi said. "Cali would love to do a makeover."

"A makeover?"

"Just bring money," she grinned.

{2}
Cyberspace Knows No Bounds

IT WAS NEARLY midnight and I was back on the cyberstreets. There's a whole virtual world hidden behind the one we see with our eyes. In my mind, that virtual world is more real than the spring rain that had returned late tonight. April showers bring May flowers as the saying goes. In cyberspace I could have flowers whenever I wanted them.

I was working on a contract that I'd put off while we were tracking the identity thief. I regretted ever having taken the job. But she'd been so convincing and so vulnerable.

It's one thing if an abused wife comes to me and asks me to investigate her husband's online activities so she'll have evidence that he bragged about hurting her and can justifiably sue for divorce or even press charges. I'd had one case like that in the past year. I was only too happy to help her nail her shit-bag of a husband.

But the young widow who came to me with her deceased husband's laptop seemed so sweet. She was hanging on to the dream of her husband and wanted anything of his that she could get.

Better to stay living in her own virtual world instead of his, I say.

It was a sad story. Her husband was killed in action during his second tour of duty, just days before he was scheduled to come home. What they shipped instead was not her living, breathing love, but a flag-draped coffin and a footlocker full of personal belongings. In the trunk was her husband's laptop computer.

It was password-protected, of course. There's an military regulation on basic security measures in the field. I suppose a soldier's laptop could be a security risk if it fell into the enemy's hands. But the army is surprisingly lax about giving the same device to the family of the deceased. Apparently they place a lot of faith in the family of fallen soldiers, or in the impossibility of breaking the password.

Of course, that's false assurance. If *I* have the computer, I own everything on it.

That's what she said she wanted.

"WE'VE BEEN MARRIED two years. We were together as much as possible for four years before that. He was my high school sweetheart," she told me. Twenty-two or twenty-three years old. Pretty in the way that all young women are pretty. Maybe fresh is a better word. The makeup she wore amounted to a little foundation to conceal the bags under her eyes. It had been a month, but her eyes were still red from crying. "We got married after his first tour of duty. We didn't have the money before that. I thought we'd have a normal life after that. But they offered a big bonus for him to take a second hitch. It was enough that when he got back we could put a down payment on a house. It was our dream."

I let her play out the story the way she wanted it to happen. I've had dreams myself—and disappointment.

"They called me last week and told me I could pick up his effects. I had to drive down to Lewis-McChord to get them. They didn't even deliver them." The tears dried in a streak down her cheek. She was suddenly very angry. "Isn't that a stupid word? Effects? I gave them my husband and all they could give back was a stupid trunk full of 'effects!' I hate them!"

"Why do you want to do this?" I asked. "Your memories are happy. Why do you want to dig into the computer?"

"Because… I can't help but believe that somewhere in there… he's… he's still alive."

I took the laptop from her hands. I had a bad feeling. People live double lives all the time. Was he really as wonderful as she thought? Or when I opened the laptop, would I find the Sergeant Mason that was still living there was someone different than his young widow imagined?

"You know I could find out something bad. I'm not suggesting that I will, but what will you do if the husband you remember is not the same as the one I discover?" I asked.

"It doesn't make a difference. Back it all up so I can see it and then wipe the disk and reformat it. I brought all the software. I'm going back to school and I'll need a computer."

"What else?" I asked softly. She hadn't told me everything yet.

"Mike was an avid gamer and was real into social media. We used to joke about all his virtual friends. But… it really is a community, isn't it? They deserve to know he's gone and that he gave his life for his country." She paused and dabbed at her eyes before she went on. "I don't want to know who they are. I don't need a hundred or a thousand unknown people telling me about Mike. But please tell them that I thank them for being his friend and that he is at rest."

I suggested she see a counselor before she made a final decision. She was adamant and suggested that if I was unwilling to do the job, she would find someone else. Since she'd come on the recommendation of a mutual friend, I didn't want to blow her off. So now, just a couple of days from when I told her I'd have it ready for her, I pulled the laptop out of its case and set it on my desk. I pulled the drapes and turned off all the lights except the keyboard lamp at my desk. The world around me went dark.

WHEN I'D RECOVERED from being dumped six year ago—at least recovered sufficiently to function again—I found this efficiency apartment on Capitol Hill. The SoDo loft I moved from had been designed to show off a rising star in the tech world—someone who had loud parties and beautiful artifacts. Like Hope. The little apartment I moved to was a cave where I could hide and lick my wounds. In the intervening years it had become a refuge from the real world and a gateway into whatever I wanted in the virtual world.

My new neighbor, Eric, helped move my meager possessions into the room. There was some television show about gay guys helping straight guys look good. Eric could have run that show. He made decorating suggestions. He would be very pissed that Cali was doing my makeover. His efficiency apartment the floor below mine was identical. He'd explored dozens of tricks to optimize the space.

Then he saw that all the furnishing I had was a recliner. My box of clothing, computer equipment, stereo, and one painting made the room look huge and empty.

"We need to go shopping," he said brightly. "I have a pickup truck. Let's go to Ikea!" I declined, politely.

"First, I want to paint."

"Oh yes. I see you in pastels. Blue would go so well with your eyes."

"Black."

"Oh Honey, she really did a number on you, didn't she?" I just shrugged my shoulders back at him, so he continued. "All right, Hamlet. Black it is. But you do *not* want to paint these walls."

"Why?"

"You'll never get them white again and your lease specifically states that you *will* leave the apartment in the same condition as you found it, including white walls. Just ask Jared." I remembered my apartment manager having pointed that out when I signed the lease. I sighed.

"But I need it to be black."

"Okay. Here's what we do…"

It was a genius solution, a little more complex than just painting the walls, but worth it. During the decorating that followed, Eric and I became good friends. Jared even approved the plan with the stipulation that I had to restore the apartment to original condition before I left. He collected an additional month's rent as a damage deposit in case I skipped and he had to hire painters.

We hung paintable, strippable wallpaper and painted the room. We hung black drapes. We tacked black fabric to the ceiling. When we were done, I had a black room in which even the glow of the monitor was absorbed and sound was muted by the soft surfaces.

I had my 'mantuary,' as Eric pointed out. He warned me that no woman in her right mind would spend the night there. I asked if there was a way to ensure that no men would, either. He had the good grace to laugh. And leave.

I was in my own little womb, and it was my gateway to cyberspace.

WHO ARE YOU *really, Sergeant Mason?*

His widow had filled out an extensive questionnaire. She didn't understand at first why I wanted things like names of brothers, sisters, parents, pets, schools, mascots, and hobbies in addition to social security numbers, serial number, addresses, and birthdates. Once I explained that passwords were rarely random, she filled out the form with more information than I was sure was necessary. In an effort to make a password memorable, people often use familiar names, numbers, or terms for their password.

I was prepared to enter all the information in a database and let my software do the work of cracking the password. I set the computer up on a wired network and then attempted to access it with my own computer, plugging in each potential password in succession from the database. I have secondary software that will write variants of words, substituting numbers for letters and capitalizing first letters of syllables, among other things.

I never needed to run the software.

Elaine831, his wife's name and birthday. Testing shows a 72% strong password rating. Unless you happen to know his wife's name and birthday and the fact that Army regulations stipulate that "passwords must be at least an eight-character string using the thirty-six alphabetic-numeric characters. At least two of the characters should be numeric." Just like the Navy.

I entered the virtual world of Sergeant Mike Mason.

THROUGH HIS JOURNAL and photos, I followed him down streets I'd never walked where every shadow could be a sniper. He ducked into a doorway, swinging his rifle left and right as the light on his helmet swept the room. In the empty silence that greeted him, he allowed himself a deep breath, shook the sweat out of his eyes, and then moved back into the street.

By the time I tracked him for a quarter of a mile, sweat was running down my own forehead. My heart was racing when I heard shots fired. He slammed himself against the wall, trying to disappear against the rough surface behind him. The shots were a street over. Not his responsibility. Another deep breath and he forced himself to move forward again.

At the next door he repeated the process. Enter. Sweep. Breathe. I was no longer certain if the droplets running down our cheeks were sweat or tears.

At the end of the street, a Humvee with a man in the turret waited for him. The door opened and he dove in. Two others joined him. They moved out, returning to base. They joked and laughed. There had been no one there in the empty buildings waiting to attack them. *Got them on the run now, don't we? They'll never show their faces here again.*

Being in a computer is more real to me than watching a movie. I grew up in the age of text-based gaming, long before virtual reality put avatars on screen and made digital constructs of cities, zoos, and planets common. I see everything, just based on a few words or even a line of code that I read.

I tailed Mike Mason through his journal, his email, his photos—watching, seeing for the first time the threats the young soldiers saw in every shadow, every bump in the road. It took me back to my own time in the service, though I was always in the bowels of the ship whenever it saw action.

When he came off duty, he sought the comforts all soldiers seek. He read email from home and talked to Elaine on Skype. There was no beer to be had in the Muslim country and base security was tight. There was no way he was leaving the safety of his base when he was off-duty.

All he wanted was someone to talk to.

The time difference meant that Elaine had to go to work soon after he got off duty. They had to break off their conversation before he was finished talking. Again. He had lots of online friends, but there was only so much he could tell them. Every day he was frightened. Every night he was awakened by any noise. Every minute he missed his home and his wife. He was exhausted and there was no hope of rest.

"If I could just see her for a few minutes—hold her and put my face against her hair—I'd be able to sleep again. God, of course I want to make love to her, but I don't know if I could do that—right away, at least. I'd be so caught up in just being with her that I'd fall asleep in her arms before I could do anything else. This tour is so much worse than the last one. I should never have re-upped."

I was surprised to find that I recognized one of his aliases on a gaming site that I played. There are several million casual and hardcore gamers online at any given time, but there are comparably few of us who still do old-fashioned text-based gaming. Finding he was one of them forged a deeper kinship with him. I wondered how a guy almost twenty years younger than me got into text playing. In one way or another, we could all track our legacy to John Patterson, a local game developer who made it big, building an online empire. Patterson still maintained the biggest text-based gaming site in the world and, being officially retired, manages a huge charitable foundation. I have half a dozen sub-domains on his network to run my own games from. Instead of fancy branding and graphics, all Patterson's text game sites bear the legend, "Remember guys, it's just a game." It's the kind of guy he is.

I tapped into his game identity and told Sergeant Mason's online friends that he had been killed in action and that his wife thanked them for being his friend during his final days. The forums were flooded with messages, condolences, memories. I set up a memorial website so that people could see a few of his pictures and leave messages. I'd ask Elaine if she wanted the address, but it was really for the benefit of the friends, not her. A few messages I downloaded onto the backup. Most I let go. I set his other online pages and forum registrations to expire in 30 days so his friends could continue their tributes and comfort each other.

But, of course, not every social forum is innocuous.

The chat room he'd chosen was like any other in the long line of sleazy and dark holes where he could get lost. His online friends were prone to joke and ask him if he'd had any bacon lately. But people shy away from too much information when an online buddy starts showing his weaknesses, fears, depression. In the stark anonymity of a not-so-popular webcam site, he'd found a confidante. *She* was special. The first time he saw her webcam he thought he'd just seen Elaine. Of course, Elaine would never do the things this woman did. She'd never dance like this in front of so many men. But every time he saw her, he imagined for just a moment that it was Elaine.

He was going to stop coming here. He wouldn't come back tomorrow night. The dancer wouldn't miss him, and if she did, he wouldn't know about it. He just needed to spend a few more minutes with her.

⌗◳⌖⌅⌾⌇⌁⌔⌰⌸⌶⌺⌽⌍⌎⌹⌻

I WATCHED THE public area of Angelique's site for a few minutes, the message area saying, "your nick is guest256." She relaxed on a bed with a college pennant hanging on the wall behind her. I saw a poster for a popular band just to the side come into view when she shifted the position of her webcam a little. She held a stuffed monkey doll in her lap, occasionally using him to bat at the camera or manipulating his long arms and legs to pet her own breasts. She wore a dark bra and panty set, not quite as trashy as some of the girls I'd seen while making my way to this room.

I watched the flow of text next to the image as she typed out messages to a dozen people who were on-line with her—the visual equivalent of a group talking around the dinner table, only she was dinner. The messages ranged from banal to risqué to rude.

"r u rl?"

"u lik cox?"

"nice ass"

Occasionally she would respond to a message if there was anything said that could be responded to. Otherwise she just read the screen and occasionally shifted her position to give the voyeurs a different angle. I'd have left without a second thought if she hadn't looked so much like Elaine. She might not remember Mike since it had been over a month since the last time they talked according to his log. But his log had shown hours spent on the site. That wasn't cheap.

I logged in.

"OneTinSoldier just joined the conversation."

"Mikey! I missed you! Wanna go private?" Her response was immediate and it looked like real excitement on her face.

"Yes, please."

In a moment the public screen went blank with a message that said "In private session." Then the screen cleared and her image came back on. It was a higher resolution camera for the private session, and audio came on as well. I was hoping no video feed from my end came on automatically.

"Mikey, I've been so worried. You just dropped off the face of the earth. Tell me what's happening."

I pasted the message I'd prepared into the text box and pressed send.

"I regret having to inform you that Sergeant Mike Mason, whom you know as 'OneTinSoldier' was killed in action on March 10. On behalf of his wife, I've been asked to locate Mike's online friends and let them know. She has also asked me to express her appreciation for your friendship with Mike over the course of his final days. I'm sorry to have to bring you this unpleasant news."

I'm pretty good at reading people for genuine feelings… at least I tell myself that. What I saw on her face was an instant transformation. She looked square into the camera with tears running down her cheeks.

"That's not funny, Mikey. Please, don't be mean to me," she said.

"I'm sorry to have to bring you such bad news," I typed. "There is a memorial website at this URL." I gave her the address and watched while she typed at her keyboard. I could tell that Angelique believed it was a practical joke until she actually saw the story. She was crying when she looked back at the camera.

"Who are you?"

"I'm just a hacker his wife hired to let online friends know he was gone."

"She knows about me?"

"I don't think so."

"I look like her. He told me that, but he never showed me pictures."

"From what I can tell on his computer, you helped him get through his loneliness while he was overseas," I said. "That means a lot to everyone."

"I'm just a performer. But I really liked Mikey. He wasn't rude like most of the assholes on here. He just wanted someone to talk to. Of course, he didn't mind if I was naked while we talked." She smiled a little even though the tears were still flowing freely. "Sometimes I was jealous of his wife," she continued. "I won't leave any messages. But thank you for letting me know. I thought he was just tired of me."

SERGEANT MIKE MASON'S life came to an end before his story was finished. He'd gone where I could not follow. I was snapped back into the reality of my black room, my armpits sweating and my head aching with fatigue. In front of me, only the glowing screen of his computer, the connections severed.

I finished backing up his email, his daily journal, and his photos and music onto a thumb drive and put an install disk in the drive. Then I turned to my own computer to write my report.

"Completion of project. Attached is a backup of Sergeant Mason's personal files. Hard drive has been wiped and original system restored and updated. Additional software provided by the client has been installed. Computer is fully usable or salable with a current value estimated at $450."

There was little chance that Sergeant Mason's virtual life would ever impinge on the memory of his real life.

Now they could both be at peace.

{3}
Not What It Appears To Be

THE POUNDING ON my door started at ten a.m. sharp. I wasn't happy. I'd only been asleep about two hours, having spent most of the night living another man's life half a world away. What sleep I'd had was restless as the dreams kept flooding my sleeping brain—dreams made so vivid in my mind through his laptop computer.

People don't realize how much of their lives are on their personal computers. Photos, email, links, music… lovers—it's all a part of who they are. When I dive into a computer, or ferret out information on the Internet, they become so real that I can talk to them in my head and it feels like they're answering. Getting that deep into someone else's head makes it hard to keep track of your own. It takes a while to decompress and I do that best while I'm sleeping.

The knocking continued and I finally dragged myself out of bed, pulled on a pair of sweats, and went to the door.

A little blonde bundle of energy almost poked me in the nose with her fist as she raised it to knock again. About five-three and weighing about a buck ten, she glowed with scarcely contained élan. She smelled of something fruity that I guessed must be her shampoo and I was instantly thankful that it wasn't floral. I'd be sneezing all over her.

"You're not up? It's time to go!"

"Why would I be up at ten on a Saturday morning, Cali? And how did you get into the apartment building? Go where?" I know. I wasn't giving her an opportunity to answer as I kept asking question after question, but once she started talking, I was pretty sure I wouldn't get another chance to say anything.

"Your makeover! Mom says you should meet us at the Analog by ten-twenty. Your hair appointment is at eleven o'clock." She wrinkled up her nose as she looked at me. My eyes weren't quite open yet. "And shower and brush your teeth before you come down. Did you stay up all night again?" My nod was all I got out. "Mom says that kind of schedule will age you prematurely. That's what she tells me. If I keep staying up late at night, I'll get wrinkly. She might as well say, 'Cali, go to bed or you'll end up looking like Dag.'" She giggled. "Anyway, Mom's heading down to the Analog and is going to order coffee for everyone, so you need to be there in—let's see—twelve minutes. 'Bye!" With that she skipped off down the back stairs outside my door and was gone.

Makeover? Oh. Yeah. Bring money. *Damn.*

I read somewhere that on average women who have been dumped spend $800 on a makeover. When Hope left me and cleaned out my loft, I spent $12.95 on a case of beer and didn't change clothes for two weeks. That was the last makeover I'd had. When you do most of your work in cyberspace, who cares what color your t-shirt is?

My self-image is a cross between the dark intensity of Sam Spade and the suave sophistication of Nick Charles. Really? I'm a tall, skinny, rumpled Columbo in faded jeans and a t-shirt. I showered quickly, brushed my teeth, pulled on said jeans and t-shirt, and headed out the door to meet the mother and daughter—all the while feeling like the golden sun logo on my shirt was turning into a massive target on my chest.

On the street corner outside the Analog Café, a guy dressed almost like me was tacking posters to a utility pole. The broadsides were stapled from the ground to as high as he could reach and all the way around the pole. About twenty posters, I guessed, each for a different band or venue. He stepped back and took pictures of the pole from all sides on his cell phone, then closed up his kit and walked over toward Denny. I shook my head, knowing that by noon, Jared would come out and tear them all down while muttering about how he'd call the police if they didn't already have too much to do. He and the owner of the Analog, across the street from our apartment, were vigilantes when it came to keeping the neighborhood clear of flyers and playbills.

Just inside the door of the Analog, a couple in matching, studious black-rimmed glasses, tight black jeans, and army surplus jackets sipped coffee and read. He was reading Tolstoy. For pleasure. Intellectual. She read *Still Life with Woodpecker*. She typed messages into her phone one-handed without looking. She might have been transcribing the book for all I could tell.

Andi turned away from her conversation with the barista and held out a cup of coffee for me. Hot, strong, and black. Cali was right beside her, sipping something that looked sweet and chocolaty with a big dollop of whipped cream on top.

"Finally," Cali declared. "Let's go!"

Andi smiled and greeted me. "She's kind of excited about the shopping expedition today."

"Why would she be excited about getting me a new pair of pants?"

"Oh, she just figures that if we are shopping there is a high likelihood that she'll be able to divert the purpose to her own benefit. I know she has her eye on a sweater she saw at Candy's. And Candy's just happens to be next door to the Men's Wearhouse." Andi pulled her keys out of her purse as we left the café. "I'll drive. Nothing we want is within walking distance of here."

I tried to think of what was around. Well, there were more costume shops per capita on Capitol Hill than anyplace except Reno, but aside from a few vintage clothing stores there isn't much in the way of actual clothing—at least not if you're over twenty. Granted, if you wanted to dress like a vampire or a zombie, this was the place to come, but neither of those would go over well at a finance company.

Fifteen minutes later we walked into an upscale hair salon in a fancy hotel. I was pushed into a chair in the waiting room while Andi and Cali walked back to where I could see half a dozen stylists clipping at their customers. I was trying to remember when I'd last had a haircut. I usually kept it pulled back in a ponytail and just whacked enough off the ends to keep it above my shoulder blades. I hadn't really been into short hair since my Navy days, though I'd gone through various lengths when I was a rising star. I just quit caring about it a few years ago.

My beard was thin. Blondes have lousy beards. My Swedish heritage showed up in my skin and hair tones. Granted, the beard wasn't *really* long. I had a pair of hair clippers my mother gave me years ago and once a month I put the longest attachment on them and buzzed my face. I picked up one of the magazines and flipped through it. The pictures were of men that all looked fifteen years younger than me and several millions richer. They'd all either walked off the pages of GQ or had just come from performing with the Chippendales. My boney ass wasn't going to measure up to these guys no matter how they cut my hair.

Andi and Cali came out to sit with me and said it would be a few minutes before Sinclair was ready to see me. Somehow I pictured a big green dinosaur lumbering around grazing off what was once on my head. Andi and Cali got busy with the magazines, pointing and then shaking a head and turning the page. Before long a middle aged woman just over five feet tall and just under that wide came into the waiting room from the studio. She was not, however, green. When she said my name it sounded like a frog had dragged itself out of a particularly filthy swamp and taken up residence in her throat.

"Dag Hamar?" I stood. She looked at me and then threw a questioning look at Andi. "Turn around." I rotated. She pushed on my arms to make me turn further. Then she motioned me to follow her as she lumbered back into the salon and pointed to a chair in front of a sink. "I should have scheduled a longer appointment," she muttered.

It was an hour and forty minutes later that I was finally allowed to look in a mirror after having been scrubbed, scraped, clipped, dyed, massaged, and blown dry.

I almost didn't recognize the face that looked back at me. It was shaved completely smooth except for a pencil thin mustache. Even that had been darkened slightly. Sinclair called it chestnut, but that made me feel like a horse. My hair was short and I'd forgotten that at that length it curled slightly. It didn't have a part, but was just swept back. My nose twitched a bit and I realized my chin was cold. And a little lopsided. Cali reached up and felt my cheek.

"Ooo. Baby smooth," she giggled.

"I don't know what to say," I said. "It looks great, thank you."

"Be back here in two weeks and I'll keep it looking that way," Sinclair rasped. "You've got a good head. If it weren't for that…" She shook her head sadly. "…disaster." Two weeks? Fortunately, Sinclair took a credit card because in spite of what Andi said about bringing money, I was nowhere near prepared to pay $160 for a haircut. Plus tip. But I had to admit, I was beginning to feel a bit more like Nick Charles. If only I liked martinis…

WE STOPPED FOR lunch before serious shopping. I'd been to Andi and Cali's house with friends when Cali was watching a makeover show on television, and I could tell by the way she kept eying me over lunch that she was calculating what she was going to do to me. Andi and I were having a reasonably adult conversation during the meal—she asking me test interview questions. I bit into my BLT and saw Cali with her cell phone sending text messages.

"No phones at the table," Andi reminded her daughter.

"I was just sending myself a note," Cali replied. "I didn't want to forget the colors I see him in."

"Wait a minute," I said, coming to full attention. I could see where this was going if I didn't set some boundaries. "You are not turning me into a fashion plate. Neither I nor anyone I might work for would be impressed or comfortable with that. I don't want to stand out. I want to blend in."

"Even conservative business wear has some things you can do to make it a little edgy," Cali said. "You'd be so cool in…"

"No."

"What?"

"No edgy. No colors. Simple blacks or grays and white shirts. Blend in, don't stand out."

"Can we at least have colored ties?" she pled.

"Only if it doesn't make any difference what I wear it with," I said adamantly. "I don't want to have to think about what I'm pulling out of the closet to wear. I reach in, pull out pants, shirt, tie, and I'm dressed. It should make no difference which of each I put on." I didn't want to mention the fact that I'm colorblind. If the girl put different colored clothes in my closet, there was no question that I'd end up wearing the wrong ones. People would notice.

"Boring!"

"Cali," Andi jumped in, "it is his life and his image. We're only making over his appearance, not who he is."

"I like who he is, but all that black clothing he wears is just so blah."

"Hey!" I said. "*He* is right here. And he thought all you kids were into wearing black all the time."

"Men!" Cali humphed. "You just don't get it."

"Cali, we're supposed to be helping Dag. Be nice," her mother soothed. "I'm sure he won't object to *you* getting something colorful that makes up for his... uh... monochromicity." I was pretty sure Andi was going to say something like drabness or plainness, but she took a diplomatic view.

Andi and I have an easy relationship. I don't have many friends. Jordan and I are pretty close, but between his police shifts and my night-work, we don't get together that much unless it's to bring down a criminal or to study. The guys I called friends at Henderson, suddenly became scarce after I blew the whistle on our boss. They seemed to think that they wouldn't all be out of work if I had just let the CEO keep robbing the company. He ripped them off, but in their eyes, I was to blame for the company's collapse.

And Cali... Well, she was just Cali. I'd known her since she was ten and now at seventeen she was turning into a young woman, but still had the brightness and energy of the ten-year-old I'd first met. And she wasn't much bigger. I could indulge some of her whims about making me a dress-up doll. It's just that I really couldn't do colors.

I ended up with two gray suits that I could tell apart by the texture, two pairs of black slacks, and three white shirts. Cali had assured me that the five ties I bought—"You can't wear the same one every day!"—would go with any combination of the suits or slacks and that I could wear either jacket with the black slacks. She'd let her mother pick out one of the ties and I instantly found that it was my favorite. I'd picked up a nice gray cashmere sweater that I could wear when I dressed down that reminded me of petting Eric's cats.

And neither Cali nor Andi objected when I paid Cali for her fashion-consulting services by buying the sweater at Candy's that she'd had her eye on.

I still couldn't get used to my naked chin, though.

I WAS RAISED in a traditional family. My father went to work every day of his working life at the same company and had risen from a wiper on a fishing vessel to dock foreman. He'd retired with a pension and was rewarded for his many years of service. And when he died the next year, he left my mother with a modest but comfortable nest egg that ensured her security for the rest of her life. It was the American ideal.

Well, the dying part sucked.

I was among those who held that same dream when I came out of college. I joined a firm, and worked my butt off to ascend to my level of incompetence. My years of loyalty were rewarded with a bankrupt company from which the bastards at the top had stripped out every cent of our retirement plans, most of which was held in company stock.

I swore I'd never work for a corporation again, unless I owned it. The only thing that made this situation palatable at all was that I would only be pretending to work for them.

I spent the better part of Sunday with Lars, getting briefed on the job and the background of the company I was going into. He was suitably impressed with my new look, though I cringed when he suggested I looked just like "one of them" in my black slacks and gray cashmere pullover. Lars reminded me, however, that I needed to keep up with the shaving. I realized I didn't currently have any shaving equipment, just my clippers. That was going to take some getting used to.

Not to mention that I hadn't been on a job interview in fifteen years.

{4}
A Sheep in Wolf's Clothing

EVERGREEN FINANCIAL CORP., or EFC, was one of a number of independent credit card issuers that had sprung up about twenty-five or thirty years ago. It had never made it as big as its chief rival, because it adamantly refused to align itself with any mainline bank. Instead, it issued credit cards under private labels for various associations, unions, and even churches. It looked like a prime take-over candidate to me, but miraculously it had staved off attempts by big banks during the great consolidation wave. It kept to its niche market, offered good services, and was semi-privately held. Though technically a publicly traded company, the vast majority of its stock was held by a small number of large investors who seemed of like mind when it came to maintaining their independence.

To those in the right circles, it was also held to be a fortress regarding personal information and computer security. The very thought that the company had become vulnerable to cyber-attack grated on the nerves of management and IT. Lars suspected the company's unusually proactive movement had other motivations as well. Financial organizations are not required to report incursions into their systems unless customer data has been compromised. Most do what they can to cut off the threat and silently swallow the losses rather than have them made public. The fact that EFC was calling in a consultant meant they thought the threat might be internal.

MONDAY MORNING, I was up and dressed by eight, having taken care not to cut myself with my new razor. It was going to be difficult to maintain the little strip of whiskers on my upper lip. Shaving close to it without cutting it off would be a daily challenge.

At half past nine, I was sitting in the plush twenty-third floor offices of Evergreen Financial Corp. on 3rd Avenue in Seattle. I'd checked in with the receptionist, a woman about my age with an extraordinarily pleasant voice. She asked me to have a seat and I heard her call to say I was in the lobby. Her tone in dealing with the person on the other end of the line was one that would calm a tornado. I heard her answer another line in the same calm, reassuring tone.

"Evergreen Financial. I'm sorry, Mr. Drake is out of the office until two o'clock today. May I take a message?"

Take a message? No connecting to voicemail? If I ever have a business that involves a lot of incoming phone calls, I want her *answering them.* Well, that day was so far away I couldn't even see it on the horizon.

A woman came through the security doors on the left and stopped to speak to the receptionist. They conversed in low tones for a minute before she approached me. She wore a dark suit and white blouse with one of those long collars that tie into a bow at the neck. Her skirt was cut scarcely above her knee and the one-inch heels she wore clearly stated that she was here on business. I silently thanked Cali for my new suit and stylish tie as I stood to greet her.

"Mr. Hamar? I'm Darlene Alexander, Mr. Dennis's admin." Well, that answered my first question. She wasn't the executive I was interviewing with. "His meeting is taking a few minutes longer than expected and he asked that I get you situated in his conference room. Would you come with me, please?" I acknowledged her greeting and agreed to follow—almost before she turned and marched back to the security door. She waved her badge at a black box on the frame and the door clicked to allow us through. On the way to the conference room we passed a small kitchen and she asked if I would like a cup of coffee. I stopped myself from automatically saying yes. I asked if I might have a glass of water instead and she quickly showed me the cooler and glasses. I filled a glass and continued to follow her to a room next to the corner office with a round table and four chairs. I selected the chair that faced the door and after I sat down the admin departed. It was a great view, out across the Sound. I turned away from it and faced the door, relaxing in my chair.

The executive who was going to walk through that door any minute now was the crook. I'd decided that even before being told exactly what the job was. As far as I was concerned, the guy was guilty just because he was a vice president. That's my version of "the butler did it." I supposed I'd have to investigate everybody in the company in order to prove it.

I didn't have long to stew about it. The door opened and a slightly balding man a little shorter than me strode through the door with purpose. He closed the door and then turned to me.

"Hamar? I'm Arnold Dennis. Don't get up." I'd begun to rise when he entered the room, but settled back. This was not a man who beat around the bush. I needed to hang on for the ride. "Good references. Let's talk about Henderson."

"Okay." That wasn't what I expected. Why would he be interested in my former employer?

"It's one thing to identify that a fraud is taking place. How did you pinpoint who was moving the money?"

"I see," I said. "Officially, I held the encryption key to the back-up data at Henderson. When the police took the disks, I decrypted them. The evidence was there."

"Data isn't knowledge. What led you to believe it was the C-levels who were doing the work?"

"There are confidentialities involved."

"You don't want me to know the how."

I looked at the guy. This was not the interview I was prepared for. I didn't really want to go into my techniques for nailing the CEO. Evidence appeared. It was turned over to the police.

"I use a combination of techniques that fit the parameters of the job I'm assigned. If one technique fails to produce results, there are others that I can fall back on. The real question is what you want me to find and what you don't want me to find," I said. I kept my voice even and pitched low. Arnie Dennis was leaning forward to hear me better. He was buying and I was selling. He didn't strike me as a man that many people stood up to. He paused as he considered me and I looked him in the eye.

He smiled.

"Good. Here's the situation. Our losses due to fraud are increasing. Every credit card company assumes some risk of fraudulent card usage. We expect it and plan for it. Most fraud losses would cost us more to prosecute than the loss itself. Frankly, you can't even call it fraud most of the time. Usually it's a spur of the moment decision by someone who is desperate and sees what they think is an opportunity. Could be as simple as finding a credit card and charging a shopping spree to it. Sometimes we still get the captured number and signature used by an unauthorized person. Occasionally it's something more serious like a raid on a series of card numbers for charging porn. The Internet makes it more difficult to track some of those uses, but we are vigilant about protecting the customer and where we can make an impact we prosecute the offender."

It was what I expected. Both State and Federal Laws are specific about the responsibility of financial institutions to protect their customers from fraud. But they weren't required to press charges. Business crimes occur every day and wasting their money on small cases isn't profitable for an institution's shareholders. But losses are something every manager at every level is responsible for—whether they are in banking, designing software, or selling shoes. If losses were increasing, however moderately, it was going to raise red flags.

"A basis point is one-hundredth of a percent of the company profit. It is a tough market out there and a downward shift of a single basis point could mean millions of dollars in losses. I've been given the authority to investigate and remedy the situation."

"Why, if I may ask, does that fall to the Chief Technology Officer and not to the Chief Financial Officer?" I asked.

"Good question, with two answers. First, we believe our losses are specifically tied to incursion into our systems. It's my job to plug that kind of leak. Secondly, technology is now fundamental to every job in our company. Every single employee has a computer and is tied into our network. Our employees and our network are our greatest vulnerability. Finance will be watching my every move on this, but Tech has the ball."

"Don't you have inside people who can trace network use?" I asked.

"Yes. But anyone inside the company could be a suspect. And that pisses me off. It pisses me off that *I'm* a suspect. You are here to get into the network and sniff out the vulnerabilities," he said. Apparently, I'd been hired. "I'll call you my Technical Assistant. That will give you unfettered access to everything on the network. Everything. You will have read access for every single computer and server on the network. I want to know whose pocket every missing penny lands in."

I'm licensed and bonded, but it was sounding like I was just being given the keys to the kingdom. What company was going to give an outsider complete access to their financial documents, strategies, marketing, and technology? Not only that, but this company had an entire division that handled fraud. Those folks certainly wouldn't be happy about having an outsider looking over their shoulders. There had to be a catch somewhere. Arnold's smile was back on his face. He looked like he'd just caught me with my fingers in the till.

"You'll be watched," he said simply. "I'm not about to launch anything like this without safeguards that I have personally put in place. *I* will know where you go and every file you touch. I can't do the investigation myself, but I can be damn sure that you will be monitored. And challenged." I nodded. That made sense. I'd spend the next few hours pondering exactly how they were going to watch me. Then I'd figure out how to get around it. I don't like being watched.

"If you are ready to go to work, I'll have Darlene get you down to HR. She'll introduce you to my Director of Network Security, Don Abrams. He'll get you a computer and logon. You're going to be an employee—full benefits and the works. Of course, I'll pay your agency a fee as well, but no one in the company is to know that you are an outside consultant or the precise nature of your job. As far as anyone else is concerned, you are doing specific technical investigations on my behalf regarding the impact of new technology on the financial world. There's a cross-departmental team that does that and you'll become a member. I hope you can hold your own in a conversation about the Fed's new policies on electronic record maintenance. Darlene has the position number and employee job req."

He stood to leave but turned to look at me once again.

"Zack Henderson was a personal friend of mine."

Damn! Zack was my former boss's father and the founder of Henderson Associates. And my new boss was his friend? Zack committed suicide two months after his son was arrested.

"It wasn't what you did that killed him. It was what you found. If you find that one of my partners in this company is raiding the bank, it'll kill me, too," he said. Did I believe him? "I've been here twenty-three years and I expect to be here another ten before I retire. Just remember this company is twenty times the size of Henderson. It'll take twenty times the work."

All right. Maybe I was too quick to condemn corporate executives. Maybe.

IT WAS TWO o'clock by the time I was actually seated at a desk and staring at a computer. The morning had been filled with paperwork and briefings by Human Resources. I had forms for filling out 401k deductions, health insurance, and membership in the Puget Sound Health Club. I'd received my security badge/keycard, and as soon as I arrived back at Darlene's desk she made a quick tour of the office and gathered together the other members of Arnold's 'team' to head out for lunch. Wild Ginger has great food, but it's never a quick lunch, especially when trying to meet and memorize the faces of half a dozen new people.

I paid close attention. These were the insiders and as such, prime suspects. I'd met Don Abrams earlier in the day and he assured me there would be a computer waiting on my desk as soon as I finished with HR. He was Director of Network Security and Arnold's go-to man. Allen Yarborough sat across from me at lunch and asked an endless stream of questions that probed my knowledge of system administration. That figured since he was the Systems Admin Manager. It turned out that he was the one directly responsible for issuing my laptop and having me registered on the network. Within a few minutes, I realized I was being interviewed by Arnie's staff, which hadn't been given the usual opportunity before I was hired. They were testing my mettle. When Allen finished hammering me about systems admin, Phil Jackson, Manager of Fraud Detection, took over. His questions focused on my knowledge of attacks that were specific to credit fraud. As it turned out, my work on the Henderson case came in handy. Part of what brought the company down was the default on a sizable loan they'd received from a private lending company. If the loan had been through a mainline bank, there would have been a long waiting period while the wheels of justice spun up. Since the lending company was privately held, the default action went from zero to sixty in ten seconds. It didn't give the execs enough time to hide their tracks before the police were called in.

Ford McCall took over the questioning at that point. Ford was a low-level employee compared to the managers at the table. I was still curious as to how this so-called team was put together. They didn't seem to have a common manager below Arnold himself. They were at a number of different hierarchical levels. Ford was a researcher. His level of interpersonal skills had probably kept him from being on a management track, but it turned out that he knew something about just about every development in technology that had taken place in the past twenty years. His questions were random, sometimes asking about the credit industry and sometimes about programming in C#. He asked questions about the breakability of different operating systems and went so far as to ask me point-blank if I'd ever hacked a UNIX system. I was going to be watching this guy like a hawk.

That left the two women at the table, the admin, Darlene Alexander, and Jen Roberts. Jen didn't give her title when she introduced herself and no one seemed inclined to fill in the blank. She asked if I was familiar with matrix management techniques. Things started to click. Most companies have a purely hierarchical structure. If you are an engineer, you work for an engineering manager who works for an engineering director who works for an engineering vice president. You know exactly how many levels separate you from the president of the company. In matrix systems, there may be a hierarchical structure on the boards, but teams are organized according to projects and the individuals on the team might be from several different departments. It turned out that Evergreen Financial Corp. was a hybrid system, but that most of the high level work was done by matrix teams who reported to a team manager and had little to do with the hierarchical structure. In fact, some team members had titles of "Director" but had no direct reports. It was far more typical of the financial industry in which directors and vice presidents were given their titles to show status and not line management. A vice president had higher decision-making authority than a director. Jen Roberts—title unknown—was our team lead.

And that brought me back to Darlene. The rest of the team jumped up from the table before the check arrived, scurrying off to various meetings, appointments, and tasks. Darlene motioned for me to stay while she took care of the check with a Platinum card.

"So, what do you think of your team, Mr. Hamar?" she asked as we left the restaurant.

"Do you prefer to be called Ms. Alexander?" I asked.

"Oh, no. Darlene is just fine."

"Then please call me Dag."

"Okay, Dag. But the question still stands."

"My team. Exactly what is my role on this team? It's not something that Arnold mentioned to me," I said. In fact, I was beginning to wonder how I was going to carry out a covert mission in this company if I was going to be assigned a bunch of random investigations on the part of the team. I'd imagined that I would work in relative isolation—like I prefer.

"Your team is a SWAT team. It's cross-functional and is responsible for identifying and neutralizing threats before they occur. You have a long-term project assigned by Arnie Dennis. The results of your research will be delivered to your teammates in regular weekly reports. You'll show progress for however long it takes to accomplish the real task that he's assigned you." She paused and looked at me expectantly, but I decided to do no more than nod. I didn't know yet how much she actually knew about my mission. Arnold had led me to believe that no one knew the real reason I was brought on, and certainly the lunch conversations seemed to confirm that. Seeing that I wasn't going to provide any input at this stage, Darlene sighed.

"Well, I should have expected that," she said. "I won't press you for details. I've had stranger job requests. Here's how it's going to work. My job is to make sure that there is nothing standing in the way of Mr. Dennis doing *his* job. That means that it is also making sure there is nothing impeding your progress. I know only that your real job has nothing to do with the position on the team that you've been introduced to. Every morning I'll give you a brief email synopsis of what your 'research' is revealing. That way if you encounter any of your teammates, you'll have something to say when they ask you questions. Each Thursday night I'll provide you with a short paper discussing the progress. You'll study it that night and be able to talk intelligently about it during your Friday morning team meeting and one-on-one with Jen. Your project is Internet Protocol Security, which I take it you are reasonably well-versed in anyway, so you should be able to fill in at least a few of the blanks. Just watch out for Ford. Somehow that guy knows everything that has ever been published on every subject. I think his brain is wired to the Internet."

"So what you are saying is that you are going to be doing my official job while I'm doing my real job?" I asked. She nodded. "Isn't that a little beyond what an admin would normally be, uh…"

"Qualified to do?" she asked, raising an eyebrow. I hadn't wanted to go there, but yeah. How exposed was I going to be if an office administrator was supplying all the research that I was supposed to be doing because of my high level of expertise?

"I've worked with Arnie for years. We were hired at the same level. Only one could rise and I hitched my wagon to his star. I left my position as programming developer to become his administrator as soon as he reached a level that allowed him to have one. We've been talking about hiring a technical assistant for the past three months. No matter what it might look like on the outside, the job you are filling had to be defined, vetted, a position number assigned through HR, a job description agreed upon by the executives, and budget approved for hiring. Everyone knew he had someone in mind for the position before he announced plans to hire."

That was news to me. I'd only known about this for three days. Arnold Dennis was rising on my list of suspects again. If he was devious enough to plan three months ahead of time, then he would have had plenty of time to hide his tracks, or even point evidence at someone else in the company.

"During that time, he also directed me to research the latest in Internet Security Protocols and I have an unending list of resources and papers. I'm familiar with all the data and I'll be cross-checking it against any new developments over the past three months, but all the heavy lifting has already been done." Darlene paused and we walked the rest of the block in silence. Before we entered the building, though, she stopped me.

"Something has been bugging Arnie for the past six—maybe eight— months," she said. It was the first time I'd heard her use his first name. She looked at me with an intensity that I found unsettling. "Whatever you are here to do, it's supposed to put his mind at ease. I will do everything in my power to make you successful at that. Don't you dare let him—or me—down."

TWICE TODAY, I'D been admonished to not let someone down—the second time with a passion that I thought of as intimate. I'd seldom seen such intense devotion to an employer and I wondered if there was more to their relationship than met the eye. It would bear investigation. But more, I'd realized that people here liked to meddle in other people's business. Every person I'd met today could potentially be the person "keeping an eye on me," and most of them had the ability to use techniques that would be hard to spot. Whatever I did, someone would be watching me, just as I was watching them.

Darlene showed me to my desk. I had a small but comfortable window office just down the hall from Darlene and Arnold. That made sense, I supposed. I was his direct report, even if my team functioned in a matrix. What really surprised me was that my name and title were already on a placard on the door. On the desk was a large laptop computer docked to an even larger flat-screen monitor. A sheet of instructions for initial registration on the network was next to the computer. The rest of the room was sparsely furnished. One desk. One desk chair. One guest chair. One credenza. One lamp. The view out my window was not of the Sound, though if I looked as far left as I could out the window, I could get a glimpse between the buildings. Directly out the window, across the street, was another tall office building and I could faintly see movement behind some of the windows.

It wasn't an executive desk. Like most tech companies, EFC issued the same basic furnishings for every office and every cubicle. It was a flat surface with metal legs and a wrench that would adjust the height by cranking a bolt in a hole on the top. The desk faced the window so my back would be to the door when I sat at it. That was the first thing that would change. I swung the desk around perpendicular to the window with my back to the wall. The window was on my right and the door on my left. I could see both. I pushed the credenza against the other wall and pulled the guest chair around to the end of my desk so visitors would sit beside me with their back to the door.

In the process of moving the furniture, I surreptitiously checked under the surface of the desk for any listening devices or electronics that might go unnoticed. That's a nice thing about this kind of furniture—there's really no place to hide anything unless they hollowed out the desktop and inserted something or it was hidden in a leg. I tapped on the solid surface just to make sure.

Satisfied that the furniture was secure, I turned to the computer itself. I suppose I was being paranoid, but after my lunch and briefing with Darlene, I was inclined to distrust everyone. I turned the device over and examined it closely, from the RFID asset tag on the back to the stickiness of the keys. Without actually starting the computer, I opened it and began typing on the keyboard, testing the touch of the keys to see if the keyboard had been tampered with. When I turned the computer on, I made sure no fields were selected before entering my alias and a fake password. After a moment, I typed Darlene's alias and a brief note: "Thank you for lunch today and for introducing me to the rest of the team. I've got my team meeting and one-on-one with Jen on my calendar. Could you set up a weekly one-on-one with Arnold for me? I'll keep my schedule clear, but will not be in the office on Wednesdays. Please let me know what would be convenient." I figured that would be an adequate amount to be picked up if there was a sensing device attached to the keyboard of my computer. I shut the computer down and popped the battery out of the computer to examined it and the channel it fit in. I carry a toolkit in my briefcase, so I grabbed a screwdriver and opened the memory slot. The computer was well-equipped with RAM, but that's where I found the bug.

It was tiny. Whoever had planted it knew a lot about electronics and cutting edge tech. I suspected this baby might even be black market. The device was just below the keyboard and could record and transmit every keystroke.

It confirmed my suspicion that *someone* was watching me electronically. All that someone needed was a computer set up to receive my keystrokes and they would be able to see on screen everything I typed.

By the time I'd finished my physical examination of my office and computer, it was nearly five. I suspected that this group would be looser about the hours they kept, but we were in the financial industry and experience told me that most of the office would close up and go home before six at the latest. Someplace in the building, people would just be arriving who were in synch with the Japanese markets. I was pretty sure a contingent was leaving about the time we got back from lunch, indicating a shift that was synchronized with New York. And then there were the twenty-four-hour customer service and security teams. Tomorrow I'd do a floor-by-floor tour of the entire building. But I was about ready to call it quits for today.

"Dag? Excuse me, but I couldn't help but notice you haven't logged into the network yet. Is there a problem with your computer?" Allen Yarborough was poking his head through my doorway. *Couldn't help but notice? Right!* As Systems Admin Manager, he would know who had logged into the network if he was watching. That he'd been watching for *me* to log in gave me the creeps.

"No problem, Allen. HR just gave me a ton of paper to go over after orientation this morning. You know, benefit elections, policies and procedures, all that. I just never got around to logging in."

"Well, it's almost quitting time for today. Let's get you logged in so I know everything works and go have a beer." I'll bet he wanted to know everything works. *Okay, I can play this game.* I powered up the computer again and it came immediately to the log-in screen. "It goes more quickly if you use your smartcard the first time you log in. You've already set a password when you got your ID," Allen said helpfully. I slotted my ID card into the reader on the computer. It identified my user name and I typed in the password. The screen went directly to the official EFC desktop and I was on the network. I smiled at Allen.

"Looks like everything works."

"Great. The first time you open email, it will install and record your settings. Takes about five minutes to get the test message sent through. By this time, you probably already have a day's worth of email backlog, so you'll have your work cut out for you tomorrow. Now let's go get that beer."

"Oh. Hey, sorry about that. I can't make it tonight. I've got an appointment at six to... uh... see a dog I'm thinking of adopting. Let's make it another evening. Anytime but Wednesday or Friday."

"No problem! I'll see if there's some other guys I can introduce you to. Maybe Thursday. What kind of dog?"

"A, uh... greyhound. Rescue, you know?"

"Oh yeah. I've heard about that. Let me know how it goes." He left, looking for all the world like he was just a helpful teammate. Hmm. New candidate at the top of my list.

As soon as he was out of sight, I changed my password. There are easy passwords to remember that are almost impossible for a computer to guess. I called up a virtual keyboard on screen and used the mouse to click on each character. My physical keyboard was bugged, but it was a lot harder to track mouse clicks.

When I was satisfied that I had thwarted any attempts to capture my log-in information, I sat back in my chair to contemplate my first day at work. I had a whole list of suspects, and I had a feeling Arnold had put this team together specifically for me to watch. It probably included his entire list of suspects plus whoever was assigned to keep an eye on me. I decided to leave the keyboard bug in place in the computer and to bring a detachable keyboard into the office with me tomorrow. I'd just let my spy stare at a blank screen for a day and see if anyone poked his head in to find out what was wrong. While I was contemplating this, my screen went dark and then switched to screen-saver mode. Didn't take long—less than five minutes. One of the company policies that had been driven into my head during orientation this morning was the importance of not leaving your desk with an active screen. The screen saver, however, surprised me.

In place of my desktop, I saw a video feed. Of me. Sitting at my desk. Right now. I didn't immediately swivel around. I could see the direction of where the camera was located as it was shooting straight through the glass door and sidelight of my office. What I was looking at was a live feed from a security camera in the hallway just outside. After about twenty seconds, the camera panned to the right thirty degrees and held that position. Then right another thirty degrees so I was looking across the cubicles across the hall.

If I had left my desk in the position it was in when I arrived, whoever monitored that camera could have seen everything that appeared on my screen. Someone was serious about watching.

But why show me the video?

{5}
Once a Hacker

BEING A HACKER, I've always had an impulse to hide my identity. As a result, I've never put my real name on the Internet. I've never put my own photo on a social site. I've never indicated in my profile where I live, how old I am, or even my sex. I have very few 'friends' online and they mostly know me by one of my aliases and not by name.

Amazingly, I'm still pretty active and think of myself as even a little vulnerable online. I have a dozen email addresses, carefully concealed behind various identities. My passwords for those accounts are changed every thirty days. I create temporary email addresses through anonymous host sites and then create permanent addresses using the temporary one as a reference. Then I delete the temporary account. My security software is the best I can find, but because I've cracked it myself, I place little trust in its ability to keep my systems safe.

I don't use WiFi in my office or my home. I use a cellular modem to connect my computers through encrypted packet data on a virtual private network. That makes my activities almost undetectable as my IP address changes with every location from which I connect.

It also makes everything damned inconvenient.

I am a digital fortress, and even so, I am afraid of being spied upon. It really irritated me that in my first day at EFC, I'd found two devices set to spy on me as I worked. And I figured there would be more.

I hadn't opened email after logging. I'd simply stared at the computer screen watching the security camera outside my office continue its 360 degree pan every four minutes. Who monitored that camera? As I left for the day, I wandered aimlessly down the corridor. All through the office I could see monitors on people's desktops displaying images from security cameras. Occasionally, I would see myself on a screen as I walked by, which meant the cameras were located all through the building. That amount of visual data would take truckloads of digital space to store, even after high compression. But I had to admit, the simple reminder that I was being watched at all times had a Big Brother effect on my willingness to commit any grave sin in the office. It probably had the same effect on every other employee.

I left the building and wasn't sure that I ever wanted to go back.

The keyboard was tapped. The camera was watching. What other types of surveillance were in place? I had to bet that the laptop I was assigned had monitoring software installed on it—very likely in places that I couldn't touch. So, Tuesday morning when I went into the office at half past eight, I swiped my ID against the reader and went straight to my desk. I attached a portable keyboard to the laptop and did a network boot, avoiding accessing the hard drive at all. As soon as I reached the 'repair' screen, I slotted in my smartcard and gave the commands to format the hard drive and reinstall the operating system and standard company issued software. That should take care of any malicious software on the computer that was directed only at me. The fact that I'd never know what was there was irritating, but not worth bothering over if I wanted to start exploring the company networks. Of course, EFC might be monitoring *everyone's* computers and have software built into the network install. *Que sera, sera.*

After the disk was formatted and the system was up and operating again, I'd have to figure out how to put my own protection on the computer. I was pretty sure the network security protocols would prevent me from installing any software that wasn't on the official list—that was typical of both financial and government offices—but I was confident I could find an unprotected network computer where I could install and run it remotely. If not, I had a way of running the programs that I'd use remotely, although I'd rather have it right here.

While the system was installing, I tapped into my own VPN on my cell phone and started a series of probes at the company's firewalls from outside. If there was someone getting through from outside, then the fraud they were worried about might not be employee-based at all.

I timed the rotation of the camera outside my office and while it was turned away, I used a small bug detector to sweep the rest of my office. There were two—a listening device in the lamp and a bug on the phone. Those, I simply wouldn't tolerate. I removed them and went out of my office to the restrooms and flushed the two devices down the toilet. With luck, no one would have been listening that early in the morning and they'd just hear silence from that point on. But I didn't care. They would all know by now that I'd detected the devices and cleaned house. And good luck to them trying to break my password to reinstall.

I wasn't surprised to find that when the screen-saver kicked in on the computer, I was once again viewing a security camera, but it wasn't the same one. I'd read my company handbook the night before. EFC had security camera feeds as the standard screen-saver for all network computers. The feeds were randomly assigned and changed to a different camera each time the screen-saver kicked in. I was willing to bet, though, that the feed I'd seen on my screen the previous day had not been chosen randomly. Someone was making sure I knew I was monitored. The question was, "Who?" After all, Arnold had told me when he hired me that I'd be watched. Throwing me the camera might simply have been a way of driving the point home. There was no reason to believe I had a strong ally anywhere in this company. Yet.

They'd as much as challenged me to show I could get around them. I was going to do it.

I opened my email and scanned through the messages that came through yesterday and early today. If the number of messages in my inbox was any indication, it was a wonder anyone got any actual work done. I set my mailbox up on a removable drive. I wasn't keeping anything on the company computer. When I turned it back into them after I was done here, it would look unused.

It was time to start earning my keep.

THE EFC NETWORK was a new city and the streets were unfamiliar to me. Usually when I track someone, I know the streets and I can eliminate the background noise. Here, everyone I saw looked like a threat, and everyone I couldn't see was suspect.

I could randomly pick virtual doors and walk in hoping to find something interesting, but I was pretty sure some of the doors I could see had security systems that would sound alarms all over if I just busted in. And being random wasn't a good plan. I needed to learn how this city was organized. Where did people live and where did they play? And most importantly, where did they keep their treasures? If I was going to catch a thief, I needed to know where there was something worth stealing.

Every bit of information on the Internet—every file on a company server—has value. The problem is making it transactionable. If I buy artwork for my home for $1,000, one day it might be worth $10,000, but only if I can find a buyer who will pay that much. The same thing is true of information. It is worth what a buyer will pay for it. So, when looking for something to steal, the first place to look is not at what people are guarding most heavily, but at what people are most willing to buy.

I headed for the vast underground marketplace of the Internet.

Most people think of the Internet marketplace as big storefronts that house multinational companies or auction houses. Those are the ones with a dotcom address. Most of the places I visited were identified by IP addresses without even a domain name. In my mind, it was more like a medieval village than a shopping mall. Random booths were set up throughout the square offering goods for sale. Auction blocks competed for attention as everything from slaves, to weapons, to food was offered to the highest bidder. Hawkers barked out their wares and the benefits of their products. Crowds pushed and shoved, individuals clamoring for attention. But these were the sellers. The buyers stood around the perimeter, usually silent. Occasionally one would step up to buy, often haggling over the price. Those were bargain-hunters. I wasn't interested. Demand drove prices up. If the price was going down, it wasn't worth stealing.

In the side streets off the market I found people asking for goods and services. They weren't there to bicker about a price. What they wanted had value to them. It was worth going after. These were the people who could inspire theft.

I wasn't there to engage, but lurked in the shadows watching transactions and proposals taking place. Nonetheless, a shadowy figure attached itself to me and spoke quietly.

"Buying or selling?"

"Depends," I answered. "What do you need?"

"Bank accounts would be nice."

"Wouldn't they though?"

"You don't have any to sell? Go away."

"I didn't come to you. You came to me."

"Go away."

I decided it was in my best interest to go away. I left the alley and circled around to it by a different direction. I could feel the presence nearby, though it didn't approach. I moved out again and came back a different way. It was definite. I was being watched.

I HIT ESC and dropped into the real world a moment before a tousled redhead with black rimmed glasses poked through my doorway. Ford McCall was trying to get my attention. I waved him in.

"I like your furniture arrangement," he started. "It's good feng shui. These offices make it difficult to find a position where your back is neither to the door nor the window. Nice solution."

"Thanks. You a decorator?" I'd had nearly the same conversation with Eric after we'd painted my apartment black and he'd convinced me to go to IKEA for furniture. When there are windows or doors on three sides of a room, it gives few options for positioning yourself so that you don't have your back to one or the other. I guess that would make Wild Bill Hickock a feng shui expert because legend said he never sat with his back to a door or window while playing poker.

"No. Just read a lot. Speaking of which, did you see the article in TechCrunch on the upcoming meeting of the standards committee for IPSec? You should put in for a field trip. Arnie's serious about improving security all the way around, so I'm sure he'd fund the travel." I could see that Darlene's assessment of Ford's connection to the Internet and reading every article on every subject was probably true. I'd have to be careful what subject I engaged him on as I was sure he probably knew more about anything than I did. Still, the fact that he was standing in my doorway as I was being followed through cyberspace meant that it wasn't him that was following me—didn't it?

"Thanks, Ford. I'll check it out and see what Jen thinks."

"That's a lost cause," Ford snickered. "If you talk to her, put together a spreadsheet that shows how much the whole venture will cost, where you'll stay, who you expect to talk to, and a list of objectives for the trip with a dollar value attached to each one. She may look like a woman, but she's just a suit. If there isn't a bottom line, there isn't a reason." There was a little bitterness showing through Ford's comments, as if he'd tried to convince her of a venture with no success. "Oh, Allen says we're going out for a beer Thursday night. I understand you aren't in on Wednesdays, so I'll see you then."

With that, the smartest and most socially inept man I'd ever met left the room. I glanced at my clock and was surprised to find it was already past five. I'd been so absorbed in my exploration of the network that I hadn't had lunch. My stomach growled. I shut down my computer, unlocked the security cable that fastened it to my desk, and packed it in my briefcase.

I wouldn't be in the office tomorrow, but I'd be doing a lot of work before I showed up here on Thursday morning.

{6}
Dealing with Teens

WEDNESDAY MORNING, I had an appointment to keep. It almost felt normal to get up, shave, and head to the office by eight. This time, though, it was my own office up on 15th Avenue. I have a room and a half in a war-era house rezoned for commercial use. My upstairs co-tenants include two children's counselors and an accountant. One of the counselors specialized in testing and study habits for ADD and learning disabilities. From what I understand, most of the kids he sees are bright but can't focus in school. The other counselor works with kids who just need help coping with life. I was amazed at the age range of the kids that came through the front doors—some with parents and some just dropped off out front and sent in alone. My office is on the main floor, so I have a clear view of the entry when my door is open.

Bernie, the accountant in the third upstairs office, helped with my incorporation, does my taxes, and generally keeps me honest in my bookkeeping. Whether he has any clients other than the three he shares the house with, I don't know.

I have direct access to the kitchen from my office. It's a nice setup, but we're all waiting for our landlord to announce that the building will be torn down to make way for a real office building.

I like the space. I need an office where I can actually meet with potential clients, even though I do as much real work in my darkened apartment at night.

Monday night I'd received a referral from the counselor upstairs and he was waiting on the front porch when I got there at eight-thirty. Actually, they. A boy about fourteen and his father. I motioned them into my office and asked if they would like coffee or chocolate or tea or a soft drink. The dad took coffee with sugar and his son, after getting approval from his father, opted for the hot chocolate. Once we had our drinks, we settled in and I asked how I could help them. They fidgeted a bit, the boy looking at his father.

"Son, it's okay. He won't judge. You just have to tell him what's happening or he can't help." The boy nodded, took another sip of chocolate then looked up at me.

"I... I'm being harassed. Online." It was apparent that there was more than he was saying. After a minute I decided on a way to help him.

"Can you show me an example?" He pulled out his tablet and in a few gestures had a popular social network on the screen. He handed it to me. There were a few of the normal messages between friends, but not as many as I expected kids his age would have. Two out of every three posts, however, were derogatory. There were links posted to everything from "Save the Faggot" to "Gay porn." There were a couple of messages that were subtly threatening—warnings about where not to walk and where fairies weren't welcome. It was vile and I couldn't believe the network had allowed this kind of behavior.

"We've tried everything," the father said. "We reported it to the network, flagged the posts, blocked various users. Every time one goes away, another pops up. Now it's spreading on video sites and other networks."

"My friends aren't posting anymore because they're afraid they'll get harassed too."

"Is it all online, or are you getting real life harassment, too?" I asked. I could deal with taming a cyberbully, but if he was getting pushed around after school, it was a matter for the police.

"No," the boy said quietly. "I'm just always afraid. I just came out a few weeks ago." He looked down.

"Is that going to be a problem for you?" his father asked me.

"Not at all," I said.

"Good. Daniel didn't want us to interfere, but how can we say 'it gets better,' if we don't do something to *make* it better?" I nodded and smiled at Daniel.

"What would you like me to do, Daniel?" I asked. "If I can get results, what would you like them to be?"

"I'd just like the flaming to stop so my friends will come around again," he said. "I've been talking to Cora, upstairs, about this for a while now. She said I should talk to you and see if you could make it stop."

I thought about it a few minutes as I scanned through more of the messages. It was sick. If there is anything I dislike as much as a thief, it's a bully. I was relieved to see a few messages that I took to be signs of support for Daniel. I was ready to take on the case pro bono, just to get a crack at the bastard behind the cyberattack. At the same time, I couldn't help but think how lucky this kid was. His father was sitting beside him, ready to fight for him. A strong family could keep a kid from becoming a statistic. I got out a contract, filled out the necessary blanks, and then handed it to the father to fill in name and contact information.

"Daniel, I'm giving this to your dad to fill out because legally you can't sign a contract," I said. "But I'm working for you."

Daniel watched as I used his account to friend one of my own aliases on that network.

"This is me. I won't be using our connection to post on your page or anything like that. As much as possible, I'm going to lurk rather than take control of your account, which I might have to do later if I find something that I can work with. You can contact me with a direct message if you think of anything else I should know, like a list of any other sites that you are a member of—even if they are embarrassing. I'll need your aliases and passwords. And if your friends start getting messages, I need to know. Got it?"

He looked at me a little quizzically and then nodded his head. If the kid was registered on a gay chat room or even had a login for gay porn, it could be where his information was leaking out. He understood.

"Yes sir," he said. "Will you be able to make it stop?"

"Worst case, we'll have to set up clean accounts for you and only invite your trusted friends. I'll put some software into place that will block specific kinds of content. If I can't make a positive ID on the person and turn the information over to the police, I might still be able to make contact and... uh... negotiate a stop."

"Thank you."

"Yes," said the father. "Thank you very much." They left. I was already angry with this scum.

I WAS FINISHING up several projects and had to wait for Daniel to send me the rest of the information I needed, so I couldn't accomplish much for him that morning. I really wanted to wait until I had all the information he could give me before I launched my investigation. There was no sense in strong-arming information out of the net if the boy could just tell me.

I grabbed a bite of Indian food across the street from my office and was stewing over how I was going to dig through the EFC data reserves when Andi called me.

"Dag, I'm sorry to bother you but I'm in a pinch."

"What is it Andi?"

"I'm over at the University and I'm completely tied up and can't get back to pick up Cali for her rehearsal. Could you swing by the high school and take her to the theater? I know you have your new job and all, so if it's a problem, just say so and I'll have the girls catch the bus. It just takes them so long to get there on the bus."

"Andi, it's fine. In fact, it's just what I need," I said. It was really a beautiful day out—one of those April days of sunshine that makes you forget how miserable you've been all winter. "I'm working from home and I'd love to get the car out of the garage on a day like today."

"You're a dear, Dag."

"What are you doing over at the U?"

"Marcie gave me a lead on a possible opening over here. I just happened to check in at the right time and I'm going to meet with the department chair in a few minutes."

"That's wonderful!"

"Oh. Dag, you'll have both Cali and Melissa. Mel needs to be dropped at the softball field, but that's on the way to the theater. Okay?"

"Sure. I won't need to say anything with both of them in the car."

"Do what I do. Keep quiet and listen. You'll be amazed at what you can learn. Pick them up at three."

"Will do. Good luck with the interview."

I WAS WAITING out front at 3:00 when Cali and her best friend Melissa came down the steps. Cali hesitated a moment looking for her mom's van, then squealed when she saw my yellow Mustang with the top down. She and Melissa came running toward the car with Cali yelling, "Shotgun!" as she tagged the door first. Melissa piled into the back seat and sat sideways since there was so little leg room, even for a high school girl. It would have been fairer for Cali to sit in back since she was so much smaller, but I wasn't going to interfere.

IT WAS FIVE-PLUS years ago that I moved into the apartment on The Hill. Even before I'd painted the room, I remember standing at the window with my suitcase and box of books, one chair and a mattress, watching two twelve-year-old girls playing an elaborate game in the postage-stamp yard of the duplex next door. The game somehow involved a tennis ball, a Frisbee, two croquet wickets, and capes. Then I saw the door open and a perfectly lovely young woman came out with lemonade for the girls. From the angle high up where I was watching, it took me a minute to realize that I was looking at my friend Andi Marx from the faculty lounge. I'd had no idea I was moving next door to her.

It wasn't long before the carefree childhood games were put aside by the girls as they started playing real sports, acting in plays, and—let's not forget—being interested in boys. Now they were juniors in high school. Cali was playing Lady Macbeth, opening in two weeks, and Melissa was pitching for a city league softball team. Still the two girls were almost inseparable and I listened to their nonstop banter as I pulled away from the curb.

"OH, HE'LL NEVER go out with you," Mel said. "He's totally gaga over Barbara. He can't even see another bitch."

"Nobody loves me," Cali moaned dramatically.

"I fuckin' love you baby!"

"Yeah, but you're a slut so you don't count!" The girls howled and I kept my own counsel about not acting like an adult and chastising the language. I didn't see Melissa often, but I'd noticed that her language had been getting riper each year. Cali listened and laughed, but I seldom heard her swear.

"I'm not a slut. I'm lubricious," Mel said haughtily. They laughed.

"Look! There he is," Cali said pointing at a car in the next lane. "What do I do?"

"Ignore him!" Mel snapped. Cali twisted in her seat to turn on my radio. "Woohoo!" Mel screamed as she waved her hands in the air. The boy in the next car over turned to look at her. He was stuck behind a guy waiting for a pedestrian so he could make a right turn. I pressed down on the accelerator and was half a block away before he cleared the intersection.

"Why did you do that?" Cali screamed. "I'm so embarrassed."

"Now he knows you're out with a cool guy in a convertible and too busy to notice him," Mel answered. "He'll ask you out this week."

"That's insane!" Cali continued to fiddle with the radio. "Thanks for picking me up, Dag. Sorry I brought *her* with me."

"No problem," I answered. "Just the price of seeing your mom." I regretted that statement instantly. What was I thinking?

"Oh? You're dating now?"

"No, no. You know what I mean. We all go out with our friends. We're friends. We're not involved."

"Yeah, right!" Mel scoffed. "You're dating."

"He can't be dating mom," Cali answered. "He's gay."

"I'm what?" Cali's eyes got big and she covered her mouth with her hands.

"I'm sorry, Dag. Aren't you out?" she whispered.

"What makes you think I'm gay?" This was a real revelation to me. I couldn't imagine why she'd think that.

"Well, you live on Capitol Hill—with Eric and Jared."

"Since when can only gays live on Capitol Hill? And I don't live *with* Eric or Jared. They're neighbors."

"Yeah but, you're like my mom's best friend in the world. Straight men can't be best friends with women." She really thought I was gay? Hmm. There was a bit of fun to be had here.

"Well," I said, sounding almost like I was going to confess. "Did you ever think that maybe *she's* gay? I might just be her beard." We pulled up in the parking lot at the softball field and I noticed that both girls were staring at each other with their mouths open. I smirked a little. "This is your stop, Mel."

"Oh, yeah. Thanks. Uh… and uh… sorry about the language thing. I get carried away."

"I didn't notice."

"You're cool," she said and jumped out over the top of the door with her duffle in tow. "Thanks for meeting me at school. See you tomorrow, Sweetie!" she said kissing Cali on the cheek. Then she was off. Cali punched a button on the radio. Electronica came blasting over the speakers.

"Dubstep? You listen to dubstep?"

"I listen to all kinds of music," I said. "Is that what you call this?" I'm a lousy dancer, but when I'm driving around in the Mustang, sometimes that heavy electronic dance beat is just what I need. She fiddled with the dial until she found the local jazz station.

"There. Real detectives listen to jazz. It's in all the books." I chuckled, but let it slide. She was quiet for a few minutes.

I THOUGHT BACK to those early days in the apartment and why Cali could be confused. I was good friends with Eric and Jared. They'd both, in their way, helped me through those first months after Hope left. "She really did a number on you," I remember Eric saying. He was a little tipsy from all the wine we'd been drinking and he'd brought a CD up to play on my new stereo.

"So, Eric, why are you here on a Saturday night? Are you between boyfriends?"

"Oh honey, don't I wish. I don't even have *one* right now." It took a second before he started laughing at my open mouth. "I don't suppose you're just a little gay curious are you?" he smiled.

"No," I answered truthfully. "I can't say it's ever even crossed my mind." He shrugged it off and had never mentioned it again. He was just a good, if sometimes flaky, friend.

"IT'S OKAY, YOU know," Cali said just above the sound of the wind and the radio. I was pulled out of my reverie, trying to think what she was talking about.

"What's okay? If I'm gay?"

"Yeah, sure, but… I mean… It's okay if you date my mom, I guess."

"Cali, your mom is really just my friend," I said smiling at her.

"Okay. But still—" She left it hanging. It was quiet the rest of the way to the theater. I dropped her off and drove back to the apartment.

Yeah. But still…

{7}
Little Fish

I'D TAKEN APART the laptop I was issued at the office, used peripherals for entering data, wiped the hard drive, reinstalled everything, and stored all my data, including my email, on a removable drive. But I still wasn't satisfied with the device. My personal laptop was faster, had more memory, and had all the software on it I couldn't install on the company laptop. So the last thing I did before I got home Wednesday was buy a smartcard reader for my personal laptop and head to my cozy apartment to try using remote access from my personal computer. My laptop wouldn't be recognized by the network, but my smartcard should let me through. Then, maybe I could explore the databanks of Evergreen Financial Corp. while others were asleep and unaware.

About ten Wednesday night my phone buzzed and I snapped it open. "Hamar."

"Nails," came the response, followed by a suppressed giggle.

"Sorry. Hi Andi. I didn't mean to sound snappish."

"I must have caught you in Nowhere Land. Do you have a minute?"

"Sure. I was just working on a computer and didn't pay attention to who was calling."

"I thought I had a custom ring."

"The phone's on vibrate. But I'm happy to chat anyway. Any break from the demons of the corporate world is welcome." I smiled and left my desk so I wouldn't be tempted to keep looking at the screen while we talked. It's a bad habit. I plopped down in my recliner and clicked the light on over my one painting—a man looking out across the sea. It was painted by a dear friend back in high school and always makes me feel peaceful.

"Cali has been going on nonstop about how cool it was of you to pick them up in the Mustang. Everyone they know is insanely jealous. She and Mel want to know if you would chauffeur them every day."

"Well…"

"I'm kidding, Dag. But seriously, Cali has a big-time crush on that car. She's actually talking about wanting to get a driver's license. You know Mel has had hers for over a year, but Cali just wasn't interested until now."

"Tell her a driver's license isn't enough to get her into the driver's seat of my baby."

"I'm sure. But the girls want to pay you back and asked me to invite you to the movies Friday night."

"What movie?"

"They've got tickets for us all to go see *Once a Hero* at Harvard Exit. It's a new film with a PG rating. Please save me from being the lone adult with these two wild ones."

"That sounds like fun. I can't take four in my car, though. Mel was folded like a pretzel in the back seat this afternoon."

"Not to worry. Mel's parents approved the movie and suggested she drive her guests. They're pretty conservative and even though Mel is seventeen, they still hold a tight rein on what she sees and with whom. I think they approved because I said I'd go with them."

"From what I've seen, having Mel around would turn me into a very conservative parent as well," I laughed. "What a wild child."

"It might have worked the other way around," Andi sighed. "I worry that all their rules have pushed her to act out in ways that aren't always appropriate. At least it makes me look like the world's coolest mom by comparison."

"That you are. What time Friday?"

"The girls will pick us up from the faculty lounge at seven if you are going to be there."

"Sounds good. I'll see you Friday." I could hear cheers in the background as apparently Cali had been close enough to get the gist of our conversation.

"Good night, Dag. I seem to have a happy girl on my hands."

"Good night, Andi."

I was a pretty happy guy, too. I was going to take three lovely women to the movies. Or be taken. What difference did it make? I sat for a few minutes just staring out at the ocean in the painting on my wall. Finally, I snapped out the light and settled back in front of my computer. The night was still young.

THE MOST INTRIGUING part of the EFC information highway was the fraud line. Computer gurus don't analyze threats on the fraud hotline. It's a place where consumers report problems with their accounts. I guessed that only one out of ten people who suspect a problem with their accounts actually report it. That would be comparable to the number of consumers who actually send in rebate coupons when they buy something at a store.

Half the time, credit card statements aren't even examined unless there's an expense report to be filed. An unfamiliar charge might be passed off as just another expense. A married person might assume something was charged by the spouse. There are those who call the phone number associated with the purchase. They could find that "according to the on-line agreement you signed, this renews automatically at the first of every month unless we are notified in writing of your intention to withdraw." Or they might sit on hold with a message that customer service is helping another customer, playing over and over for hours. An especially tenacious customer might fight it out with the vendor, but still not report it to the credit card issuer.

But occasionally, a person will see something that is out of the ordinary and challenge it. Very rarely, it will be done in such a timely manner that the company can actually do something about it. "My electronic statement shows six charges for $29.95 late last night. I didn't charge anything. What's going on?" In that instance, the call gets bumped to the head of the queue. The database of vendors is searched. An off-shore porn company? Over a hundred cards charged for six items by that company just before midnight?

A calling force is organized to call all the affected cardholders to warn them that unauthorized charges have been made and their card information could be compromised. New cards are issued. Refunds are made, and the unit sent out to investigate the fraudulent vendor reports back that the company's accounts have all been closed and the vendor has disappeared.

Net loss absorbed by the credit card company of over $25,000 plus time. There is no one to prosecute. Perhaps the company's fraud losses move from two basis points to two-point-one basis points. The fraud barely registers in the accounts as a bookkeeping error.

But someone out there just stole $25,000.

It was the fraud hotline that led me to the seamy underbelly of the EFC cyberworld.

EVERY POSSIBLE THING on earth can be bought with a credit card—drugs, prostitutes, a kidney, a trip to the space station. As long as the vendor has established a merchant bank account, credit cards are good.

Having learned from the underworld bosses of prohibition, most of these operate as respectable businesses. Their accounting is meticulous. They pay sales and income taxes—though not necessarily on the actual goods being sold. There is no reason for the IRS to investigate. On paper, they are legitimate businesses.

In reality, the purchase of web design services by a wealthy businessman may have included a web template personally delivered by a prostitute. Of course, there could be additional charges, but said businessman is not going to complain that he didn't get his prostitute with those deliveries. It wouldn't be good for his image as a church-going husband and father of three.

Here in the darkest parts of the World Wide Web, there is really only one business—greed. Any way to move money, even virtual cash, from one pocket to another is accepted.

A line of angry men pounded on a locked door demanding a refund. The door stood alone in the middle of the street and from my angle it was obvious there was nothing behind it. The vendor had closed shop and erased all traces of it.

A woman pled for help at the door of a mission in return for the years she had been donating to it. The fat pseudo-priest reminding her that she had not subscribed to a long-term care package, but described what a wonderful future she would have if she signed over her remaining assets to them.

Despicable as these were, they weren't what I was looking for. I followed winding streets looking for a back door into a corporate giant. It was easier to find than I ever anticipated.

A new shop was just being set up. It hid behind an old and respectable storefront, but once you entered, you walked directly into the scam operating behind it.

"We've noticed that you aren't receiving our current information at your home address anymore," the shopkeeper said as I entered the space. It looked pristine. The logos adorning the walls were the latest corporate color scheme, the furnishings boasted lots of flash and interactivity. It was exactly like entering the online corporate headquarters of EFC. "We'd like to make sure our information regarding your account beginning 7785 is current. Just fill out this simple form with the last twelve digits on your credit card, your expiration date, and CCV code from the back of the card. Then be sure to check which of the following items you do not want us to send to you. This is your opportunity to opt out of any of the offers on our list. Otherwise, we will renew the mailings to your home address along with our apologies for the inconvenience you've suffered by not having these valuable offers."

This guy was good. He already knew the first four digits of my credit card. Wow. Must be legit, right? And I was going to start receiving all this junk mail if I didn't opt out. I certainly didn't want that. Of course, I couldn't opt out if they didn't have the correct account information. I wondered how many people had already responded to this generous offer in the few minutes it had been open.

I walked around a bit and checked the building permits for the shop. Finally, I managed to identify the employee who was responsible. He led me into a private office where he proceeded to snow me with purchase orders, design instructions, and answers to every question but one: "Who was he?" I left the shop and circled around it. In cyberspace there are multiple entrances and exits to everything. I looked around at the foundations and understood. It had been built inside an abandoned site. The entire infrastructure was in place, but the project had been curtailed months ago. The messages waiting in the delivery room, all had a single name written on them.

An EFC employee had commandeered an abandoned subdomain to run a scam on EFC customers.

I hesitated. Was I sure this wasn't another false identity? There would be no going back. I felt a tremor and realized the shop was already being disassembled.

I pulled the trigger, sending alarms all through corporate security.

THURSDAY MORNING, I dragged myself out of bed, showered, shaved, and headed to the office in spite of feeling hung over. I'd not slept at all in the hour and a half I was in bed. I was anxious to get to the office and see if there were any results from my foray into the cyberguts of the company the night before. I grabbed coffee at the Analog on my way down the hill, caught a bus on Olive and jumped off at Third.

I was just in time.

Before I entered the building, police came out with a guy in a polo shirt and slacks, hands cuffed behind him. The officers pushed him into a waiting patrol car and then turned to address the tall, dark-haired man behind them. Don Abrams, Director of Network Security, was nodding and I could hear the tail end of his conversation as I approached.

"We will definitely press charges. We've already notified the FBI. We were lucky to catch it before there was a serious compromise of customer data."

"We'll take it from here," the officer said. "But the server unit has to be secured in order to be used as evidence."

"We've disconnected it from the network and it's ready for impound," Don said. He was so angry there was a flush about his face. The officer got in the car and Don turned back to the door, almost bumping into me.

"Hey!" I said. "What's up?"

"That scumbag heisted an abandoned subdomain and spent the night lifting credit card information from customers by posing as a marketing opt-out site. We got an alert about four this morning and I've spent the last four hours tying down the site and corralling the bastard. I can't believe it."

"Somebody high up?"

"No. Just a damn web designer who stumbled on a vulnerability that we'd never closed."

"A lot of publicity coming out about this?"

"Fortunately we were alerted almost as the guy started operating. We were able to stop the flow of data before it got offsite, so technically we don't have to go public. But we'll do whatever is necessary to put the bastard behind bars." Don and I went up to the twenty-third floor in silence. "I'm sure I'll hear about this from Arnie this morning, though. He's been here since seven."

"Wish I'd been here for all the fun." Don looked at me a little strangely and then nodded as he turned down a different hallway.

"Later."

CORPORATIONS THE SIZE of EFC have hundreds of websites, but usually only a few domains. Additional pages that are needed for promotions, products, departments, or other legitimate purposes are often subdomains. Subdomains do not have to be registered with any naming authority. A company might, for example have a site that is Promotion.CompanyName.com where "CompanyName.com" is the domain and "promotion" is the subdomain.

Until a few years ago, it was common practice for entrepreneurs to buy up domain names and hold them, especially if they could get the names of major corporations. Eventually the companies would want the domains that matched their company name both for convenience for the customer and to protect themselves from being spoofed. Now it's illegal to camp on a domain name someone else might have a legitimate claim to, but there are other methods of making consumers believe they are viewing legitimate sites that are scams.

More insidious with the rise of social media sites were subdomains that looked like the company. For example, "We're giving away a $200 shopping spree to the first ten visitors. Register at CompanyName.freeoffers.com. If the information was reversed and it was freeoffers.CompanyName.com, the request would come to the corporate domain. But this one had no connection to the company at all. People fell for it every day and the fraud detection group had scans going all the time to locate subdomains on other websites that looked like their company.

Buying domain names for illegal purposes is a risky proposition. The names have to be registered and the owners can be located. But since a subdomain is not registered, it could be used for less ethical purposes. In the case of EFC, the web designer had gained access to an abandoned subdomain that still had server space. He sent an email to several thousand customers informing them that they need to opt-out of various mailings related to their accounts. It all looked legitimate except for three things. Legally a user must opt-IN to promotional use of their information and never be required to opt-OUT in order to avoid getting mailings. The first four digits of every card issued by a specific bank or bank system are the same. Therefore, having the first four digits of your account does not indicate the sender knows anything about you. And banks and credit card issuers do not ask for account information. They already have it. They might ask for proof of identity, a password that has been set up (not the ATM PIN), or last four digits of the SSN. But they'll never ask for the account number.

The trickiest part of my late-night foray into the company's intranet was identifying the perp without identifying myself. I was feeling pretty proud of myself for having solved the problem. I was ready to return to my life as a private investigator.

When I got to my desk, and logged into my laptop, I fully intended to email Arnie and resign, having fulfilled my contract. But as soon as my screen connected to the company network an alert box showed up in the middle of it. The message was simple.

"Little fishy in a brook. Little fishy on a hook. Just a little fishy."

{8}
A Shining City

I SLAMMED MY LAPTOP shut and charged out of my office. I went straight for Arnie's office, but Darlene blocked my way.

"He's out," she said. I saw his laptop sitting on his desk before she closed his door.

"Where?"

"He's with Don." I headed off in the direction of Don's office but Darlene grabbed hold of my sleeve. I pretty much dragged her with me. "I wouldn't interrupt him. You haven't been here long enough to go charging in when he's dressing down another employee." We were at the door to Don's office and I could see the two men standing nearly toe to toe. It was a heated exchange, but I couldn't hear through the door. A screen saver of one of the security cameras playing on his laptop.

"Damn!"

"Ford's office is next. Just down the hall," she said, this time taking the lead and dragging me along. I stopped outside the door. Ford was asleep at his desk, his head thrown back. I imagined the snores I couldn't hear. These offices were pretty soundproof. Another camera played on his computer monitor. I turned away from his office.

"Allen?" I asked.

"Not in yet. Phil is out of town. He had some time off coming and is taking a long weekend," Darlene ticked off my team members on her fingers.

"And Jen?" I asked. I still didn't know exactly what Jen did.

"She's in conference with Mr. Davenport." Darlene stood and waited for that information to soak in.

"Davenport?"

"As in CEO."

"What does she do here, anyway?"

"Same thing as you, apparently. She reports directly to a C-level and runs around putting her nose in everyone else's business. When you figure it out, let me know. I'm not sure I like her all that much." I stopped and thought about that. My heart rate was slowing down and I didn't feel like I was going to explode anymore.

"Thanks, Darlene. I appreciate knowing what you think of me."

"Putting your nose in other people's business is a company policy. Let's go get a cup of coffee." We went out the main doors to the elevator. I thought we'd just head for the cafeteria, but she went straight out onto the street and headed for the waterfront. Two blocks from the office she went into the Daybreak Coffee Shop. "I know you're used to better coffee up on Capitol Hill, but this is as good as it gets downtown." I ordered a double short Americano and savored the warmth as it settled into my system. Somehow, just holding the cup in my hands brought a sense of peace and tranquility to me. I smiled at Darlene who had given me a respectful moment with my brew.

"Sorry," I said. She nodded and we sat at the counter in the back of the shop with a view overlooking the Sound.

"Was it you?" she asked when we were settled.

"What?"

"Was it you that blew the whistle on that kid in Web Services?"

"Why would you think that?" I evaded. Darlene might be an ally in this whole thing, but I wasn't ready to spill my guts to her.

"Crap. Even bringing you two blocks away from the office I'm not going to get any information out of you, am I?"

I just smiled in response.

"If you were easy, he wouldn't have hired you. You're a strange man, Dag Hamar. Almost no Internet presence. At all. No public profile. I had to raid the personnel file to find out what little I know about you. I'm suspecting that Dag Hamar isn't even your real name. Not only that, but you are in disguise. Not your real hair color. I can already see a bit of your natural mustache color at the roots. You wear suits that beg not to be noticed. And even though you're a fulltime employee, you have tacit permission to work offsite at will. And I'm supposed to brief you on a subject you probably know more about than I do so you can face your team meeting tomorrow."

"You're in a hard place," I said. "I've already apologized enough, though. I don't think there's anything I can do to make it easier."

"Oh, you could, but you won't."

"What could I do?"

"Take me to dinner tomorrow evening."

"I can't."

"You won't."

"I have a date."

"Just my luck."

We walked back to the office companionably, but she stopped while we were still half a block away.

"Dag, I like you." I must have sighed. "Not in the 'take me to dinner' way. I'm too old for you. I've worked here my entire career—twenty-four years. I just want to tell you that nothing at this company is what it appears to be. Whatever you think you're doing here, it's really something else."

"Maybe my best bet is to just do nothing at all, then," I said.

"I've heard worse ideas," she laughed.

We both dutifully swiped our smartcards against the security door—one card, one entry—and got back as far as my office. A yellow sticky note was on my door with the words "C ME NOW! AD"

"Your turn in the hot seat," Darlene said. "Good luck."

I went on to Arnie's door and knocked. He looked up and waved me in. I closed the door, on the spat we were about to have. Our conversation took a turn for the worse as soon as the door clicked shut.

"Was it you?" Arnie snapped.

"What?" It was the second time I'd been asked that.

"Was it you that reported that breach this morning?"

"You mean you didn't know? Yes, it was me."

"I wouldn't ask you if I already knew. Now Don is scrubbing the entire system trying to track down who intruded to alert his team. He knows for sure it was someone with top clearance in the company. Do you think that was the threat I hired you to find?"

"I thought it might be. I happened to stumble on it while it was in progress. It's pretty rare to catch something like that in real time."

"But he was no one. The damage could have been eradicated in twenty-four hours with no losses. Instead, we've got a federal case and a witch-hunt going on."

"What did you want me to do?" My own voice was rising.

"I thought you'd be subtle. No one else is supposed to know you are on this." He ran his hand through what was left of his hair. I took a moment to really see his office. It was all chrome and glass with no drawers or doors where anything could be concealed. The only paper in the room was a pad of sticky notes next to a pen. I thought about it a moment and realized I'd seen very little paper anywhere in the building. They had truly gone paperless. If you had access to the network, you could have access to everything.

"Someone already knows," I said, lowering my voice. He looked up and raised one eyebrow. "Either that, or they just got lucky. In my mind that doesn't happen often. I thought it was you, but it's obvious to me now that it isn't." I told him what I'd found when I started the job, from the desk position with the security camera to the bugs on my keyboard, phone, and lamp, to the message on my screen this morning. Finally, I suggested that it seemed pretty common knowledge that I wasn't here to do what my job title said and I told him about my conversation with Darlene. I left out her warning, though.

"Darlene shouldn't be prying, but you're right she knows you are working on something different than your job. I had to have assistance and I trust her. She'll divert suspicion away from you and keep you supplied with a cover. But that doesn't mean she knows what you are doing, so don't give her any more information than you have to. Just treat her nicely. She's sticking her neck out on our behalf."

"I'll bring her flowers."

"That's not a bad idea. Tomorrow is Secretaries' Day—er… Administrative Professionals Day. But yeah, show her you appreciate her. And show *me* you can get some real results." He waved his hand in dismissal and went back to his computer keyboard.

No paper. Where did people keep their personal items? Surely not everyone in the company was so tech savvy they didn't need notebooks or calendars. I thought about my own life as I went back to my office. I'd stripped my life down to bare essentials when I moved into the apartment. But I still get a daily newspaper. I still get enough political flyers and advertisements to fill my recycling bin each week. And I distinctly remembered filling out a batch of paperwork in Human Resources just Monday, which apparently Darlene got access to. Where did that paper go?

I walked on past my office and continued to the stairwell at the end of the hall. I hadn't done a physical survey of the office yet. When images from security cameras flashed on my screen, I didn't know where they were. I was going to take a look around.

The building is twenty-six floors. It took me the rest of the morning.

WHEN I GOT back to my office after lunch, I opened my computer and scanned the long list of emails I'd received in the past thirty-six hours. I'd set up a filtering system so that only mail from my team showed up in my inbox. That cut the volume to only fifty or sixty messages. Three-quarters of those I could ignore. I had the meeting requests for the team meeting on Friday morning and my one-on-one with Jen following it. That should be interesting. I accepted them and read through the remaining email. The last message was my weekly work briefing from Darlene.

That reminded me. I flipped to a local florist website and ordered flowers to be delivered to her tomorrow morning. I paid the extra to get express delivery. I'll bet every boss and staff member in town was hitting the emergency button to get flowers for their admins tomorrow. Then I settled in to read Darlene's report.

She'd done a good job. It was just the right amount of material to assume that a knowledgeable employee could uncover in his first week at work. I could study this and speak intelligently about it tomorrow. So, what remained was to conduct an investigation into people who were near me while one or more of them watched me doing it. I decided on a different tack.

'Decide' might be too strong a word. In spite of several cups of coffee, my lack of sleep was catching up with me, so it was more of a drift into P.I. mode without thinking about it.

I'd told Darlene that perhaps my best bet was to do nothing. Maybe that really *was* a good idea. I started doing searches on cyberbullying. I pulled up the social networks my young client had given me and started tracking the messages that were posted to his accounts. Some of the material I was pulling up was definitely NSFO—'not safe for office.' Employees could be fired for viewing pornography at work, but I was using my own laptop and not the one issued by the company, and I wasn't interested in the picture sites. I was interested in the forums. I was especially interested in the number of anti-gay posters in the gay forums. Sometimes these erupted into all out flame wars, and sometimes the offending thread was locked so no one could comment on it. Whoever managed these forums had to have a really huge staff monitoring their site to keep it under control as well as they did.

Still there were certain signature phrases that kept repeating. Sometimes a phrase is passed around amongst a group of people with a common connection, but sometimes a person who changes names, even IP addresses, will continue to use the same phrasing wherever they post. That's what I was watching for. Using keywords that I gleaned from Daniel's bullies, I modified a shareware spam-filtering software to search out the same phrases and IP addresses on various forums. There were even a few track-backs to websites that became progressively more conservative and religious. I was discounting the further-out sites. I was looking for someone with an axe to grind against gays, and a platform from which he (or she) could spout hatred.

I couldn't execute a command on my software from behind the company firewall because of the restrictions that were on computers on the network. So I uploaded my program to a remote Internet server and executed the command from there. Just before I closed up my computer for the night, I downloaded the log of websites visited from within the company. I didn't think there was any connection between Daniel's case and what I was working on at EFC, but if someone thought I was investigating inappropriate web behavior on company computers, it might chase them out of the woodwork.

I left the office intent on getting a sandwich and some sleep. I'd completely forgotten about the after-work beer with the guys.

ALLEN AND FORD caught up with me on the way down the hall and there was no way to escape being dragged to a preppy bar downtown. Don eventually dragged himself in and I was surprised to see Jen and Darlene approach as well. I was dead on my feet, but showing that would just make people suspicious of my late night activities the night before, so I bravely laughed and chatted with the guys as I sipped a beer. I don't drink much, but I wasn't planning on doing anything tonight but sleep, so I decided one wouldn't hurt.

It was after ten when I left the bar, leaving a wake of co-workers behind me. We'd been joined by nearly a dozen other people from associated departments and I was introduced to everyone. Everyone had questions for me and at one point it occurred to me that a person who interviewed everyone at the bar could put together a passable profile on me. No one asked the same question as anyone else and I had the feeling I was being passed from person to person, each having an assigned task. I feigned too much to drink and caught one of those rare cabs that swing down Third at night. I'd managed to nurse just one beer all evening.

When I got home I automatically plugged my computer in and turned it on. As soon as I logged in, I knew this was not going to be a night for sleep. An identical message had been posted to each of the forums I was investigating. It was a direct, private message, not a general topic posting. The message said simply, "You missed this one," and included an IP address. The messages were all from the same user name, registered to each of the networks. "IGotUrBak."

I put water on to boil and fixed a strong cup of coffee. It was going to be a long night.

EVERY COMPUTER CONNECTED to the Internet is assigned an IP address. Originally the numeric identifiers were 32-bit codes which allowed a little over four billion unique addresses, but the Internet got so big that a new system was introduced with 128 bit codes that allowed more than 300 undecillion addresses. That's a real number and it's a lot bigger than the national debt. The IP address in the message was one of the new ones.

This was shiny. I had to sit down and investigate.

THE WORLD I entered was as different from the slums of cyberspace as bottled water was to the brackish slime of Puget Sound. I couldn't help but think of *The Wizard of Oz* and the Emerald City as I began exploring its coded streets. I was so excited about getting into this alternate reality that I hadn't even stopped to think about who had been tracking my movements at EFC so closely that they knew my alias at every one of the forums I'd investigated. If I'd thought about that, I might have been a little slower to plunge in.

At first glance, I was impressed with the orderliness of this world. The streets were neatly laid out in straight lines with clear markers as to where each one led. This path to administration; this one to finance; this one to social services; the next one to health and welfare. The thoroughfare I was traveling was clearly marked 'Religion', and seemed to be the broadest path available.

The street name made my blood run cold. At least three of the hits on my search of people flaming gays came from domains owned by big religious organizations. Yet, absurdly enough, they were also organizations that had incredibly strong family services programs. Sure enough, the first cross-street I encountered was labeled 'Children's Welfare.'

When I turned off the Religion thoroughfare, my virtual world tilted on its side.

The streets were just as orderly if more narrowly defined. After a moment's disorientation, I started identifying passages marked Food, Health, Population Control, Abuse, Education, Adoption, and just about anything that you could name that had to do with children.

I randomly walked through the door marked 'Food' and found a con-stant pressure to feed the hungry. It was like a big soup kitchen attempting solve world hunger. Around the kitchen there were doors that led to other kitchens marked, with the type of clientele they served: Homeless, Third World, Civic, and Science, for example. One door caught my attention. I've always believed in the old detective adage, 'Follow the money,' so when I spotted a door marked 'Executive', I boldly went through.

Once the momentary disorientation of shifting to a new angle and perspective dissipated, I was able to assess my surroundings.

I glanced at the exits, some leading to other kitchens and several leading to executive offices. I chose one marked 'Board Room.' Might as well start at the top and work my way down from there.

The adjustment to a new set of input settled as I found myself in what was more reminiscent of King Arthur and the Knights of the Round Table than a corporate board room. There were dozens of seats around the table and I was stunned when I started reading the names. Some of the great philanthropists of the world were listed here. It was a hub of charitable giving. These people included some of my personal heroes. I don't know why my source suggested I come here because I was damn sure none of these people would be involved in gay bullying. I looked around at the various exits, some that led to other corporate-sounding destinations, like 'Treasury,' and some that had the names of streets I'd seen before I went indoors.

It was time to start over. I chose the door marked Religion and walked out on the broad street down which I had originally entered this world. I realized the exit had not taken me to the same location on the street. I was apparently much deeper in the city center than my initial entry. There were a wide variety of temples and churches on streets I came to, many that had their own international hierarchies. I decided to enter the first church I came to.

Inside, I discovered the now familiar structure of the city's buildings. Off the large central sanctuary, a number of passageways and doors led off to the various missions, donors, programs, staff, and members of the congregation. I was beginning to get a mental map of what I was thinking of as *Philanthropolis* when I exited the church.

In fact, I realized that the entire complex of domains was laid out as a mind-map. The city was mapped by relationships. Someone had done an amazing job of organizing the most disorganized activity in the world—charity.

All the streets were connections between kinds of organizations. The buildings were specific organizations, and the rooms were activities within the organization. Sometimes, only the doorway to an organization was within Philanthropolis. But many were linked through several different activities as well. As a result, the kitchen could lead me to kitchens in any organization that had one. It was like the secret passage in the game of *Clue*.

With the overall structure in my head, I had to admire whoever had designed this domain. There was a lot of programming talent at work here. But it was an Internet portal. It might go on forever. If there was a cyberbully hiding in this environment, I was going to need assistance in ferreting out where.

I needed spiders.

I HAD SOFTWARE that I could modify to search the Internet for specific combinations of terms, not unlike what I used to locate users who were attacking Daniel. Setting it up was going to take me the rest of the night.

Search engines generally are keyed into a specific association of terms that are searched for. But that is what yields millions of results. A search for 'gay bashing' on any given search engine will yield over two million results in less than two tenths of a second. 'Cyberbully' yields nearly 700,000 results in the same time. That's simply too many results to sift through. And people aren't likely to put 'stalker' in their profile. The search engine looks at the entire page code, not just the part that is displayed on-screen. Keywords, descriptions, and other information, called metadata, are in the file but are not displayed when the web page is loaded.

Sending search spiders into the Internet, or in this case into a particular complex of domains, would let me explore every avenue in Philanthropolis and should yield only the specific information I wanted to have. Was anyone hiding in this cybercity actively engaged in harassing Daniel?

Like most jobs, the work that took the most time was designing the search parameters. I spent most of the night programming my spiders and then the first time I sent them out I discovered a flaw in the code that took me another hour to track down. Since my spiders were nowhere near as well optimized as a major search engine and had no catalog or index to work with, the search would take considerably longer than the three-tenths of a second a general search engine search would take. I executed the search and then flopped on my bed, still dressed in my suit pants and white shirt. I was asleep before the first results started showing up.

{9}
Changing Tactics

THE PHONE VIBRATING on my desk eventually woke me up. I snatched it up and answered before I looked to see who was calling.

"Hamar."

"Where the hell are you? Your team meeting started ten minutes ago," Darlene snapped at me.

"Damn!" The clock on my computer screen read 9:42. I'd only slept a couple of hours, but I'd forgotten entirely about the team meeting this morning. "Tell them I got caught in traffic. I'll be there in fifteen minutes."

"Wait! Shower, shave, and dress right. It's business casual on Fridays. Slacks, no ties. You can tell them I sent you home to change."

"That's better than traffic?"

"Trust me. Oh. And thanks for the flowers."

"Okay. Half an hour. I'm moving." The line went dead. I stripped and headed for the shower. I took just enough time to shave carefully. I was beginning to get the hang of it, but one bad move and I'd have no facial hair at all. I chose black slacks, a white Oxford shirt, and my gray sweater.

I skipped coffee and was at the office ready to enter the conference room in twenty-eight minutes. I was lucky with the bus. Before I was visible from the conference room windows, Arnie caught up with me and called me to a stop.

"I almost missed you," he said as he pulled me to a stop.

"Sorry, I was rushing to the team meeting. I'm late."

"I know. That's why I'm here. Please don't make a habit of this. You and I have been talking for the past hour. I'll apologize for keeping you away from the meeting."

"Darlene said she'd tell them she sent me home to change clothes."

"That would have worked, but this is more plausible. I didn't come into the office until after the meeting started, so none of them know we weren't together off-site. Just listen closely and follow along." I nodded and Arnie pulled the door open and pushed me through.

"You're late," Jen barked. She halted suddenly as Arnie pushed through behind me.

"My fault," he said. "I intercepted Dag on the way in this morning and asked to go over his report with him. We got into a discussion about the viability of IPv6 as a security mechanism and lost track of time. If Darlene hadn't buzzed us, we'd still be down at the Daybreak." Now why had he suggested that scenario for our discussion? Was he the one who suggested the IP address as 'IGotUrBak' on all those forums? He either had my back this morning or he was changing the game and throwing me to the wolves. It made sense that he might have been the one sending me the message since he hadn't shown up for the beer bash last night. I knew everyone else in the room was with me up until I headed home. I was reluctant to have Arnie as an ally.

"What's IPv6 got to do with IPSec?" Ford asked.

"Ford, you know the answer to that question better than I do. I know you've read the spec. Is this another interview question?" I asked.

Ford grinned at me.

"For the benefit of the Neanderthals," he said.

"Well, technically, the spec only provides for a few gazillion unique web addresses," I said. "Part of the network discovery protocol spec emphasizes the use of IPSec to protect NDP messages, but there's no instruction manual for using it. That means we could be vulnerable to a massive security hole if we don't do some R&D in the next year to eighteen months. It's part of a proposal I'm putting together to attend the IPSec Working Committee Conference coming up in July. Actually Ford, you suggested that in the first place if you recall."

"I'll leave you folks to it, since I've heard all this before. Sorry to have made Dag late for your team meeting."

When Arnie walked out the door, all eyes turned back to me and they started bombarding me with questions. I professed that I'd just come across this information and that I'd been up a good bit of the night exploring an IPv6 site. I watched for reactions to that comment, but no one showed a sign of being complicit. I commented about how orderly everything seemed, but how difficult it was to protect with so many IPv4 portals connecting into it. When we broke up the meeting, it was noon and I'd talked myself hoarse. It was a good thing I'd spent so much time exploring that site last night or I wouldn't have known a thing about what I was talking about. Of course, if I hadn't been up all night trying to break into the site in the first place, I wouldn't have slept late and been late for the meeting.

I went to the cafeteria for lunch and when I sat to eat, Jen pulled up a chair and sat across from me.

"Do you mind?" she asked pleasantly.

"No. Please, have a seat."

"That was a nice bit of work this morning. I fail to see how it's going to be relevant, though," she started in on me. *What's her problem?* "We aren't going to do that R&D here. They'll get around to doing it in Redmond or Silicon Valley and we'll buy a package off the shelf. But, it was still a great way to distract everyone from what you're really doing."

"Why does everyone assume I'm not here to do the job I was hired for?"

"Part of this team's charter is subterfuge. We have projects we work on and show results to each other, but no one on the team is focused on our team. Everyone's up to something."

"Is that official or your personal observation?" I asked. "As the team lead isn't guiding the team your responsibility?"

"My responsibility is to give the team a reason to exist. I have no idea what any of them are really doing."

"Isn't that a little counter-productive?" I looked at her curiously. We hadn't had much one-on-one time since I got here. Last night she'd been affable, but just part of a group. Today she wore her version of business casual, which was a simple skirt that fell just below her knees and a silk blouse with a black camisole keeping her from exposing more than a business-acceptable amount of cleavage. It was quite an appealing look.

"It could be, but I'm inclined to trust my boss on this one. We really do have security problems and pitting our best and brightest minds against each other is one way of pushing them to the limits." She seemed to be assessing me in much the same way. "You know, by the way, that the size tag is still running down your left pants leg?"

I looked down. I hadn't even seen the tag. I wondered if there was one on the other pair I'd bought as well. I stripped the transparent, sticky strip off the leg and folded it up on my tray.

"So now I at least know you wear a 34x36 pair of slacks. Am I going to have to figure out everything else about you the hard way?"

"Why don't you start with what you know and then ask what you want to know?" I asked. "If I can help you, I will."

"Okay. Why did Arnie hire a private investigator?"

Whoa! That was too off the wall to be a random guess.

"What makes you think I'm a P.I.?"

"I'm pretty good at searching for information. I searched state records for your name and discovered your P.I. license."

"You're a pretty good hacker then, too," I said. "Those records aren't open to the public."

"I have my ways."

"Then suffice it to say that anything I'm hired to do as a private investigator is covered under client privilege and I can't say anything about it to anyone, including you."

"Okay. So maybe you could tell me what kind of work you do in your private investigation business so that I will know if I ever need someone," she asked coyly. I'd almost say she was flirting, but perhaps she was just trying to lighten up the mood a little.

"Mostly, I fix computers," I said, trying to make it sound as boring as possible. "I'm also an expert, I suppose, on data recovery. That could either be erased files or damaged media."

"Sounds like a waste of your skills. Who is Lars Anderson?"

"You can't hold an agency license until you have three years of experience in this state. Lars owns the investigative agency that holds my license. He's an old friend from my Navy days." I felt confident in mentioning the Navy since that was on my resume and I was sure she'd read it.

"Why do you need a P.I. license to recover hard drives?"

"I don't, technically. But it gives me latitude to handle investigative cases. Let's say you suspect your husband..."

"I'm not married." That came out rather quickly. She was looking at me intently. I wasn't going to bite.

"Let's say a married woman suspects her husband of hiding assets. In divorce court, she might demand the record of his private email. When the court issues a civil warrant, she discovers the email has all been erased. Her attorney might bring me the computer and ask me to recover the deleted email." I saw her nodding. "It's part of digital forensic science and has very specific practices that have to be adhered to. Since I would be handling legal evidence, I need to be licensed and bonded."

"Fascinating," she smiled. "I could just listen to you talk about digital forensics all day." I could hear the sarcasm in her voice. I knew my description didn't impress her, but I wasn't prepared for what came next. "Why don't we continue the discussion over dinner tonight?"

Damn!

"Um…" I couldn't believe I was almost tongue-tied, but this was definitely going no further. "Do you suppose any of the guys on the team want to ask me out, too? I mean, both women have. It would only be fair for the men to have a chance, too." She went scarlet.

"It was just a friendly invitation," she said coldly. "I think we've covered everything we need to for our one-on-one today, so there's no need to come by my office this afternoon. It's such a nice day, I think I'll knock off and start my weekend early. See you Monday."

She was gone. I was relieved. I didn't even have to tell her I had a date tonight.

<hr/>

WITH MY LACK of sleep for the past two days, the idea of knocking off early was appealing. I headed back to my office and stopped to thank Darlene for covering for me this morning. Her office had enough flowers in it to be a funeral parlor.

"Darlene? Are you in there?"

"Hi Dag. Thank you for the flowers."

"You're welcome, but I didn't send all these."

"I know. Yours got here first thing this morning. I picked them up at reception on my way in," she said. "Just about noon, all the others arrived. One from Allen, one from Don, one from Ford, one from Phil, and even one from Jen. Wasn't that nice of her? Of course, the fact that I paraded your flowers around the office before your meeting this morning, telling everyone how nice you were to have remembered Administrative Professionals Day, might have had something to do with inspiring everyone else. I don't think anyone else had a clue."

"What about Arnie? Didn't he send you flowers?"

"Oh no. I just had a card from him… a little cash card kind of thing to use at Nordstrom." She smiled and I could see exactly how devious a person she was. "This day almost makes putting up with their crap the rest of the year worthwhile." She was definitely being sarcastic. She even rolled her eyes in a way that reminded me of Cali and Mel.

"I'll try to make sure you are shown proper appreciation for all the crap I throw at you. I really do appreciate you running interference. Say, did Arnie tell you the new direction my research is going? I'm afraid it might mean some extra work for you," I said, thinking of all the new security stuff we came up with on the fly.

"Yes. Fortunately, I just make the reports look good. He has to do the research."

"You mean I just caused more work for him?"

"Don't worry, he loves it. It gives him something to look forward to when he's in executive staff meetings and poring over spreadsheets," she paused and looked up at me. "Nice sweater, by the way. Don't you need to go get ready for your big date tonight?" It was only two in the afternoon, but if I could get a nap before faculty lounge, the whole evening would be better.

"I was just stopping to tell you I was taking off for the rest of the day. Frankly, I do some of my best work at night, which was why I overslept this morning."

"Well, if you go home and nap, set an alarm so you'll wake up in time for your date." She waved at me. "Go on!"

I had used the excuse of having a date tonight to such good effect, that I was even beginning to think of the outing with Andi, Mel, and Cali as a date.

I needed to get a handle on that. It was just a thank you for picking up the girls.

{10}
Date Night

EVEN THOUGH SHORT, it had been an intense day and I was exhausted. I stumbled into my apartment, stripped off my clothes and a moment before I went to sleep, followed Darlene's advice and set an alarm. Two hours later it woke me as though I hadn't slept at all.

I stepped into the shower and for good measure shaved again, though my beard can go two days without being noticed. I felt revived and set off at a brisk pace up the hill to the faculty lounge. I nearly tripped over the leash stretched across the sidewalk. The little shih tzu squeaked and, as I came to a precarious stop, began to dance around me. Attached to the other end of the leash was a cute blonde in a yellow sweater and form-emphasizing black leggings. Her high-heeled boots stopped just above the ankle and her smile lit up the block.

"Sorry," I said. "I didn't see the leash."

"They said a dog would help me meet people," She laughed and reached down to pick up the little dog. "I wasn't planning the rope and hogtie method, though. Really, I just got her and we haven't learned to stay together and not block the sidewalk. It's me who should be apologizing."

I smiled back at her. I had seen her in the neighborhood before, but it seemed only recently.

"Are you new in the neighborhood?" I asked politely.

"Just a month. I moved over here especially because it's a pet-friendly neighborhood. I've always wanted a dog."

"Well, you almost got one there," I joked. "You are right, though. There are lots of animal-lovers in the neighborhood. Hang out outside the Analog on Sundays and you'll see lots of them."

"Hmm. Maybe I'll try that. Will I see you?"

"I like the coffee but my building doesn't allow dogs. Have a nice evening."

"Ta-ta. See you around."

Get it together, Dag. She wasn't flirting. She did have the right idea, though. Pets in this neighborhood were magnets. Two people walking dogs meet and if the dogs like each other, the people become a couple. It's unbelievable.

When I moved into the neighborhood a few years ago, Eric tried to convince me to get a pet. Then I met his cats. Two three-legged cats. It was my official introduction to pet-crazy Capitol Hill. Every time I saw the poor things, though, I thought about Velcroing them together.

I finally got up to the Blue Bastion and realized I was huffing. I was obviously not getting enough exercise. *You're getting old, Dag.* I stood around outside waiting for my heart to get back to normal. I spotted Andi at the table with our crew and my heart sped up again. We'd known each other how long? Six years? Almost seven? It must be the fact that I turned down two sure dates and one open flirtation to spend the evening with her and two seventeen-year-olds that was making my body react this way. Maybe I did need to get a pet.

Jan's wife Donna had joined the group this evening. Donna works in a real estate office, but she makes it a practice to 'hang with the intelligentsia' at least once a month. Lisa was there, of course, and so was Sara Gates, a musician who teaches music theory at PCAD during the week and plays in a Celtic fiddle band on weekends. Her boyfriend, Sandy tends bar during the week at a nearby watering hole and joins her in the band on the weekends if he isn't pressured into working. I recognized Laura Hersey sitting next to Andi. Laura is another English prof but seldom joins us for the lounge.

Laura greeted me first and stood to kiss me on each cheek. She'd spent the summer in Italy two years ago and hadn't stopped kissing people since.

"Dag! I heard you weren't teaching this year. They still let you come to the faculty lounge?" she asked.

"We grandfathered him in," Jan said. "There's still a chance he'll come back to teaching."

"Not a very big chance, I'm afraid," I answered. "Haven't you heard? I've got a day job now."

"You had a day job when you started teaching if I recall," Andi smiled. "That didn't stop you from getting a job at the college. Or from dating your students." The smile turned to a smirk. Everyone at the table knew the story of Hope's and my romance and its disastrous conclusion. What most of them didn't know was that I'd ended up putting her new husband behind bars and that she was now living in Costa Rica.

"I know, I know," I said. "I learned my lesson. Never date a person less than half your age…"

"Plus seven," they joined in.

"So, tonight I'm going out with two women," I added.

"Two?" Andi asked. "There are supposed to be three of us."

"Yes, but I have to add Cali and Mel together in order to get them over 30!"

"So, are you two seeing each other now?" Laura asked. Andi blushed a little. *Damn!* Maybe I did, too. We stumbled over each other explaining how I'd rescued the girls on Wednesday and they insisted on taking me to the movies tonight. Then we got involved in a lengthy discussion of the indie film we were seeing tonight and the upcoming Seattle International Film Festival line-up. We laughed and talked while we ate our burgers.

"Spring is here," Andi declared at last. "Let's have a barbecue tomorrow. We can commandeer my front yard for the grill and spread out into the park across the street. Can you all make it?" There was general agreement and by the time we had compiled the guest list and who was inviting whom and who was bringing what, it was time to catch our ride to the theater. Melissa pulled up in front of the Blue Bastion at exactly seven with Cali in the seat beside her.

"Cali, let Dag have the front seat. His legs are longer," Andi said as she opened the back door.

"That's okay," I said. "It's only a few blocks. We could have walked it. I can ride in back for that distance. Besides, I'm sure Mel wants to pay me back for folding her up in the back seat of the Mustang."

"It was great," Mel gushed. "I couldn't believe you had the top down. Everybody at school was *so* jealous."

"Mel kept trying to tell everyone that you were her boyfriend."

"Oh no!" I said in mock horror.

"Yeah. When that didn't work, I told them you were really Cali's long lost daddy and you'd come to spoil her senseless."

"Mel, you didn't!" Andi and Cali exclaimed at the same time.

"Just kidding," she sang. It really was only a few blocks to the theater and Mel pulled up outside. "I'll drop you guys off and go find a parking spot."

"Yeah. Here's your tickets. You don't have to wait for us to go in. We'll be there in a jiff," Cali said handing the tickets to her mother as I held the door open for her. They waved as they pulled away from the curb and turned down Broadway.

"I guess they don't want to be seen with the adults," Andi said as we went inside. I bought a bucket of popcorn but we both decided to forgo the massively overpriced drinks. If I drank one of their large sodas, I wouldn't be able to concentrate on the movie. Speaking of which, I gave Andi the popcorn and excused myself to go use the restroom.

When I got back, I found Andi with her cell phone in hand staring at the screen. That reminded me to silence mine, which I did as I sat down. Andi continued to look at the screen and then turned sharply toward me.

"We've been set up." She showed me the text message on her phone.

"Mom, we're going to see *Mad Men* at the Neptune. We'll see you at McHenry's for pizza after the show. Enjoy your date!"

"Oh," I said. What could I say? *Oh, gee! Let's leave? I don't want to date you?* We'd met for lunches before. We hung out together with our friends. Why should this be any different? "What do you want to do?" I asked. She snapped her phone off muttering that she'd deal with her daughter later. Then she turned to look me square in the eyes.

"I haven't been on a date in ages," she said, smiling. She reached over and took my hand, holding it firmly in her own. "I'm going to enjoy myself."

That sounded like a really good plan to me.

⸻⸻⸻

THE MOVIE WAS enjoyable. It was about what you'd expect eight to twelve-year-old superheroes to come up with—belching toxic gas and walking on their hands. And for just an instant—when most needed—their pretend superpowers became real. It was sweet, innocent, and a really good date movie. After the movie we walked over to McHenry's and found a quiet table for four. We ordered a small pizza and a couple of cokes. We figured we'd let the girls order their own when they got there. Andi and I had been laughing about the movie ever since we left the theater and talking about how literature, movies, music, and art didn't have to be great to be enjoyed.

"So what's your superpower, Dag Hamar?" she asked me. Now I was on the spot. I could code a cyberattack in under two hours? No. I needed something just ridiculous enough that it fit with the movie, but still be something that I could actually do. Now the Navy had taught me one trick my shipmates had said always got the girls' attention in bars. I practiced until I could do it. Then I tried it out. The results were unspectacular, but it was all I had to go with.

"I can tie a cherry stem in a knot with my tongue," I answered with a straight face. I could see her face fall. I was afraid it was too coarse.

"Oh?" A long pause. Her eyes got wide. "Oh!"

"Now, Ms. Marx," I pressed before she could question me further. "What is your superpower?" I could see the wheels turning in her head.

"Hmm. I can swim two lengths of the pool underwater." I did some quick calculations.

"That would mean you can hold your breath for…"

"A little less than two minutes—while exercising."

"Oh?" It was my turn to be taken aback. "Oh!"

Had we just inadvertently changed our relationship? All these years we'd been friends, I'd never felt there was anything I couldn't talk to Andi about. I'd been a wreck when Hope left me and Andi was both sage and comforter. She'd told me about hard problems she had as a single parent and I'd listened and given support—even babysitting when Cali was younger. We'd each come through our various crises intact. Our friendship had continued to get stronger. We'd teased each other, but we'd never crossed the line into openly flirting. They say that love, like murder, requires means, motive, and opportunity. Since I'd known Andi, there'd never been a time when all three of those came together. Until…

"Where are those girls?" Andi said suddenly. She pulled her cell phone out. "I didn't turn my phone on after the movie." As soon as the phone came to life, it chimed with a text message. She read it and smiled. "Little minx," she whispered. She held the phone out for me to see the message.

"Mom, I've got really bad cramps so I had Mel drop me off at home. Don't hurry. I'm fine. Hope you enjoy your date."

"I am, you know." she said as we left the restaurant and started the walk down the hill toward our homes.

"Am what?"

"Enjoying my date." She slipped her hand back into mine and reached across with her other hand to hold my upper arm while she hugged herself close to me.

"Are you cold?" I asked.

"It's a little brisk," she confessed. I extracted my arm, pulled my jacket off and wrapped it around her. Then I took her hand in my left and wrapped my other arm around her shoulders. She reached up to hold the hand on her shoulder and we walked on in a promenade. Unless you are dancing, that particular position means that you move slowly. That was just fine for both of us.

▭▯▮▯▭▮▯▭▮▯▭▮▯▭▮▯▭▮▯▭▮▯

A KISS IS really a simple thing. The popular movie kiss is all tongues fighting with each other. But a kiss isn't about the tongue. It's the lips—soft, warm, welcoming lips that hold you with no more effort than the lightest touch. The tongue might convey passion, but the lips reveal true emotion.

We stood on her front porch like two teenagers experiencing a kiss for the first time—neither of us willing to break the contact, but softly caressing the mouth of a new love, wrapped up in the sensation of some ten thousand nerve endings making contact with each other for the first time.

We looked into each other's eyes as we touched our lips together, neither of us certain how the other would respond. I watched Andi's eyelids slowly drift closed and then felt the tip of her tongue caress every one of those nerves. Our tongues touched and then darted back into our own mouths, leaving our lips together for another brief eternity.

She pulled away, slowly, then handed me my jacket. I'd forgotten I'd worn one. She sighed and then she whispered, "Goodnight."

"Goodnight," I said. I backed up off her porch and crossed the postage stamp yard to the alley where I mounted the back stairs to the third floor. I savored her kiss, a smile still on my lips where hers had so recently played. I turned and looked back down from the third floor landing before I went into the building. Andi was still standing there looking up at me, smiling. We stood a moment, connected by our eyes and then she waved and went into her house.

I stood there lost in thought; my hand lifted toward where she'd been. I turned and unlocked the door. I caught a glimpse of myself in the bathroom mirror as I hung up my coat. I'd almost become used to the naked face now, but I hadn't seen that silly grin on it since I was a teenager.

I was falling in love.

{11}
A New Client

THE BRUNETTE IN front of me at the Analog had her hair pulled up in a Saturday-morning-and-I-don't-care knot on top of her head. I saw her often. You get to recognize people in a neighborhood like this. Usually, her hair fell straight below her shoulders and was brushed so silkily shiny you could almost see through it. This morning, as she leaned on the counter chatting with our friendly barista, she was wearing a short jeans jacket that left several inches of grey t-shirt exposed, cutting enticingly across her butt over black skin-tight jeans. Her white socks were pulled up over the legs above her Converse high tops, nearly to her calves. I was noticing everything female and feminine this morning, as if my own senses had just been awakened to the opposite sex. But even when she turned away from the counter and looked at me with a smile almost as big as the bag slung over one shoulder, my mind was on Andi.

The barista, Lonnie, had already started pulling my regular double short Americano and kept up a running conversation asking me how my weekend was going and how the new job was working out. Seems that everyone knows a little about everyone in this town—especially Lonnie. His sandy hair and two-day beard were as much a part of the atmosphere here as the fact that he pulled the best shots on Capitol Hill. I'd just answered with a quick, "Fine," when I felt two delicate hands cover my eyes and a voice whisper "Guess who."

My heart skipped a couple beats and instead of answering I reached up and slid the hands down to my lips and kissed the fingertips. "Morning," I said softly as I turned toward her.

If my heart had skipped beats before, it stopped cold now.

"So that's how it is?"

"Cali! I… I'm sorry. I thought…" *Damn!*

"I know. You thought I was Mom. Must have been a pretty good date last night." I was still spluttering. The last thing I wanted was for anyone here to think I was involved with a seventeen-year-old. How could I have not realized it wasn't Andi?

"Here's your coffee, Dag," Lonnie said.

"Did you want anything?" I asked Cali. My voice cracked and I realized the question could be interpreted in different ways.

"Tall mocha, please." Lonnie turned and made the drink while I slid money across the counter. There were a few stools at a bar under the corner windows and a church pew cobbled together into a corner seat opposite. On the rough wooden table, a selection of fringe comic books were scattered among the remains of today's newspaper. Cali picked up her drink and I waved off the change Lonnie offered me. We stepped outside and sat at one of the sidewalk tables, taking advantage of the fourth sunny April day in a row. Sunny April. Now, that was an oxymoron.

"Where's your mom?" I asked.

"Still asleep with a smile on her face that covers the entire pillow. I just had to make sure the feeling was mutual."

"That was really wicked of you."

"Surprising you this morning?"

"That, and setting up that little date last night. You don't look like a girl with cramps."

"Oh, they come and go. And it worked, didn't it? You really are dating now, right?" She was a little anxious, but all I could do was grin.

"I certainly hope so."

"Good!" We sat sipping our coffees for a minute. I have a hard time concentrating on anything else when I'm drinking my first cup of coffee in the morning. Years ago, when I got out of the Navy, I adopted the Seattle fascination with lattes. But somewhere along the line I realized that I didn't really like milk that much. It didn't make sense to force myself to drink milk by flavoring it with coffee when what I really liked was the coffee. That first cup in the morning—the hotter, the stronger, the blacker, the better. Cali's big sigh cut through my momentary reverie.

"I need a fake ID."

"Excuse me?"

This girl could knock me for a loop with a word. How the heck did her mother manage?

"Do you know how to get a fake ID? I'd hire you to get me one."

"Cali, that's illegal. Besides which there are reasons for the laws against underage drinking. Your body isn't equipped to handle alcohol at your age and especially at your size." I realized I had adopted the tone of a lecturing parent and I cringed in spite of myself.

"Oh, really! If I wanted to get drunk I'd have said, 'I need a bottle of booze,' or something. What do you think I am? I don't drink and I don't do drugs. I don't do a lot of other stuff, either, not that it's any of your business."

"Ok, sorry," I said. This was my girlfriend's daughter and I really needed to think about keeping lines of communication open. Hmm… Girlfriend. I liked the sound of that and just hoped it was true. It could be a long-term thing. "Why do you think you need a fake ID?"

"Because all the good music venues are twenty-one and older. I can't get in to see any of the bands I want to see. It's just so unfair." Music? She wanted a fake ID so she could go to concerts? Man, I really had to catch up with the times. But right now, I had to sympathize while still steering her clear of the notion of doing something illegal and stupid.

My coursework with Lars included a lot of information on covert operations. That was his Navy Intelligence background and he required it of his staff. Twenty years ago he'd taught me how to create a second skin as he called it. Yes, I had a driver's license, credit cards, social security number, and even a passport locked in a safe deposit box at the bank that had my picture but a different identity. It took years of planning and maintenance to establish a good cover, and secrecy above all else. Lars had suggested that he would be assigning the same task for his undercover operations class in the fall. Not even he knew I had maintained my cover identity all these years.

Today, I knew, college kids were ordering passable IDs on-line from an 'entertainment' company in China. They wouldn't stand up to careful government scrutiny, but most bouncers couldn't tell the difference and even the police had stumbled over finding the telltale marks.

"I see the problem," I said calmly. "Do any of your friends have these or is this your own solution?" She looked at me a little warily.

"Maybe."

I've got to learn to ask one question at a time. I just waited.

"It just seemed like an easy way to get in to see the groups I want to see. All the cutting edge music gets played in bars after ten. Even when there's an all-age venue, they usually cut it off before the good stuff comes on. And Mel said—well, she sort of suggested it would work because…"

Andi had told me a few days ago to just be quiet and listen and I'd learn a lot. The wild child of ultra-strict parents, who got permission to go to the movies last night because it was a PG film and she'd be with Andi, Cali, and me but then went to an R movie when she ditched us, used whatever means she needed to stretch her wings. I assumed that meant she had already acquired a fake ID.

"Oh, poo! It was a stupid idea and I told Mel that to start with. Here. I won't be needing these." She pushed a computer printout of tickets across the table to me. I listen to a lot of music when I'm alone in my room. This was one of my favorite groups, playing at an over-twenty-one venue next Friday. "I'm sure you could find *someone* to go with you," she smirked.

I'd been had again! She couldn't keep the smile off her face; her eyes were so bright you could hear the laughter. This whole ID thing was just… Well, maybe there was some truth to it, but that wasn't the point.

I became just as devious.

"Wow. Thanks, Cali. I'll pay you for them. There's this lady at the office who kinda dropped some hints—"

Cali's expression collapsed on her face and she reached to snatch back the tickets, but I held the paper back out of reach. I grinned at her.

"You!" she snarled before breaking down in a fit of giggling. After she settled down, she looked me in the eye and I could tell she was a little worried. "You won't hurt her, will you?"

I knew the question was coming from the heart of a girl who loved her mother more than anything in the world and was truly trying to make her happy.

"Cali, whether we are dating or not, I would never intentionally do anything to hurt her. Or you." Her expression relaxed. "But wait a minute," I said. "These tickets are for Friday. Doesn't your show open Friday night?"

"Mmm. Yeah, so I guess I couldn't have used them anyway, huh."

"But don't you want your mom at opening night?"

"Well, it's gonna be a big flop and I'd rather you guys came Saturday instead of Friday. I couldn't think of any other way to kind of tell Mom and you not to come to opening." She shook her head and smiled as if it were the most logical thing in the world.

I glanced at my cell phone for the time and stood up.

"I need to get to work so I'm back in time for the barbecue this evening." She looked at me skeptically.

"You're going to work looking like that? Didn't you just buy new clothes?"

"I'm just going up to my office on 15th. I'm not going into EFC."

"Okay. That's good, I'll walk up there with you."

"Maybe we should get a cup of coffee to take to your mom."

"Maybe we should just let her sleep. It looked like she was having really nice dreams." I chuckled and nodded my head, dropped my coffee cup in the compost bin, and turned up the street.

"Why are you headed up the hill?"

"Well, for one, I'm going to rehearsal. It's wet tech today and I have to be a living body under the lights. It takes me about an hour to get to the theater by bus, but it's a little quicker if I catch the one on 15th. And for another thing, I'm not done talking to you yet." She had her shoulder bag slung over her back and held onto it with one hand while she continued to slurp her drink rather noisily through a straw. I was carrying only my laptop, so I offered to carry her bag. "Aren't you a schoolboy! Thank you Dag." I wasn't sure I liked that, but when I picked up her bag, I regretted the offer.

"What do you carry in this?"

"My life. My life. My life."

"You should consider only carrying one."

We walked up most of the hill in silence. That's pretty normal for me. As often as I walk the ten blocks to my office, I still get winded. Walking to an office ten blocks away was supposed to get me in shape. I guess I needed to go there more often. Carrying her bag didn't help.

"Dag, you really are a private detective, aren't you?" We were almost to my office when she popped that question out.

"I'm licensed."

"Do you have a lot of… what do you call it? Caseload?"

"I have a couple of clients. The office downtown is pretty much full-time right now."

"Could you take another?"

"I often take multiple clients. You can't really work non-stop on most projects. You have to give them time to sit sometimes."

"I'd like to hire you."

That threw me. I looked at her as we went up the steps to my little office and I unlocked the door. Cali was a little shorter than Andi—about five-three. As long as I'd known her, she'd been blonde, but occasionally she put a temporary rinse in her hair to try something different. Like most teens I'd known in my life, Cali could go from frivolous to intense in three-tenths of a second. It didn't pay to take what she said lightly.

"Come in and tell me about your problem, Miss Marx," I said seriously.

I had no idea what she wanted, but it was obvious that she was serious and I didn't want to brush her off. If I was going to date the mother, it behooved me to stay in the daughter's good graces. She sat down across my desk from me. I decided my best bet was just to wait and let her take her time. Finally, she started.

"Okay. Here it is. My mom lied to me. God, that sounds terrible. I don't mean it to sound so serious, but she told me something that I found out wasn't true and I really want to know why and I want to know the truth, but I don't dare confront her with it because I'm afraid she'll be hurt by the fact that I didn't trust her. I'll keep whatever I find out a secret and will never let her know. But it's about me and I just have to find out."

Once the floodgates were open, Cali was off and running. All I had to do was give her a little nudge occasionally to keep the story flowing.

"My mom was totally in love with my dad. She was in college when they met and he swept her off her feet. He was a salesman, but not a sleazy one. He was really nice and so outgoing. He loved to party and took Mom to all kinds of nice places. They were married during her senior year in college and she got pregnant almost immediately. Just after graduation, he took her to a big convention and was showing off his young beautiful wife who was very pregnant. Then, all of a sudden he just collapsed. He died in her arms with a smile on his lips, a martini in his hand, and me in her tummy. Mom never married again. In fact, she's hardly ever dated anyone. She just takes care of me."

"I've heard the story before. It's very sweet."

"Yeah. Except it isn't true."

I was taken aback. We all knew the story of Andi's tragic marriage. Cali started rummaging around in her bag.

"One of the sophomore U.S. History projects in school last year was to compile a family tree. I asked Mom for help and she kind of stalled. The next day after school, she pulls out a box of papers and says everything I needed should be in that box. It had her marriage certificate, birth certificate, my birth certificate and some papers about her parents and grandparents. It went back three generations. Just three! Then everything was listed as unknown, or 'came from Germany,' or some stuff. It was pretty pathetic. So I decided I'd try to push it back a little further. I did a bunch of searches and sure enough I found more information. I thought it would be cool to show it all to Mom, so I was going to do this big family tree for Christmas and I thought I'd try to get something that would help, so I started searching around and posted some things on a college site trying to get a copy of her senior yearbook. I managed to buy one for like twenty dollars, but it cost about as much to ship it to me." She finally pulled a black and gold yearbook out of her bag. She plopped it on my desk as if I was supposed to know what to look for.

"Here," she said, opening the yearbook to the senior pictures pages. I glanced down the pictures. There were about 400 of them.

"What am I looking for?" I asked.

"Anne Doreen Sullivan."

"Was that your mom's maiden name?" Now I got it. Anne Doreen. Anne D. Andi. Cute nickname.

"It's what was on her birth certificate."

I kept scanning down the pages. There she was. Anne Doreen Sullivan.

"I don't think that's your mom, Cali."

"Not unless I'm some kind of albino black person," she said. "But she's got a diploma and everything. Why would she lie about something like this? I can't find her picture in the stupid yearbook at all, under any name and I've looked at every single picture. I thought I was just going to find more about my mom, but now I don't know who my mother really is. That means I don't know who I am." Cali's eyes were glistening.

This had been eating at her for a year. She hadn't told anyone about it. It must have taken a lot of courage for her to tell me about it. I wasn't sure what I'd done to deserve that trust. And I wasn't sure that I wanted the information she'd just given me.

"Cali, I don't think I can do this."

"I need to know. I keep thinking of all the terrible things that it could be and *nothing* you find out could be that bad."

"Cali, what you have is a thread of information. It could have been a mistake on the part of the yearbook staff—putting the wrong picture in the book—even a practical joke. Maybe that's why your mom didn't have one already. But whenever you find the end of a string, there's another end somewhere. You have to be ready to deal with all the tangles between them."

"I'm sorry, Dag. I love my mom. Nothing in the world would ever make me stop loving her. And I would never, ever, do anything to hurt her. But it's driving me crazy. I have to know."

There was no question now. She was dripping tears even though she was holding her voice steady.

"I shouldn't do this, Cali."

"If you don't, I'll find some sleazy detective on-line and pay him. But I trust you, Dag."

"Let me think about it. This could be very painful for all of us. I might not be... well, my relationship with Andi isn't like yours, but I care for her very much. And for you. If she has maintained a false identity for all your life, there's not much chance that I'll find anything."

"I understand. You have a contract?" That took me by surprise. "I want this to be clear that I hired you. I have two hundred dollars I can give you in advance. If it costs more, I'll find a way to pay you."

We'd gone from zero to ninety in a heartbeat. I wanted to just refuse her money, but she was determined and I really didn't want her finding an investigator online. I'd find a way to get the money back to her. I pulled out a standard contract and made a couple of edits lowering my standard rate by half and estimating about half the hours I figured it would actually take if I did anything. There wouldn't be any further payments and maybe I could refund some of her money legitimately. She signed the document and handed me the two hundred dollars. I signed the receipt and gave her a copy along with fifty dollars in change.

"What's that for?"

"To pay for the tickets. You may be conniving to get Andi and me together, but I can pay for my own dates."

"Okay," she said, reluctantly. "Now if you could just tell me what my evil friend is up to for prom, I'd feel great."

"Does Mel have a surprise for you?"

"I suppose so. She's insisting I get a prom dress, even though I don't have a date and really am not interested. I'm afraid she's going to embarrass me to death."

"Oh, surely she wouldn't do anything to embarrass you. You've been friends for what, ten years?"

"Yeah, but she's really getting weird. I know her parents bug her, but I'm getting kind of worried about her. And I'm afraid she's going to try to fix me up with one of her freaky on-line friends or something. Some days—"

She stopped with a quick intake of breath, realizing that she was talking too much and not really wanting to put her friend down.

"Cali, if there's something that's genuinely worrying you then you should say something to your mom or to Mel's mom. I know they are strict, but they do love her."

"I know. I can't just betray her confidence though. It wouldn't be right."

It amazes me how the teenage mind works. She wasn't going to betray her best friend's confidence because that would be against some unwritten code that said it wouldn't be right, but she wanted to dig into her mother's secret. I was thinking that maybe I should talk to Andi about all this myself. But even if I didn't say anything, I was definitely going to check up on Mel and make sure Cali was safe.

{12}
Broken Idols

I HAD WORK TO do. I'd been so caught up in sleeplessness, office politics, and relational bliss for the past thirty hours that I'd not yet examined the results of my search for the cyberbully. Once Cali left my office to go to rehearsal, I settled in. Working at the office has advantages since I have a lot more computing power there.

I pulled the drapes and turned out the lights. I cranked up the music and started following my leads. It wasn't quite as dark as the apartment, but the level of adrenaline I felt pumping through my veins as I plunged into Philanthropolis was enough to block out all distractions.

IP ADDRESSES ARE assigned to devices participating in a network, in this instance, the World Wide Web. Philanthropolis was hosted on multiple computers, with backup and mirroring on dozens more. Many of those computers functioned as virtual devices, meaning they answered to several different addresses, and pretended to be wholly different devices for each one. When I added in the problem that Philanthropolis was a composite of numerous organizations and domains that had been grouped together, I was dealing with a problem of incredible proportions. My automated searches, however, led me deeper into this morass than I thought possible.

The domain my searches all seemed to lead to was a massive structure in its own right. It housed such a reputable charitable organization that my first inclination was to ignore it and look elsewhere. I didn't even want my search to lead me here. Not only is the Internet a great place to find things, it is a great place to hide things. The cyberbully I was after wanted to stay hidden.

Off the main portal I entered an antechamber that held a number of awards and certificates of appreciation. Each award and certificate could open a portal into the organization that issued it. That wasn't where my spider was leading, though. In the back of the room was an unmarked passage and that is where I went.

The momentary disorientation of crossing from room to room was caused by the shift from domain to domain. This was leading me now through different countries as well. Being immersed in the U.S. Internet structure, it is sometimes easy for me to forget that there are over two hundred different domain suffixes, many specific to countries. Some countries found it profitable at the dawn of the Internet to sell domain names at prices significantly lower than the familiar U.S. domain names. Tonga—dot-TO—was a popular place for teens to get domains in the nineties because they charged only ten dollars to register. In the U.S. at that time, domains were $80 per year. I found that there was still a sizable market in country-specific domains available.

It's common for a major company to buy the .com, .org, and .net domains for their businesses. International organizations often buy up the country specific domains in which they do business. But why would an organization that doesn't have a business presence in a country own a domain in that country? There is no regulation regarding who can own a domain. If you want to contact the President, go to whitehouse.gov. If you go to whitehouse.net, you will find a parody owned by a couple of comedians. There are thousands of ways to hide on the Internet.

Buried in a backroom of an organization that didn't exist in a politically turbulent African nation, I found the name of an owner. I'd been at it for two hours, but now that I had one, following the spiders to a dozen others went more quickly. I compiled search criteria for each of the names I found and sent the spiders out again. This time, I dove into the data.

The Internet is a real place to me, with real people, buildings, streets, and rooms. When I'm searching as I was now, it's as if I am driving, walking, or running down those streets. A casual observer would see me mesmerized in front of my computer, tapping out commands on my keyboard as thousands of lines of code fly by. I learned a long time ago that I couldn't comprehend what I saw as the lines scrolled across the screen. What I looked for were anomalies. If I saw string of numbers—for example: 1', 3', 7', 10", 15', 22', 47"—I would immediately recognize that the 10 and 47 were out of order. All the other numbers are in feet. The 10 and 47 are in inches and should be ordered first and fourth in the list. Many computer programs could not even put them in ascending order of the numbers that a human would recognize. It's just how my brain works. Matching a single word, phrase, or string on the fly or spotting one that is out of order is less difficult for me than sitting down to study a segment of code in detail. I could see the difference as though driving down a street of bungalows and spotting the Taj Mahal.

IN SIX HOURS, I had seventeen names—aliases for the same person. I sat back at my desk shaking. I hadn't eaten, drunk, or gone to the bathroom. My neck, arms, and back were cramped and my head was throbbing. I pushed myself away from the computer in disgust and went to relieve myself. I washed my hands and then washed them again. I looked at myself in the mirror. Tears were running out of my eyes and I splashed water on my face to wash them away. I glanced into my office and just pulled the door closed and locked it. I couldn't face looking at the screen again. I left the building, locked the door and wished I could burn it down rather than face what I'd left inside.

I'd walked two blocks before I grabbed my cell phone out of my pocket I wanted to call John Patterson and tell him someone was spoofing his identity. As if he'd pick up a call from a nobody gamer. But somehow I didn't believe it was a spoof. I angrily punched in the speed-dial command for Jordan. It was his private phone, not the office, and he picked up on second ring.

"Dag! How's the undercover adventure going? Put them straight yet?"

"It's going okay, Jordan, but I need to talk to you about something else. I've got another client." I quickly described my encounter with Daniel and his father, the bullying on the Internet forums and my searches through cyberspace. I skimmed through my adventures in Philanthropolis. Jordan knew I dealt with searches and results; he didn't know what my mental imagery was.

"The net result is that I've found something that I can't handle, Jordan. This is a job for the police." I was still having trouble getting to the point. I didn't want to believe what I'd found. I didn't want any of it to be true. The work on credit card fraud, in fact my whole obsession with thieves, seemed insignificant and mundane.

"Dag, you know I have a lot of sympathy for victims of cyberbullying, but mostly we have to tell them to cancel their accounts and stay away from the Internet for a while. We've got a caseload that's too big to handle as it is. The chance we could make charges stick on a case of bullying are remote. You're better off trying to get the school to take disciplinary action."

"Jordan." I measured my words carefully. "We don't have a cyberbully. We've got a predator. And he's high up the food chain."

I GOT TO Andi's house at half past four with the barbecue slated to start at five-thirty. I'd promised I would come to get the grill going. The police had been to my office and my computers—in fact, my whole office—had been impounded. The entire trace on my searches was subject to rules of evidence and they had to certify that I broke no laws in finding what I had. As far as I knew, I hadn't even encountered a security measure that might be considered suspect. I don't maintain data on my computers, and the police only had warrants for what was resident on the computer itself. Besides, Jordan was leading the investigation and I knew he would be circumspect, so I felt safe having the police in control of my office.

But I was totally drained. The discovery left me doubting basic humanity.

Four teenaged boys. God knew how many others had been near. But three had been lured away from their families and later found mutilated and dead. The fourth had never been found. The messages had come, first flaming them on the Internet, destroying their friendships, warning them away from certain parks, restaurants, bars, and—finally—one offering help. The boys had sought out the kind voice, and gone to meet with the friend. They'd never been seen again. It was never about sex or orientation. Like always, it was about power—about winning. To him, it was *just a game*.

I'D BEEN LOOKING forward to seeing Andi ever since I left her last night. In fact, even in the depths of the discoveries I'd made, I had flashes of her smile flit across my mind—tastes of her lips on my lips. Then I was standing at her door. I raised my hand to knock, but couldn't bring myself to do it. I felt so foul, just having discovered what I did.

The door opened before I'd had time to retreat. She stood there, smiling at me, welcoming me into her home and into her arms. We both had a moment's hesitation before we lost ourselves in the embrace. I smothered myself in her hair, yearning to wipe away all the memories of the day past and start again from where I kissed her last night.

She seemed of like mind and when our embrace loosened, she raised her lips and sought mine.

We were still tentative. The newness of this relationship was still overwhelming and neither of us wanted to miss one bit of the way it developed. She stepped back away from me and looked me in the eye. She must have seen the fatigue and pain there. Her eyes fell.

"Are you okay?" she faltered. "Are *we* okay?" *My God!* She thought my fatigue and pain were because of her! I hastened to correct her.

"*We* are great. *We* are the best thing about my day. *We* are just beginning. *I*, on the other hand, just had a very bad day."

"Oh dear. Poor baby. Did the bad guys get away?"

"Not yet." She took my hand and I followed her into the living room where we sat down together on the sofa. She cuddled up next to me, an intimacy we hadn't dared express before today.

"Tell me about it." I couldn't give her specifics because of police investigations. I told her of the boy and father who had come to me, about getting a clue about where to look for the cyberbully, and then about the revelation of the predator and involvement of the police. Like the boy's father, Andi wanted to go directly to her computer and pull the plug out of the wall. She stroked my cheek and soothed me and in a moment we were kissing again. I didn't think we'd break this time. I was breathless when our lips parted. She was scarcely breathing heavily when she pushed me lightly away.

"We have company coming," she said softly.

"It's a good thing," I answered, breathing deeply.

"We need to get ready. Uh… I bought a treat for you. There are ginger snaps on the kitchen counter."

I confess; I've had a weakness for ginger snaps for years. When I was a little kid, my dad carried ginger snaps in his lunch. Three. It was really no problem for a big Swede like my dad to eat his lunch and polish it off with three ginger snaps and a big cup of black coffee. But every once in a while, Dad would bring one home in his lunch pail. He'd catch me up in his arms and say, "I went fishing today."

"What did you catch?" I'd ask.

"A ginger fish." I'd wrinkle up my nose. "I made it into a cookie. Want to try it?" I'd pretend to be doubtful, but nod. Out of the pail he would pull the one last ginger snap and offer it to me. My eyes would light up and I'd take a bite. If I was very lucky, Dad would pour the last spoonful of coffee out of his thermos and I'd sip it as if I, too, were working on the docks like my father. Ginger snaps have had a special place on my taste buds ever since.

I went into the kitchen, intent on grabbing a couple cookies before I lit the coals in the grill. I glanced around, finally lighting upon a cookie jar under the cabinets. I lifted the lid and reached in for a couple of cookies and pulled out two foil packets. I thought it must be a new brand of cookie that was individually wrapped, but when I looked in my hand, I froze. I heard a sudden intake of breath behind me and spun to see Andi with her hand over her mouth and her eyes wide. I quickly shoved the condoms back in the cookie jar and put the lid on.

"Cookies," I whispered. My mouth was dry and my voice cracked.

"On this counter," Andi squeaked. She pointed at an unopened bag on the opposite counter.

"Sorry. I didn't mean to… I thought… I just… I'll go start the coals."

"They're Cali's!" she almost shouted. My jaw dropped and I rushed out into the yard. I'm sure I used more lighter fluid on the coals than is strictly legal in the City of Seattle.

◆◆◆◆◆◆◆◆◆◆◆◆◆◆◆◆◆◆◆◆◆◆◆◆

"So Dag got the surprise of his life when he reached into the cookie jar!" Everyone started laughing. I blushed, but was thankful that Andi had not included the part about how embarrassed we both were. The story was shared by several people who had been in at the actual start.

"We invited Andi and Cali over to join us one weekend. What was that? Five years ago? Cali was twelve or thirteen. There were eight of us total and we were playing Pictionary with two teams of four," Jan started. "It was Cali's turn to draw."

"She looked at the card and just stared at it for the longest time and we started saying, 'Cali we can't guess if you don't draw. You should have seen Andi's face as the drawing took shape," added Laura. "Eyes wide and mouth hanging open."

"She drew a penis!" Andi said.

"Not just a penis," Jan continued. "A textbook quality illustration of a flaccid penis. Circumcised. There were a few guesses, but we just knew there was no way it could be one of the words any of us was thinking."

"The thing is that she didn't stop there. She drew a line around the whole thing, balls and all, and closed it like a circle," Laura said. "It was definite that she was calling specific attention to the genitalia. Thank God, someone noticed the sand had run out of the timer!"

"Andi said, 'Cali, honey, let me see your word, please.' When she looked at it she almost choked!"

"The word was 'rubber'," Andi laughed. "I said, 'Oh, I see, honey. But a rubber is usually put on an erect penis and doesn't cover the testicles, too.'"

"Cali got embarrassed, which is what we were all trying not to do to her, and she said, 'Well how was I to know? They told us about them in health, but I've never actually seen one!' Everyone was howling by this time, and I was wiping the tears out of my eyes.

"The thing is," Andi said, "I realized that what they call Sex Ed in Middle School simply isn't. They were tossing out a bunch of crap and not really explaining what anything meant. So I decided to take matters into my own hands, so to speak, and teach her myself. I bought a pack of condoms and explained them to her. We practiced rolling them onto a ketchup bottle. It kind of got started as a joke and I'd leave a condom randomly around the house. If she didn't find it while we were cleaning, I'd make her clean again. Then, I told her that she'd never have to feel embarrassed talking to me about that again and if the time ever came when she actually needed one, she would know there was a supply in the house. We finally decided to put them in the cookie jar and over the years we just kept adding to them. When she turned sixteen, I made her go to the drugstore and buy one herself so she would know it was okay. That one went in the cookie jar, too."

So that was what I'd walked into. A cookie jar full of condoms that six of the guests tonight already knew about.

"You should probably check the expiration dates on them," Jan said. "It wouldn't do to have her get one in an emergency and then have it fall apart."

"They have expiration dates?" Andi exclaimed.

"Yeah. I knew a guy who put one in his wallet when he was a freshman in high school because he had heard guys should always be prepared. Boy Scout I think. Anyway, he didn't get a chance to use it until he was a senior in college. When he pulled it out it was torn to shreds."

"That was probably just from being in his wallet for that long."

"Maybe I should check."

■▸▶◦▸◦▾◦▾◦▾◦▾◦▾◦▾◦▾◦

WHEN CALI AND Mel arrived after her rehearsal, the entire room went silent with no one wanting to say anything about the discussion. We were sidetracked by Cali's rant in answer to her mother's simple question, "How was rehearsal?"

"I can't believe it! I hate this play!" Cali shouted.

Uh-oh.

"Everybody for act one, scene one. Places!" Cali shouted.

"Thank you, places," Mel responded.

"Cue one. Cue two. Cue three. Cue four," Cali recited, moving to pose differently for each cue. "Okay, cut to Macbeth's line. Cue five. Cue six. Positions for end of scene. Cue seven. Cue eight. Scene two. Actors."

"No, no, no, no," Mel chimed in. "We have to go back to cue five; there's a light out. Electrician!"

"Now, Cali, let's go over your mad scene on the parapet again. You just aren't selling it. You're looking angry, not mad." Cali growled and stomped around the room. "As if it's not enough to be a slab of meat getting dragged around under the lights so tech can practice over and over again, I can't even get my lines right. I just don't get her. Why'd she go mad? What did she think? You stab someone, there's going to be bloody blood. She's in medieval Scotland. She has to know what blood looks like. Probably kills her own chickens."

"Wow," I interjected. The English teachers were huddled. I slipped out of the room and into the kitchen, ostensibly to go out to check on the grill—which I did. On the way through the kitchen, I grabbed a freezer bag that was lying out waiting for leftovers and squirted a bunch of ketchup in it, then filled it with water. It was weak blood, but I figured that would be easier to clean up in the long run. I grabbed a plastic butter knife and opened my own pen knife in my hand. For good measure, I squirted a little ketchup in my mouth and held it in my cheek before I went back into the dining room.

"Cali," I said. "Do you know how much blood is in the human body?"

"A few pints."

"Here," I said, handing her the plastic knife. "Stab me in the heart."

"With a plastic knife?"

"You don't think I'm going to give you a steak knife, do you?"

"What's the point?"

"You need to get into the emotion and violence of what you've done. You got Macbeth to the kill the king and then you went in and dipped your hands in the blood to smear it on the guards. You need to lose your sophistication and become the animal inside."

"How do you know so much about *Macbeth*?"

"I went to college. Now think about the one thing you want most in your life and then imagine that I'm the only thing in the world standing between you and it. All you have to do is work up enough of that anger they say you have on set and put it into action. Stab me!"

I actually saw the change in her face as she became Lady Macbeth. It was frightening. Her eyes went cold and she clenched her teeth. For a minute, I didn't think she'd do it. Then she went into action faster than I could move. She shifted the butter knife in her hand and rushed at my chest stabbing down. I was shocked and surprised to see the amount of anger she could wield at a moment's notice—so much so that I fell to one knee and then down on my back as she continued to rain blows down on me. I clutched my heart with my right hand and with the penknife cut a slit in my shirt through the bag. Her next blow squished and she brought her hand back wet. Her eyes suddenly went wide.

Cali screamed.

I pushed the rest of the red water out of the bag and let a little ketchup escape from my mouth.

She kept screaming. The plastic knife went flying.

Andi was on her feet with her arms wrapped around Cali, glaring at me as I propped myself up on one elbow. Cali was sobbing in her mother's arms.

"You would make a terrible father!" Andi yelled at me. I thought I was just going to be helpful. I was terrified. Then Cali lifted her head and I could see she wasn't sobbing, but laughing.

"No! No!" she laughed. "He's great. That was awesome! Oh my God! I thought I killed you. That was spectacular!"

"That was *so* cool!" Mel said. "How much blood is in us?"

"Four to six quarts, depending on how big the person is," I gasped. Between the onslaught of Cali and then the fear that I'd totally screwed things up, I was completely out of breath.

"I totally get it!" Cali exclaimed. "Who'd have thought the old man had so much blood in him? Oh wow. I think I can go mad now!"

"I still question whether that was smart," Andi said looking at me pointedly. "You should have asked me first. You scared me to death."

"Face it, Mom, you were more worried that I'd hurt Dag than that I was emotionally damaged."

"Well, you were convincing."

"Wait, wait," Paula said. "What's going on between Andi and Dag?"

"They're dating," Cali announced. Both Andi and I blushed. We hadn't planned to say anything to anyone. Outed by the teenager.

"Well, we were until that little stunt," Andi said, still not forgiving me, but she did slide her hand over close enough that I could reach it with my own. I took hold of her hand and brought it to my lips.

"Would it help if I volunteer to clean up the mess?" I asked.

"Well that would go a long way." Everybody in the room chorused with variations of "Aww."

◼◻▦▨▩▧▥▦▨▩▧▥▦▨◼

I DID CLEAN up. I had to run up to my apartment to change t-shirts. That was one of my favorites, too. Well, it was worth it, I thought. I cleaned up the dining room, including scrubbing the ketchup off the hardwood floor and, for good measure, I washed the entire dining room floor. I got the grill cleaned up, packaged up the leftover food, and generally made myself useful until the last guest had bid goodnight.

Finally, Andi and I stood in the entryway and I knew it was time for me to go as well.

"I am sorry I pulled that little stunt. I should have talked to you instead of jumping to my own remedy."

"It worked out okay. And Cali was right. I could see her laughing before she stopped screaming. I just wasn't sure you were okay."

"Maybe I would make a terrible father."

"With what you did today?" she asked. She wasn't talking about the stunt with Cali anymore. "You showed powerful empathy for a vulnerable child and you put the wheels in motion to bring the perpetrator to justice. Dag, you are a wonderful, caring man. You just haven't had any practice."

I leaned down to kiss her. It was brief.

"Cali and Mel are here. Will I see you tomorrow?"

"I'm taking my mother to lunch tomorrow. If I can't be a good father, maybe I can still be a good son. I'll be back about three."

"I can live with that. Let's go for a walk then."

I leaned in for one more light kiss and then mounted the steps to my apartment.

{13}
The Good Son

I WAS BORN AND raised in Seattle—well, Ballard to be specific. My parents were Swedish immigrants. My father worked on the docks and on the fishing trawlers until he retired. My mother was an education activist in the Swedish community, establishing a kindergarten program and teaching until she was forced out at 70 years old. That had been last year, and she wasn't taking it that well. It's a cruel twist of fate when a couple work all their lives toward their goal of retiring and traveling together and then something like a heart attack in the middle of the night a year after retirement dashes the dreams to pieces. Mom had been alone for nine years now.

We talk several times a week and I try to visit at least once a week, but the past two weeks had been so busy that I'd missed lunch with her last Sunday. When she saw me at the door she looked quizzically at me and asked "Yes?"

"Mom, it's me, Dag." *Is she losing it?*

"What happened to your hair?" I realized she hadn't seen me clean shaven since I got out of the Navy and I'd completely forgotten that Sinclair had dyed my hair.

"Oh. I got a job. I have to look all corporate now."

"A job? Why?"

"Well, Mom, I work for a living."

"But your business was doing so well." Now that was a twist. For the past year she'd been telling me I needed to clean up and get a job while I protested that I was in school and had started a business. She hadn't been enthusiastic about me becoming an entrepreneur and I'd downplayed the real work, choosing to tell her I repaired computers.

"Everyone has computers that need fixed. Mine never does what I tell it to," she said. That was because she'd never really wanted one and didn't bother to learn how to use it. But it was okay. As much as I thought I'd like to just jot off an email to her sometimes, she really didn't need a computer. As easily as the elderly can become prey on the Internet, I was just as glad hers sat in a corner collecting dust.

I helped her on with her jacket and we went out to the waiting cab. I don't drive my car much, and on rainy days not at all. The past four days had been beautiful but the wind and rain picked up again during the night and I nearly lost the umbrella as I opened the door for her. It was a short trip to the Fish House on the other side of Salmon Bay.

Mom always liked Salmon Bay. She could look out at the fishing boats moored at the pier. I think she liked to imagine that Dad would be getting off one of them and come to join us for brunch. I'd tried to take her to some of the other nice restaurants in town for Sunday brunch, but when asked, she always suggested the Fish House.

We talked about our lives the past week and I told her a bit about the work I was doing at EFC. I didn't tell her I was undercover, but I did suggest that it was temporary to fill a specific need and I expected I'd be back in my own business soon.

"Maybe they'll like you. You might be asked to stay."

"I doubt that, Mom. These kinds of jobs don't usually work that way." I didn't add that I wouldn't go back to work for a corporation even if they did try to hire me. The taste of independence I'd had the past year-plus made it hard for me to think about returning to a corporate grind. I'd tried that, thinking it was the road to security and wealth. Then the company I'd invested fourteen years of my life in had tanked, thanks to unscrupulous management. Why would I do that all again? I might starve, but I was happy.

"Everyone wanted to hire your father," she continued. "He was a hard worker. Of course, it wasn't always like that." That was news to me. I'd only known a father who worked long hard hours every day of his life.

"What do you mean?"

"Well…" she lowered her voice and glanced around the room conspiratorially, "when we came to America, we were hippies. We never intended to work a day in our lives."

"Mom! You're kidding!"

"No, it's true. You should know these things now that you're grown up." Grown up? I was 43. It seemed like I could have been told about this *sometime* in the past 20 years. "We got off the boat without even having a proper visa. We were just tourists on a year-long trip to see the continent like American youths went to Europe. American teens headed for Amsterdam for the drugs. We headed for San Francisco."

"What happened?"

"We met a nice couple, a little older than us, who invited us to stay with them on a ranch in Montana. They worked us hard for little food and no money, but they were very convincing. Society was about to collapse. The only ones who would survive were those who lived communally and regained a native work ethic. They could make slave labor sound like paradise."

"How did you manage to leave?"

"They took periodic trips to San Francisco to recruit new members of what they called their commune, even though they owned everything and worked the kids they brought in like slaves. They made the mistake of assuming they were so far out in the wilderness that we wouldn't try to leave on our own. But we did. We set all the animals free on the range and walked away the day they went to California. We walked seventy miles to the railroad and walked along it for two days until we came to a place where a freight train was stopped at a grain elevator. We snuck on board and the next time it stopped, we were in Seattle."

I'd never heard about this part of my parent's life. I thought they came here straight from Sweden and went to work. My mom was full of surprises.

"We couldn't find a place to live," Mom continued, "but your father found work on a fishing trawler. For the month it was at sea, I lived in the warehouse and picked up odd jobs doing cleaning and cooking. His first paycheck was enough for us to get a room in a boarding house and a permanent job offer. They weren't so particular about checking visas back then."

"You were illegal aliens?"

"You make it sound like we came from outer space," she laughed. "We discovered the Swedish-American Center and a legal aide there went to work getting us proper papers and eventually citizenship. I went to college and got my education degree while your father continued to work the fishing trawlers and then the docks. And you came along. We couldn't complain about that! The next year, Pastor Lundquist at the Swedish Lutheran Church asked me to start a kindergarten. Once we got it straight that there would be no religion taught in *my* school, I went to work."

I remembered that kindergarten in the basement of the Lutheran Church. I'd gone to it for three years with my mother as teacher.

"That's an amazing story, Mom," I said. I was too overwhelmed with the information to ask a coherent question.

"Well, it's time you reconnected with your community, Dagget. Come with me to the Center this afternoon and meet people."

"I kind of have… uh… an appointment this afternoon, Mom."

I'm not sure why I wasn't ready to tell her about Andi. It was still too new for me to be sure of what I could say. I'd really been alone now for over five years. My little black hole of an apartment wasn't exactly conducive to having women over. It was a retreat. I'd had a few trysts over that time, but I'd avoided becoming romantically involved. They'd last a few weeks at most and we'd go our separate ways, my dates having never seen the way I live. If they had, I'm sure my time with them would have been even shorter. I wondered why I was suddenly so willing to let myself go with Andi.

"You need to get back to your roots," my mother was saying.

"Mom, you always taught me to be a hundred percent American. You never wanted any of the kids in school to speak Swedish. You never took me to the SAC when I was growing up. Why should I now?"

"I mean your hair," she smiled. "Your roots are showing. If you are going to color it, you need to keep it touched up."

Damn. I couldn't afford to go back to Sinclair every week. If this was going to be a problem, the dye job would be a one-time thing.

"Although it wouldn't hurt to visit your cousins in Sweden," Mom continued. "Maybe you could take me so I can visit my sister. I miss the rest of the family." She made it sound like she missed her sister, but by the way her eyes were fixed on the fishing boats at the pier, I could tell it was Dad she was talking about.

I paid the check and our cab was waiting for us as promised. On the way to the Swedish-American Center, she turned to me very seriously.

"You are getting old, Dag."

"Gee, thanks Mom."

"You get up in the morning and shower and shave so you can go to work. That's what old men do. Young men come home from work, shower, and shave so they can go to bed."

"Mom!"

"Your father showered and shaved at night right up to the day he died." There was a glistening in her eyes and I thought she was going to cry. I reached over and hugged her. I'd always thought Dad showered and shaved when he came home from work because he worked a dirty smelly job.

"I miss him, Dag. Sometimes I hear the clock strike six and I get up out of my chair to go greet him at the door. I forget. Don't wait too long, dear." We were at the SAC and I asked the driver to wait while I escorted Mom to the door for her Sunday afternoon bingo game. I could smell cookies baking inside and my mouth watered, even though I'd just eaten. I kissed her head.

"I'll see you next week, Mom," I said.

I returned to the taxi and asked him to take me home. I'd told Andi I'd be there about three.

⬛▪️▚▞▚▞▚▞▞▞▚▞▞▞▞▞⬛

I STOOD AT Andi's door with an umbrella in hand and she came out, pulling her jacket on. She wore her brown hair down, curling in the humid air until it was less than shoulder length. She called back into the house, "We'll be back in an hour or so," and smiled up at me. At five-five she was just lip-height to my six-two frame. I only had to bow my head to meet her lips in greeting.

"That's getting to be easy," she said happily. She took hold of my right arm with both hands and we stepped off the porch into the rain together, her left hand sliding down my arm to take my hand. There was an almost giddy energy we shared, scarcely able to believe we were letting ourselves enjoy the glow of new love.

We walked north on Boylston, an unspoken agreement between us to walk around Volunteer Park. On the way, Andi asked about my brunch with Mom and I told her some of the revelations that I'd just received. I didn't mention the part about shaving at night, but I'd filed that away in my mind.

"I just can't believe that I'm 43 years old and I'm still learning things about my parents. I thought I had everything figured out. I've lived here all my life."

"It sounds wonderful. My folks died before I could find any interesting things out," Andi volunteered. "It's wonderful to have stories like that."

"How did they die?"

"Auto accident. I was only 17. They didn't get to see me graduate from high school or college and never met their granddaughter."

"Where did you live?"

"Ann Arbor, Michigan. I left the state as soon as I turned 18 and never went back. I just couldn't stand it." I remembered Andi's college was in Florida.

"To Florida?"

"Um. Yeah. There first. Until Jack died. Then wandering."

"Must have been hard."

"I was young and scared. We were well-provided for, but it's still been lonely."

Cali, why did you ever make me doubt this wonderful woman? I just wanted to be lost in the pleasure of holding Andi in my arms. I didn't want to weigh every word to see if it rang true. How could I?

We walked around the west rim of the reservoir and up past the Asian Art Museum. It was still raining, but neither of us cared. We went up the steps to the water tower observatory, but the gates to both entrances were locked. When we stepped into the archway to read the sign posted inside, the wind died and we were sheltered from the rain. I wrapped my arm around Andi and brought her close to me. She raised her face and I kissed her. There was no urgency to our kiss, but a rising sense of passion. We explored each other with all our senses, the arch and umbrella blocking us from view should anyone look up our direction. When we parted, our eyes were glued to each other, seeking affirmation in what we saw and of what we had just felt. We hugged and I buried my face in her sweet smelling hair, letting my lips glide across her cheek and neck.

"We'd better get back," she whispered. "I told Cali an hour or so."

"I think we're already into the 'or so' part of that." We laughed and held each other closely as we walked back down the steps. When we got to Broadway, Andi directed me to a drugstore. I followed along as she led me down a row of hair color products. She paused in front of a men's product line and started holding boxes up against my face.

"Your mother was right; we need to touch up your roots." I paid for the hair color—considerably less than a trip to see Sinclair—and we walked on down the hill to her duplex, forgetting to put up the umbrella.

"Cali, we're back!" she called when we went in. "How about some hot chocolate?"

Cali bounced into the room and hugged her mother. She laughed at us standing there with water dripping off our faces.

"Looks like you two stayed outside too long," she said. "Didn't you have an umbrella?" Andi and I just looked at each other and grinned. "I'll make the chocolate," Cali said, rolling her eyes. "Don't you want to change into something dry?"

"That's a good idea. Dag, run home and put on your grungy jeans and a tee shirt, then come back here and the Marx sisters will do your roots."

"I get to be Harpo! Honk honk." Cali called from the kitchen.

"You couldn't keep from talking long enough to be Harpo, brat," Andi scolded. "You'll have to be Chico. He's the fast talker."

"We could make Dag Groucho. How much of that hair color did you get? We'll have to paint most of the mustache on him."

"Okay, I'm going," I said. "I'll be back in a few minutes."

BEFORE I LEFT that evening, I'd had my roots touched up, enjoyed hot chocolate and leftover ribs from yesterday's barbecue, and shared in a huge bowl of popcorn as the three of us sat on the sofa watching old movies. I couldn't remember a day that I'd had more fun and I put all thought of Cali's contract out of my mind. *Maybe she'll just forget about it.* I could hope.

There was a tense moment halfway through *Horsefeathers* when I turned to Andi and said, "I have tickets to see Two Man Flash at SoDo Friday night. Can I convince you to go with me?"

From the corner of my eye, I saw Cali smirk.

"Aren't we too old for them?"

"Apparently there is a limited age bracket between 21 and 21-and-a-half you have to fit into, but I have a fake ID that says I'm much younger than I am." I grinned at Cali and she rolled her eyes.

"Oh, but we can't go hear a band Friday. It's Cali's opening."

"I thought…" I stopped myself and looked a silent appeal at Cali.

"Mom, I thought you wanted Saturday night tickets."

"And miss the gala?"

"Some gala. A glass of three-dollar wine and a Costco vegetable platter. We have three performances and one is a matinee. I got you guys tickets for closing on Saturday, not opening."

"Are you sure, honey? I never miss one of your openings."

"Mom, really. It's not like this is a big musical. It's Shakespeare. Go listen to some good music and then tell me all about it when you get home. I'm so jealous. Or better yet, you do Lady Macbeth and I'll go with Dag. I love Two Man Flash." Andi raised a very parental index finger at Cali and wagged it ominously up and down. "Sorry," Cali squeaked.

"Well, if you're sure, honey." She turned to me and her eyes crinkled up in merriment. "It sounds like fun!" she mouthed at me. I gave her an extra squeeze.

And before I left, I shared one more lovely kiss with Andi at the door.

I'm not getting old.

I felt young and more alive than I'd been in years.

{14}
Challenging the Enemy

MONDAY MORNING, I walked into the office at EFC feeling even more naked than my shaved face. For the first time I could remember in recent years, I wasn't carrying a computer. The police still had my office under lock and key, much to the surprise of the people who shared the house with me. I'd received a call from Daniel's counselor, Cora, before I even got to EFC, thanking me for the work I'd done and asking to be briefed on anything I could provide that didn't breach a confidence. She was stunned when I told her what I'd discovered and why my office was taped off.

"I can't believe it. I wish I'd sent him to you sooner. I just can't believe that it was a stalker and not just a bully—not that that wasn't bad enough."

"It wasn't your fault," I calmed her. "Besides, it's likely that if it had come to my attention earlier, I'd have missed the solution. It just happened that another project I was working on gave me a lead to pursue for this one."

"Nonetheless, I won't hesitate to send cases your direction. Anything I can do for you, I'll be happy to." That struck a chord with me.

"Say, now that you mention it, there is something I'd like to ask you," I said. "I don't suppose you give any classes in dealing with teenagers, do you?"

"It would take longer to teach that kind of class than for the kid to grow out of his teens. Do you have something specific?"

"I'm concerned about a friend—well, the daughter of a friend. Actually, the daughter's friend." I explained casually as I could. That certainly wasn't a great start. It sounded like I was covertly asking about myself. "I'm wondering if certain behaviors that we've observed might be indicators of something more significant or if it's just part of growing up." Cora encouraged me to tell her what was on my mind, so I plunged ahead. I explained some of what Cali told me about Mel and my own observations. This technically wasn't part of my contract with Cali and I wasn't using any names, so I felt secure that I wasn't betraying a confidence. The counselor then gave me some pointed advice.

"What you've described could simply be a part of growing up, as you said. Kids act out all the time. But you've mentioned a couple of things that I'd explore if I were counseling the kid. Ultra-strict parents aren't necessarily a sign that a kid is under duress. We see lots of kids handle the pressure of strict parents without much trouble. But sometimes, when combined with other things, we'd revise that opinion. Your teen sounds like she's an overachiever. Several sports, straight As, and a party attitude. Her vulgarity could just be her wanting to cut loose—shock people out of their view of her as perfect. But the idea that she has 'many freaky online friends,' as you said, makes me think she could be treading on dangerous ground. Sometimes a kid that aces everything and is fully self-assured will expose herself to more risks than other kids simply because she figures she can handle it. It's definitely worth looking into, especially since she might be leading a friend down the same path."

I thanked her profusely and said I'd check a few things. If I needed further advice, I'd be sure to give her a call.

When I walked into the office at EFC, I was still thinking about the conversation with Cora. I was going to need to look through Mel's social accounts. But today, I was going to have to do something about my search for fraud inside a credit card company—a company I'd already grown to dislike. And I was going to have to do it without my own computer and tools.

I STARTED THINKING about something Lars taught me back in the Navy. He set up a training drill in which we were to track down an intruder and neutralize the suspect. We—a team of six intelligence trainees—were locked in a room with our backs to each other and told to use the resources at hand to track down the culprit. We were scanning all available files on our network, looking for a breach. We quickly divided up the tasks among us and started our search. It was frantic. Lars hadn't given us an exact deadline for finding the problem, but alluded to the fact that if we didn't find the security breach soon, the damage would be irreparable. It was a typical war games scenario and we occasionally tossed information back and forth among us to help the search with others. We were nearly an hour into the search having found pointers, but not being able to locate the problem.

I suddenly became aware that the room was quieter than it had been before. I glanced to my left and right to see four of my team slumped over their computers. I spun around to see a silenced sidearm pointing in my direction. The last of my teammates was behind the gun smiling at me. The door opened and Lars walked in. The other four team members sat up at their computers.

"You all failed to achieve your mission objective," Lars stated. "All except Ensign Cooper. Why did you fail?"

"We weren't looking for a physical threat," I answered. "We were looking for an online threat."

"Which is why you were vulnerable. You let yourselves believe that because you are computer analysts, the threat you were looking for was computer-based," Lars lectured. "If at any time, any of you had looked around, you would have seen a physical threat manifested in the room. You cannot ever assume that you are safe just because you are inside a sealed room. The dangers in this game are not only digital. They are real and physical."

I'd become lax.

***

I STOPPED IN my office and booted up the laptop just to find out if there were any messages and to check my email. I wasn't paying much attention to anything that came through unless it was from one of my team or from Arnie. There was nothing on either count, so I put the computer to sleep and left the office.

"Are you done for the day already?" Darlene asked as I passed her desk. "It's only nine-thirty."

"Not done, but I need to do a little field work. I'll be nearby, but might not get back here to the office. Call me if I'm in danger of losing my job."

"Which job?" she snarked. "Never mind. If Arnie needs you, I'll call your cell."

I walked out the security doors past the receptionist and took the elevator down to the third floor. The first two floors of this building were occupied by small businesses and retail. EFC occupied the next twenty-four floors. This would take a while.

There was no receptionist on this floor, corporate offices being on the twenty-third with two floors of executive offices and conference rooms above. The elevators opened into a narrow lobby on either end of which were more security doors. I'd walked the building a few days ago, but I hadn't tested every set of doors. Third floor contained the company's computer servers. If they got any bigger, they would have to move to offsite storage at one of the huge server farms in Oregon, Idaho, or Montana that make up what is popularly known as 'the cloud.' I wasn't sure my ID would gain access, but when I passed the card over the security reader, I was rewarded with the click that allowed me to open the door.

Once inside, I wasn't sure where to go. I clipped my badge to my jacket pocket where it was clearly visible and walked confidently along a row of outside wall offices. These offices were different from those on the upper floors. There were no windows into the hallway. Each office had a solid oak door behind which, I knew, were the dozens of technicians and analysts that kept the servers running and the company network updated. If the offices had exterior windows, as I assumed they did, they would look over an alley or onto the street. No one on this floor would have a sweeping view of Puget Sound and the Olympic Mountains.

There were two doors on the inside wall of each hall, secured with a card reader. I casually passed my card over the reader on the first door I came to. There was no answering click and no green light on the reader. *Just as I thought.* Either by accident or accidentally on purpose, I was not issued a card that would automatically open every door in the company. I couldn't imagine Arnie giving me access to executive offices, Human Resources, or the server farm, though my network access had revealed no digital blocks. Technically, I should be able to access any one of the servers here without entering the room. But there were areas in the company that had information that could only be accessed physically.

I completed my circuit of the farm and emerged again in the elevator lobby. I went down and out onto the street with my cell phone already dialing the number I'd punched in. Jordan answered on second ring.

"What a can of worms you opened up this time," Jordan announced without even saying hello. "This is going to take us days just to get a case active and warrants issued. How did your client take the news?"

"He cancelled every online account he had, including his ISP, and turned off his computer," I said. "I should say that his father did. Can't blame them. I didn't want to go online again after I found that, either. In fact, I still haven't been online. That's what I wanted to ask you about."

"Sorry, friend, but I can't give you access to your computers yet," Jordan said. "I don't know how you managed to accomplish everything you did in as short a time as you were working on it. It's taking our tech hours to document it."

"I appreciate that, but I'm wondering if I can get access to the office without the computers. I need to pick up a couple of things from my file cabinet for the EFC gig."

"I don't see a problem with that. Our impound order only includes the computers currently running and equipment attached to the network. When do you need access?"

"As soon as possible. I could be at the office in half an hour."

"I'll meet you there."

JORDAN ACCOMPANIED ME into my office and I nodded to the tech who was sitting at my computer recording things into a voice-activated microphone. Behind him and to one side where he could see the screen and keyboard, sat a court-appointed observer, watching to see that all he did was read what was available and did not attempt to change anything.

One of the first purchases I made when I took this space was a fireproof locking file cabinet. I looked over the warrant for the computer impound and verified that they were not authorized to touch anything else in my office. I unlocked the cabinet, opened the third drawer, and rummaged around a bit. I finally came up with the two little tech toys I wanted and shoved them in my pocket.

I went a little overboard when I started as a private detective. I've always been into toys, but as soon as you get your license, you start getting mail of all sorts. Catalogs of high tech surveillance equipment, offers of hacking software, classes and courseware from every part of the world, and—surprisingly—an incredible number of spam emails from people who just shouldn't send that stuff to private detectives. They provided a great target for investigation with no apparent benefits to themselves. What I wanted now, however, was a tech toy that I'd picked up at SpyCon in March in Vegas. My first time there was a real eye-opener. After I'd strolled through those aisles, the volume of junk mail and email I received quadrupled.

One item was a flashlight. I could put it on a keychain if I wanted. It looked just like the one I use to illuminate the door-lock while I try to fit the key inside at night. But if I twist the light switch the other way, it changes to an infrared LED. A lot of company assets are marked with codes that can only be seen under infrared light. I might use it for investigating that, but I had another use in mind.

The other item was a miniature RFID recorder.

The ID card issued to me by EFC was a typical smartcard. In smartcards, there are three active elements. The first is the picture and identification information printed on the card itself—the human-readable part. The second is the gold-colored chip exposed on the back of the card. This exposed circuitry must be in contact with a smartcard reader in order to be activated and is almost impossible to counterfeit. When I slide my card into the reader on my laptop, it sends a randomly generated code to the computer. The computer software compares the code against its table of accepted responses and if all is well and my password matches, I get access to the network. But the third part is invisible. Inside the card is a tiny computer processor. The processor is activated by receiving ambient power from a nearby reader. Upon activation, it sends an encoded message back to the reader via a near-field radio frequency generator. Upon validation that it is a legal code, the requested action is activated. When I wave my ID card at the reader on the security door, it checks my information against the database to see if the card is valid and then unlocks the door. At EFC, the card can be used for much more. I might, for example, deposit funds in an account and when I go to the cafeteria, the account would be charged automatically for my meal. All I need to do is wave the card near the reader.

It had seemed like overkill at the time, but was so attractive that I couldn't help myself. I'd decided to put an RFID reader on my office and program a card to unlock the door. It was a project I hadn't got around to yet. Now with the reader and a few blank cards in my hands as well as a programming interface, I could essentially copy the RFID portion of my corporate security card.

Or, anyone else's.

I RESUMED MY walk in the office on the fourth floor, this time carrying a cup of coffee with me. The security cameras would simply record that I had walked the third floor and then went out for coffee—if anyone ever bothered to check them. I'd done almost the exact same thing on Thursday last week. They might think it strange that I exercised by working my way from the bottom to the top of the company, but I intended to do it every day I was in the office for a while. After the fourth floor, then the fifth. The sixth floor was a call center. I just walked the halls, then continued to the next floor.

When I reached the twelfth floor, I paced myself carefully, pausing at one point to tighten a shoelace. When I noticed the security cameras were all apparently pointing away from my target, I moved quickly to the security door ahead. I passed my card over the reader and saw, as I expected, that it did not allow admittance. I flicked on my infrared LED and held it in front of me, pointing at the security camera making its circuit toward me. I pressed the miniature reader against the bottom of the card reader. If the recording from this camera was ever reviewed, it would show a momentary white-out on the camera as I was casually walking on down the hall. There would be no picture of me at the door to manufacturing.

I continued to the fourteenth floor and on all the way up to the twenty-sixth floor. It took nearly two hours altogether.

I returned to my desk at noon and opened the laptop, logged in, and stared at the alert box on my screen. "Two down. Next? OK." The question wasn't answerable. Not that I didn't have an answer, but there was no way to answer an alert box that disappeared on any key-strike or mouse-click.

I grinned. I like games and I was beginning to think of my involvement at EFC as just being another one. I knew that at least one person here liked them, too. I was being teased and it was time to meet the opponent—or opponents—on my turf. I'd see how good they really were.

I hadn't typed a single keystroke on my laptop keyboard since I got here, but it was time now to let whoever in the company was watching me see my challenge. I sent an email addressed to an Internet alias that was automatically forwarded to my gaming forum. The message said simply, "3.2 billion in missing funds. Where is it? Finder's fee. At 7 Pacific, the game's afoot." I included the official log-in and registration information and pressed 'send.'

For good measure, I overrode the screen-saver function on my laptop and had put a scrolling message on the screen instead. It just said, "The game is tonight," and had the URL. I turned the laptop to face the security camera that still panned past my office every two-and-a-half minutes.

It was a challenge no serious gamer could refuse.

Now, let the fun begin.

{15}
The Game's Afoot

I DON'T SUPPOSE THERE is a hacker alive who hasn't spent time in the gaming world. Probably a lot of time. Gaming keeps us sharp and we develop long-term attachments and respect for each other.

Back in the good old days, online gaming was limited to Bulletin Board Systems (BBS) where the gamer entered character attributes, then chose what to do in the world that evolved. It was nearly all text-based. But just reading those lines—turn right, take two steps, strike, run—were enough to put real images in the player's mind. That's where I learned to visualize the Internet. We played on the Internet before the World Wide Web put a visual interface on it. When the world turned to animation graphics and avatars, half the fun went out of seeing it all through your own eyes. Gaming lost some of its appeal for hardcore hackers.

Most people aren't aware that there are still text-based games available online. They are run by hackers, for hackers, and half the fun is getting inside someone else's game and wreaking havoc. Most—including mine—are on the domains set up by John Patterson. That gave me the creeps just now.

I created a game over the past year that was designed to discover where my former bosses from Henderson Associates had squirreled away over a billion dollars of assets. It had been eighteen months now since I helped the police put them in jail, but there was still no sign of the money. Oh, there were the typical clues, a constantly-evolving terrain, and some very real dangers to those who played. A real reward, too, if someone happened to discover where the missing money was. It could happen.

When I posted the simple message to my gaming board, it was a challenge to all comers to play treasure-hunt. By posting it from the laptop in my office, it was a direct challenge to my watcher—or maybe to everyone on my team if they were all watching me. Now I was going to find out who showed up.

ᴍ ᴅ ᴇ

I LEFT THE office before lunch. Frankly, I was past caring who knew if I was working or not. It seemed like everyone already knew I wasn't really hired to do the job I was hired for. Like that made sense. Besides, I needed some additional equipment if I was going to run a game tonight.

I used the excuse that my computers were impounded to head out to one of the local warehouse stores and buy the biggest, baddest, gamer laptop I could find. I considered buying one of those roll-aboard suitcases to carry it in rather than trying to drag it around, but opted for an over-the-shoulder carry-all. While I was there, I ran up my credit card a little higher and bought the latest tablet model with as much memory as I could get in it and a cellular Internet account.

The nice thing is that I didn't need much in the way of software, and I didn't need my own network to run the game. All the software is in the cloud, and frankly, the entire Internet was our game board. What I needed were different IP addresses so I could jump from one to another. That meant I'd be traveling and connecting through different servers as frequently as I could. I wasn't going to be standing still so I couldn't depend on a wired connection of any kind. By five, I was sitting in a coffee shop in West Seattle, about ready to start the game.

My CELL PHONE rang and I answered Andi less abruptly than I had a few nights ago.

"Hello, girlfriend," I said. What a difference a week makes… no, make that five days.

"Ooo. A girl could get used to that."

"I hope she does."

"What are you up to tonight?" I had no qualms about doing my own thing tonight, though if Andi had suddenly offered to meet me for dinner, I'd probably have called off the whole game. I knew, though that she taught an Adult Ed class on Monday nights, so I just went with my plans.

"I'm running a game tonight online. It promises to be rather informative."

"Going to Nowhere Land," she laughed.

"You could always show me the way to Somewhere Land." There was a sequence of lands a relationship could go through. We'd already broken through Nowhere Land in our relationship, but, of course, that wasn't what she was asking about.

"You aren't going hunting for the missing money again, are you?" It was a point she disagreed with me on. I was determined to close the loop on the question of where the money went when the boss stole it. It doesn't just evaporate. What does it mean when you say you lost money on a deal? Who found it? Where did it go? I was going to be the one who found it.

Andi supported me through that latest collapse in my life, just as she had supported me when I lost Hope. But she had always challenged my thinking.

"You were awfully pleased with yourself when you brought down the company president," she'd said.

"Well, maybe I was a little too happy to find the evidence that would put him behind bars," I admitted.

"You giggled like a little kid."

"Okay, you're right. But that is nothing like the celebration that will happen when I find the money. That Costa Rican seaside mansion she's living in is going to turn into a cardboard box on the beach when I'm done." Bitter about Hope leaving me to move up the food chain and marry my CEO? Who me?

"Don't tell me things like that," Andi said. "Even in jest. They might call me in to testify against you."

"Hmm. I might have to marry you then, just so you won't have to testify against me."

"Trade my corner of Paradise for your living hell? I don't think so." She made a good point. I'd let the plundering of Henderson Associates eat at me, especially since none of my so-called friends from the company would talk to me anymore. I'd let up on the search, but I couldn't help it if occasionally it drew me back.

"IT'S DIFFERENT THIS time," I said. "I'm not really after the money, though if it shows up, I won't object. What I'm really trying to do is flush out my quarry at EFC. I've set up a pretty good proposition for the game tonight and I'm seeing who rises to the occasion. You know, that's the job I was hired to do there."

"Mmmm. Okay. You know I worry about you. There have been too many science fiction stories about people who play a game, but when they die in the game they really die. I don't believe it, but it still gives me gooseflesh."

"Well, tell me what you're doing tonight," I suggested. English Literature was always good for calming the turmoil.

"I'm pretending to teach Twentieth Century American Literature while disguising the fact that I'm doing basic language development for Adult ESL students."

"So you're playing a game?"

"That pretty well sums it up," she laughed. "They really don't know anything at this level."

"That's why they come to your classes," I admonished. She'd used the same line on me the day we met.

"Touché. I admit to being almost as human as you." We laughed. "So would you like to have dinner tomorrow after work? Cali's in dress rehearsal. I'd love company." Her voice sounded hesitant—a little shy. I smiled.

"Ms. Marx, are you asking me on a date?"

"I guess so," she said. "Damn it! Don't make this any harder than it is."

"Andi, I would love to have dinner with you. Anytime. I really can't wait to see you."

"Really?"

"Really."

"Well, I'd better get to class, and you'd better get into cyberspace. Don't forget an oxygen tank!"

"I'll see you tomorrow night. 'Bye."

"Bye." I bit my tongue as we disconnected. I'd almost said 'I love you.' Grade A number one mistake according to all the dating manuals. We'd had two dates and a group barbecue this weekend. *Don't rush it!* I lectured myself.

It was time to start the game.

By SEVEN I'D logged over a dozen players into the game. Those who were new had picked their avatars and generated their roles and power levels. I recognized several I'd played with in the past on other games. More players registered within the first half hour and set out on their quest.

I nearly canceled the game when I recognized the moniker of one player. John Patterson had joined the quest. *Damn!* I didn't want him anywhere near anything I was doing. *Why isn't he in jail yet?* I tried to calm my racing heart. I'd watch him closely and we'd see if he exposed anything I could turn over to the police. Not likely in a game, but there might be an IP address or alias I wasn't aware of.

I'd originally developed this game to send people out into an Internet multiverse searching for a combination of factors that would reveal $3.2 billion secreted in the account of some very wealthy man whose net worth read *only* $12.7 million. The lure was that it was real money and there was a ten percent finder's fee if it was recovered. Some games are written to inspire competition and some to foster cooperation. If a registered player discovered the money, even if it was done outside the game, the finder's fee was to be split among all the registered players. This meant it was to everyone's advantage for someone to find the prize. As much as I could make it, I'd ensured there was no reason beyond gaming pride to compete with each other. I was hoping that tonight the identity of who was following me at EFC would be revealed.

It was a big shock to me when two player avatars were killed.

I got two equally angry flames in my inbox almost at the same time. These were good, long-term players I'd known online for years.

"Somebody must be playing to make sure everyone loses," I answered both players. "I'm resurrecting you with a level ten power source. I'd appreciate it if you two would flank me. It looks like we've got incoming."

"I've got your six, CyberTalon," the gamer named DeepSix shot back. The other, CyClops, went silent and I wasn't sure if he'd left the game in a huff or if he was pursuing his own line. It took me a moment to realize that I'd just given John Patterson virtual immunity in the game.

It is supposed to be impossible to kill the gamemaster in a game. If the gamemaster dies, the game ends. However, it is possible to cripple or capture me, putting my power in the hands of someone else until another player comes along and frees me or until my servitude expires based on the power of the one attacking me. Online games are really nothing more than capture the flag in cyberspace.

I didn't like the look of the approaching party. Three indistinct shapes came toward us from different directions. There was no good reason in a treasure-hunt game to approach the location of the gamemaster. I threw up shields just in time to ward off a blast attack. I wrapped an invisibility cloak around myself and DeepSix and transported to my north game tower. As soon as I was there, I unplugged from the network and closed up my computer. It was time to move.

⌐▢▤⌐⌐▦▧▨ ▨⌐▦▧⌐▧⌐⌐▢▧▢▦▧⌐▦

I DIDN'T USUALLY move so far from town, but I'd spotted a bus to the airport with on-board WiFi the third time I had to move. I was working hard to log on through different networks. The game had clearly devolved into two combative armies, each trying to stymie the other's efforts to complete the quest. My own held more players and on average a little more power than the opposition. Each soldier in my army had already been killed once by the opposition and resurrected by me. The other side had collected a couple more people into its sphere, so there were nine. I had thirteen on my team, plus myself. I'd boosted each of their power levels. We split into two segments and I sent the top three gamers I knew on the quest. The rest of us continued to face off with the enemy. We could never see all of them at the same time, so there was no way to be sure if we were facing all of them at once or just a portion while the rest hunted treasure. I hadn't seen or heard from CyClops since my first encounter, but I noted that he was still logged in. *Lurking.*

I used a whirlwind dispersal just before the bus arrived at the airport, sending my troops in different directions with enough fuel to make a jump when I called them back. The attacks of the enemy were growing in power. I was getting pretty sick of them, but in the gameworld, the game ceases to exist if the gamemaster breaks the rules. Still, in spite of the diversions I was creating, it seemed that the enemy was intent on capturing me. They were picking up my trail faster than I could cover it. My ruse of jumping from network to network for access wasn't shaking them up. I was beginning to relate to Butch Cassidy and the Sundance Kid. *Who are those guys?*

After thirty minutes in the business center at baggage claim in the airport plugged into an Ethernet port under the desk and power to recharge the monster laptop, I realized I was going to have to come up with some new techniques. They were closing in again. I disconnected, ran out of the airport and headed for the train into town.

A good part about connecting on a bus or train was that you connect through a single network while on the move physically. The disadvantage was that if the opponent could identify what the network was, then they'd know your route to the next location. I elected not to log on to the Metro network as the train sped me back into town. I used the cellular connection when it was available to get messages to my troops, instructing each to head out on their own. It was obvious now that the enemy was after me. I felt it likely that the rest would not attract attention while the enemy focused its forces on me. Whoever they were, these guys were getting on my nerves and I was about to make a big leap. I shut down again until the train pulled into the University Street Station in the tunnel.

The Seattle Public Library closes at eight p.m., but I hiked up the hill anyway. I circled around to the north side and entered the parking garage under the library. Even though the library is closed, they don't shut down the computer system overnight. It was three o'clock in the morning and I was pretty tired by this time. I climbed up to the top level of the garage and positioned myself next to the elevator shaft. Then I turned on the computer and connected to the library WiFi. The battery in the laptop was about exhausted so I used the tablet to connect and tap out my commands. This time I used remote access to get back to my laptop in the EFC office and logged onto the game from there. We'd see how good these bastards were at getting through a major corporate firewall to attack me.

I had a message on my dashboard as soon as I connected. "I got my eye on you." It was CyClops' tagline, and even though I'd seen him in the game only sporadically, it was a chilling reminder that Patterson was still watching. DeepSix was nowhere around as far as I could tell.

I scanned the area around me. I was in a beautiful glass tower from which I could see infinitely in any direction. It was beginning to look like I was safe, but before long, I could see the remainder of the enemy approaching the tower. They circled it at first, but then all gathered on one side. I was monitoring the other players, many of whom were dropping out because of the lateness of the hour. I was pretty exhausted myself. I told them I'd call a time again soon and we'd focus on finding the treasure rather than fighting a war. I'd be more careful who I let register to play. This was supposed to be about identifying who in EFC had decided to come out to play. That would tell me who was reading my keyboard in the office.

A message from DeepSix flashed on my screen: "They aren't trying to capture!"

What the hell did that mean? Being preoccupied with the message caused me to miss the approaching enemy until they'd materialized right in front of my face, inside the firewall—inside my tower. There's a sequence involved in terminating the game, unlike simply going invisible. I started frantically typing in the code, but I knew it was going to be too late before I could execute it. I was about to be killed.

There was a blinding flash in front of me. My shields held, but I was pretty much crippled and in the dark. I kept entering the code to terminate play for the night. Just before I hit enter, a message appeared on my dashboard.

"IGotUrBak."

That was a player who wasn't logged into my game.

{16}
Trapped

GETTING TO WORK at nine in the morning after gaming until four is a royal pain. *I'm getting too old for this.* I was willing to bet that nearly everyone in that game last night was in his teens or twenties except me. And Patterson. I'd given up on thinking anyone from the company had been involved last night except the mysterious IGotUrBak who jumped in at the last minute. I suspected Patterson had organized the attacking team himself and sat back to watch how I handled it. The hackers were getting better all the time, and to basically turn a treasure-hunt into a first person shooter game was really rude—especially when I was the target. I wanted to find out who these guys were, but once they were destroyed, they were erased from the game system. It would have been helpful if IGotUrBak had kept them alive for interrogation instead of so completely obliterating them.

And that was reason enough to go to the office.

It was one thing to have someone in the office monitoring what I did, but to have him jump in and save me at the last minute was disconcerting. He'd proven helpful on a couple of occasions now. But still… I'd expected whoever it was to play, not to lurk until I was desperate and come to my rescue. Today was the day I was going to find out who was on my tail.

❖❖❖❖❖❖❖❖❖❖

I STARTED BY checking to see who was in and who wasn't. It looked like Ford had spent the night in his office. But his normal position was sleeping at his desk and I wasn't sure if he even had a home to go to. I swung by Arnie's office and Darlene caught my attention.

"He's in an exec meeting this morning. Can you wait till after lunch to see him?"

"Not a problem. I was just stopping by to update him," I said. Darlene stifled a yawn. "You look tired. Should we be going for coffee?"

"These meetings start at seven a.m. They just kill me. I'm supposed to get my beauty sleep, not be fetching donuts at six-thirty in the morning."

"Ouch. I barely make it to bed by that time."

"Mmmm. Hope staying up late is for pleasure."

"Sort of. About that coffee…"

"No. I have to run interference at ten when they take their ten-minute break. Phil looked like he could use coffee when I saw him. Said his three-month-old kept them up all night."

"I'll stop by and check." I headed Phil's direction, but detoured by Don Abrams' office. It would be interesting to see if anything was happening in the area of Network Security. Don was in jeans and a polo shirt, a baseball hat pulled down low as he stared at his screen. "Hey, Don," I greeted him. "Did I miss the memo on casual Tuesday?"

"I haven't been home to change yet. We had a hack attack on the network at three-thirty this morning. I got a call from my team and have been here since four. Didn't take time to shower and dress up before work."

"What area did they hit?"

"That's the thing. It looks like they were mostly interested in getting inside. Once they were in, they disappeared as quickly as they entered. It was like they all just unplugged their computers from the network at the same time."

"All? How many were there?"

"Half a dozen. Looked like they were marauding and just trying to hack through firewalls. Maybe a contest to see who could get through first. It's possible they didn't really have a reason to be there. They were gone before we got an address for them or could isolate the signatures."

"Sounds nasty," I said. So the invasion of my six pursuers had triggered an alarm in the system. It sounded like they just retreated, but the message on my dashboard led me to believe someone inside had expelled them. Still, Don seemed to have no knowledge of this. I decided to stick my head into

Allen Yarborough's office. You'd think the System Administration Manager would have been called about the security breach, but Allen's office was closed and the lights were out. It didn't look like he'd come in yet. I stopped by Phil's office and he waved me on. He was on a phone call and didn't look like he'd be off anytime soon.

There was one other person I was interested in this morning. I still didn't know what kind of work she did. I went up to the twenty-sixth floor and strolled by Jen Roberts's office. She was just walking out the door, dressed sharply in a blue pinstriped suit with a white silk blouse buttoned to the throat. She was looking at a file in her hands and nearly tripped into me.

"Oh, Dag! Just the person I wanted to see. Were you coming to see me?"

Jen was brighter and more cheerful than I'd seen her on any other occasion. She must have had a good weekend. I'd avoided her all day Monday.

"I was just stopping by to get some pointers on filling out a travel request. Ford tells me you are a stickler on setting up cost/benefit analysis and I wanted to find out how you prefer to see travel estimates put together."

"I'm a stickler with Ford because he submits a travel request every other week. If I approved half of them, that would still be four times the team's entire budget. If you have travel that will advance your work, talk to Darlene. She has signing authority for all Arnie's directs. Probably has a higher spending limit than I do. You don't need to bring it to me unless you need it to be discussed and approved in our team meeting."

"Well, that's good to know. Did you want to see me about something?"

"Yes. You wouldn't happen to have been headed out for coffee would you?"

"I was thinking about it. Most of our team seems to be whacked out of their minds with lack of sleep, but no one was interested in taking a break."

"That's what I wanted to talk to you about," she said. "Let's take a walk."

UNLIKE DARLENE AND Arnie, Jen—in her high heels—avoided the long walk down the hill to the Daybreak. Instead we entered a bank building on Third and went to the atrium where an independent vendor did a good business all day long with people in suits. I noticed the price of a cup of coffee was about thirty percent higher than down the hill. Jen had grabbed an umbrella from the stand next to our building entrance to keep the light rain off her perfectly coifed hair and silk blouse. But once we hit the marble of the atrium her wet heels slid and I caught her in a position that was neither ladylike on her part nor chivalrous on mine. I couldn't help but notice that she eschewed anything that would strap her in.

"Let's just pretend that little embarrassment didn't occur shall we?" she said once she'd straightened up.

"I'm sorry…" I started. She held a hand up to silence me.

"Didn't occur."

"Right." We got our coffees and found a wrought iron table near the three-story windows. If you were high enough, you could see the Sound out the upper part of the windows, but where we were, there was nothing outside but tree planters. "You have something in that file you wanted to go over with me?"

"No. Carrying a file is just a prop. Makes people think you have a purpose when you are walking the halls. It's like you with your smartphone." *Damn!* "I want to talk to you about last night." That was a surprise. First, she was the only person I'd seen this morning who didn't look like she'd been up all night. Second, I didn't think she could possibly have information that Don didn't have and he showed no interest in talking to me. Third, I didn't think she had the technical chops to hack the system. She seemed more like a numbers person to me.

"What about last night?"

"Forgive me, but you were behaving oddly, and I couldn't help but notice. I live in West Seattle. I went for a jog and saw you sitting in a coffee shop. I was going to stop and say hello, but you seemed intensely involved in something other than the cupcakes. You were carting around more computer hardware than most of us have on our desks."

"Oh." She didn't know about the intrusion at all. This was completely off the record. "I was setting up some new gaming equipment."

"Gaming? As in gambling?"

"No. RPG. That's a role-playing game. People from all over the country gather together online to participate in a gamemaster's storyline. I was running a game last night."

"Not just locals?"

"I don't really know where most of them are from. They sign on with their gaming alias and we play. Last night we played until quite late."

"Yes. Do you always have someone tailing you?"

"Tailing me?"

"The guy in black with a Nike jacket. Seahawks cap. Text messaging all the time."

"Didn't even see him." *There was a guy following me?* I wracked my brain trying to visualize who was in that coffee shop. I couldn't call him to mind.

"It was intriguing. Made me curious as to why he was following you, so I followed along."

"You were following me last night?"

"Oh, no. Even in running sweats, if I'd been following you, I'm sure you would have noticed. I followed him." I shivered just a little thinking about the parade of followers behind me. Was someone following Jen? I could just imagine her in sweats, jogging along. All right, I'd definitely have noticed. I put that image out of my mind.

"It must have looked pretty strange."

"I gave up when you caught the bus to the airport and called a taxi to take me home. Did you come to work straight from your game?"

She knew I went to the airport? Questions were piling up.

"No. I slept…" I didn't want to tell her exactly when I ended the game if she didn't already know. People up at certain hours of the night when other things were happening at those hours would be too easy to connect. "…a few hours before I showered and dressed for work. By the time I got on that bus, the game was beginning to wind down."

"And how many others on our team were playing your game with you?" There it was. She was suspicious.

"None that I've identified. Like I said, people log in with their gaming alias. I don't usually try to track down the real identity. Could be the whole company was playing. Were you?"

"Though I try not to be blatant, I don't play games." She looked me intently in the eyes and I could see more than a professional interest. Her lips curled into a smirk. After an awkward silence of a few seconds, she changed to a more professional tone.

"You arrived on the scene at EFC in the midst of a power struggle. The company is closely held, but the founders and majority stockholders have been at this for twenty-five years. They're getting tired of playing Caesar and are looking around every corner for potential assassins. That includes your boss and mine. It's clear to me that neither of us was brought here to do the job for which HR has a description. What's less clear is that we may not have been brought to do the job our bosses described either. Watch your back." She let me soak that in for a minute while she finished her coffee. *IGotUrBak.* A lot of what she said fit with my suspicions. "Let's get back to work," she said at last.

She stood and casually tossed her cup in a bin. She walked carefully across the marble floor, put up her umbrella and marched out into the rain.

⊓◗┇┅┱┙┝┝╳┑┱┆┲╳┱╗┏┷┶┙╳┙

IT WAS AFTER lunch that I began my exercise routine. I started on the third floor, walked the entire circuit, and then moved to the fourth floor. I stopped on each floor to examine the bulletin boards where employees posted notices of apartments for rent, puppies for sale, housekeeping services, and the mandatory HR Fair Employment Practices bulletins. EFC has a lively community of employees who post notes about community service events, multi-cultural events, and book clubs. I noticed many people walking the halls. Marketing, of course had the most elaborate displays and included notices about cookie and candy sales from various schools and clubs, and a May Day festival coming up soon.

On the other hand, floors that were mostly technical or manufacturing had little or no activity in the halls. The offices had no interior facing windows, and the core was devoted to equipment, much of which was managed remotely. That's what I encountered on the twelfth floor.

As I approached the security door where I'd concealed my miniature RFID reader, I pulled out my cell phone and launched an app for capturing the info from the device. I timed my approach so the camera was pointed away and held my infrared LED flashlight pointed at it just to make sure I wasn't caught. I waved the phone at the reader. In an instant it had captured the signal and replayed it for the security unit. The door clicked unlocked and a green light came on. I smiled and continued my exercise routine without opening the door.

⊓◗┇┅┱┙┝┝╳┑┱┆┲╳┱╗┏┷┶┙╳┙

I WAS BACK in my office by two-thirty, giving short shrift to the upper floors. There is a fundamental fact about security cameras that few people know. They aren't usually monitored. It's ridiculous to imagine a person whose job is to watch the camera feed twenty-four hours a day. Add to that the fact that there are over a hundred cameras that I had counted with at least four to a floor and you have a phenomenal amount of video to watch. I figured it would take no less than sixty people to monitor all the feeds twenty-four-seven. Instead, footage is stored for a period of time in a digital vault that holds several petabytes of data. After thirty days, the data is erased. Only if there was an intrusion into the company, a theft, or assault, would the tapes ever be reviewed. EFC's unique policy of having security cameras playing as screen-savers on every employee's desktop served more to remind people they were being watched than to monitor the cameras.

I needed to know if there was video surveillance in the manufacturing facility. I used my portable keyboard to tap out the commands and searches I needed inside the network to generate a list of video feeds. There was video surveillance at the entrances to the facility, but not inside.

Next, I needed plans for the building. I suspected there was a reason for the facility being on the twelfth floor. Unfortunately, the company plans for offices were of no help. The floor plans on the Intranet showed what offices were on which floors, where emergency exits were, and general use information regarding the large spaces that were used for the server farm and the manufacturing facility. I needed electrical, heating, and plumbing plans.

Developers making structural changes in buildings are required to obtain a building permit from the Department of Planning and Development. Applications for building permits must be accompanied by blueprints that building inspectors use to approve the work and then verify that it was done according to specification, is safe, and is habitable. Being a government office, it doesn't throw anything away. A huge microfilming project was undertaken a few years ago and development documents from the 1890s forward have been cataloged. At the same time the historical documents went into microfilming, all current projects were stored digitally. I was betting the modifications to the twelfth floor were made after digitization started.

Proper protocol for looking at these documents requires an investigator to submit a request, go to the office, and pick up the files after signing for them. The permits and drawings are a matter of public record, so technically breaking into the city's digital vault to view the plans wasn't completely illegal in my mind. I looked up the city records for the building permits on this site. The low-res digital images I found were just adequate to confirm my suspicions.

There is still something about the number thirteen that makes people jittery, even in an age supposedly beyond superstition. As a result, very few buildings acknowledge a thirteenth floor. The elevators in our building are no exception. The buttons are numbered consecutively from one to twelve and from fourteen to twenty-six. We're supposed to believe that there simply is no thirteenth floor.

The reality is that most of the building's mechanicals are located on the thirteenth floor, accessible only by a service elevator and stairs. The central core, however, had been cut out to make a single two-story room where the manufacturing equipment of the credit card company is located. It would take me some work, but I was pretty sure I could access the facility through the equipment rooms on the non-existent thirteenth floor. It was going to be a climb. It was nearly five by the time I'd finished my various searches and memorized the access points I needed. There was still one thing I wanted to check.

I STEPPED OUT to verify that Don had left for the day. If he'd been here since four a.m. he had a good excuse to bug out early. In fact, all my teammates were gone. I went back to my desk and called up the network logs for last night. I wanted to see exactly what was recorded at the time I was being attacked in cyberspace.

Network logs include screen after screen full of text lines. EFC is a twenty-four-hour company, so there is always traffic on the network. I could get close to the information I wanted by searching the time, but I was only certain that it was between three-thirty and four o'clock which left thousands of lines of log entries.

Part of being a good detective is being able to see anomalies. Take one look around a room and identify the one item that is out of place. I'd already proven how inept I was at that last night when I failed to realize I had not one but two tails on me. But it was different when I looked at code. I started scrolling through the lines of log entries, not sure what I was looking for, but watching for the anomaly. I didn't try to read the lines, just watch for the patterns. As the lines went by, I zoned out, letting them flood my mind.

It took me two passes through the entire half hour log before I saw it. The timestamps.

At 3:42:24 there was a ten second gap. The numbers had been consecutive, often multiple for a given timestamp up to that point, but between 3:42:24 and 3:42:34 there were no entries. It wasn't beyond the realm of possibility that all network traffic into and out of EFC suddenly ceased for ten seconds in the middle of the night right when half a dozen gamers broke through the firewall and were ousted by someone inside with enough power to wipe them from the system. Right. It's possible, but the likelihood is remote.

I examined the records carefully. On either side of the ten second block, an employee was surfing the Web. The network log indicated a start point and an end point for each link. Above the ten second gap the addresses moved smoothly. From a to b, from b to c, from c to d. But below the gap the transitions were suddenly from f to g. The referrals from d to e and e to f were missing. Someone had edited the network log and that took a lot of skill. The log was autogenerated from the system. If someone could blank out a portion of it or delete it, EFC's security problems were a lot more serious than a breached firewall.

Now that I knew what I was looking for, I could write search parameters and send spiders into the network. At least theoretically. First I had to locate a server in the cloud that would let me execute a program that would technically be classed as a virus by security. I could get the results, but whatever server I found would be pulled off-line and the hole patched by morning. Ah, well. That will just enhance company security. I set the little bug loose.

It was nearly six and I was supposed to meet Andi at seven. I set up both the company laptop and my big gaming machine side-by-side on my desk and put them sleep so I could wake them remotely if I needed to. Then I grabbed my tablet and my cell phone and left.

THE SERVICE STAIRWELL was accessible from the underground parking garage where some impatient mechanic had conveniently wedged the door open and left it. It had taken me nearly ten minutes to find it, even knowing from the building blueprints where to look. It took twelve minutes to climb to the thirteenth floor. Of course, it wasn't marked thirteen. The access door below was marked twelve and the access door above was marked fourteen, but this door was simply marked "Danger. High Voltage. Do Not Enter." It was secured by an old fashioned key-lock. It took me almost three minutes to pick it. That's not really my specialty.

Inside, I got my bearings as I walked up and down aisles of cable boxes, heat and air conditioning units, telephone and electrical boxes. Finally, I came to the door I wanted. This door was secured by an electronic lock that matched the ones in our office. I waved my cell phone at it with the recorded RFID and it clicked open.

It was a good thing I didn't just step through. It was an access door, no doubt on the fire department's list of emergency exits, but it was nearly twelve feet off the ground with no more than a narrow catwalk crossing in front of it. I stepped onto the catwalk and heard the door click shut behind me.

Damn.

There was no way to open the door from the inside that I could see. I was inside and I'd have to figure out how to get out later. For now, I found my way down a metal stair onto the main floor.

The room was two stories high and filled with the equipment and robotics required to make credit cards, including warehousing the stock, manufacturing, sealing, and shipping.

Sheets of plastic were fed into cutters and trimmed to credit card size. Printing on the front and back was done on a digital press, including laminating holographic images on the front of certain cards. Magnetic strips were applied to the cards and each was treated with an ink-receptive strip for the signature. The cards were then fed through a magnetic recorder that recorded the personal information of the user on the card. From there, the card was fed into a machine where the strip was read and then the card was stamped with the raised numbers and letters that identified the credit card number and customer.

I took pictures of the process with the camera built into my tablet and started cataloging the operation. EFC produced private label credit cards for various organizations, including associations and credit unions. It had also developed a side-business of manufacturing gift cards with dollar values for various restaurants and retail outlets. It even subcontracted card manufacturing for larger credit organizations and banks.

The magnetic stripe on a credit card contains the necessary information to conclude a transaction. The primary account number embossed on the card is also the leading information on the stripe. It includes the name of the cardholder, the expiration date, the Verification number or CCV Code, and the address and ZIP code of the cardholder. Of course the information is encrypted so you can't simply run it through a tape player and read the info, but one of the cleverest schemes for pirating accounts has been to have a thin card reader inserted into a regular bank station like an ATM machine or gas pump. Usually a concealed camera is focused on the keypad so that the thieves can record the keying of the PIN as they capture the information from the magnetic stripe. It's quick and efficient.

It also goes undetected for a long time. A compromised account can be hoarded by a thief for weeks or even months before use. That gives the thief time to collect a huge amount of data and then remove all trace of the illicit equipment before it is discovered. It makes it almost impossible to identify the source of the compromise.

As I watched the machines doing their thing, I observed an occasional card being rejected at one or another station. The most common rejections occurred before any data was imprinted on the card. The magnetic stripe might not have adhered. The ink might have been smeared. Any number of defects were caught by inspecting equipment in a fraction of a second and led to immediate rejection of the card.

Further down the line, a card might be rejected for failed data recording, duplication, or simply being blank when it got to a place that required data. Each of these failed cards were shuffled to a bin that led to a shredder where rejected cards were chopped to tiny bits to be recycled.

After a card passed all its tests, it was put in line for mailing. Based on the card data, a letter was printed, envelope generated, the card attached with a glue spot to the letter which was then folded, inserted in the envelope, sealed, and bundled for mailing. No human hand had touched it.

The few cameras that were in this manufacturing room were focused on the equipment so a technician could visually verify if there were production problems. If there was an equipment malfunction, service or maintenance to be done, or supplies to be refreshed, someone would come through a security door on the twelfth floor. Once inside, the operating assumption was the tech belonged there; security did not take responsibility for what authorized people did once they were inside the room.

I'd seen what I needed to in this room. I wasn't happy about exiting onto the twelfth floor but my exit back through the mechanicals room was blocked. I headed for the main door into the room and got a shock. It didn't have a RFID reader to open the door from the inside. It had crash bars that were clearly marked "Emergency Exit. Alarm will sound. Use Keypad." Next to the door was a ten-key pad with a flashing red light above it. I estimated the location of the card reader on the outside of the door and waved my cell phone at it, transmitting the code, but it was too far away and on the other side of a wall. No signal penetrated.

I was stuck.

{17}
Sweet Dreams

IT WAS TEN after seven when I called Andi. It wasn't a happy call.

"Hey! I cooked. When are you going to be here?" I loved her voice.

"Um, I got a little tied up at work," I said. "I'm not sure I'll make it."

"Tied up?" The disappointment in her voice hurt.

"Well, it's more like locked in."

"Can't you call someone to let you out?"

"I'm locked into a room that I'm probably not supposed to be in."

"Probably?"

"Definitely."

"Dag, what do you do for a living?" Andi was trying to make light of the situation while hiding her disappointment.

"I guess there's nothing for it but to tell you. I'm a spy."

"And the government has sent you undercover in a credit card company because they are suspected of manufacturing weapons of mass destruction." She was taking it well, but I had to be truthful with her. I wasn't planning to make a practice of getting locked in places I shouldn't be, but it was pretty likely that in the course of my career I'd be unable to keep some personal appointments. It was just the nature of the business.

"Andi, you know I'm contractor here and not really an employee, right?"

"Yes. I thought you were troubleshooting a computer network glitch."

"More or less, that's the story they gave out. I'm supposed to investigate ways to improve network security. But the truth is they sent me in here to find out who has their fingers in the till. I'm trying to track down someone who's stealing from the company."

"It's never going to end, is it?" she said softly. "I thought the thing with Henderson was just because it personally affected you." It was true that the Henderson case was personal. My retirement funds were part of the money that was missing. But the deeper into computer forensics I got, the more likely I'd be dealing with cases like this.

"Well, when it looks like you're an expert in a field, then others line up to use you, I guess."

"What can I do? Can I bring you dinner? No I suppose that won't work unless you're just locked in the women's restroom. You aren't, are you? I didn't think so. Is there an outside latch I could open? Should I call someone for you? I could create a distraction outside the office if you need." Andi had suddenly shifted into Cali mode. I understood now that it was a method of coping with information that was flooding her brain. I became just a little more aware of how her daughter's mind worked.

"Andi, I'll find a way out of here. It just might take me a while. I don't do a dangerous job, I just got stuck. I'm sorry I can't join you for dinner." I really was sorry. *Why the hell did I do this before my date? It could have waited until tomorrow.* It's that single-mindedness that takes over when I start working on a puzzle.

"Me, too." I could hear longing in her voice, even over the phone.

"Andi, is this serious?"

"Oh, no. I'll eat my share of dinner and the rest I'll refrigerate. Cali always comes home from rehearsal hungry."

"I don't mean dinner, Andi. I mean us. Are we really more than friends? Because I think I'm falling in love with you and if you think I shouldn't, I'd like to know that before it gets worse."

"Really?"

"Yes."

"I'm glad you said that before we had sex. I mean, not that we're going to have sex. Yet. It's just nice to know that you feel that way before, or without, or... I think I've been in love with you for a long time," she blurted out. That surprised me. Then again, maybe it shouldn't I'd been feeling closer and closer to her for months. I could feel my face stretch into a grin.

"I'm really sorry I'm not there for dinner."

"If you get lonely, all locked up there by yourself, you can call me anytime."

"Thanks. I should get started figuring out a way to get out of here. I'll talk to you later, okay?"

"Yeah. Later."

Oh, yeah. Later.

I NEEDED TO get out of this room. I was almost willing to crash the doors and let the alarm sound. Almost, but not quite. It was just that the thought of Andi saying she loved me... I really needed to get out of here.

I could see the setup pretty clearly. As with most robotic manufacturing rooms, this one was extremely clean and the air conditioning kept it between sixty-six and sixty-eight degrees if I judged the temperature correctly. Some of the equipment generated a lot of heat. The robots were controlled by their own set of computers in a room on one side that I guessed was probably kept even colder. These computers were not on the company network or a part of the cloud. I was pretty sure they could connect to get data from the network, but they'd be hidden behind another firewall inside the company. The workstations in the offices on the twelfth floor were slaves to these powerful computers. I'd have to do some investigating to find out how information on customers was eventually connected to billing and customer service.

The room with the computers was also secured behind a door with a keypad lock. With the information that I now possessed, I knew that if I had the keypad code, I could steal all the customer data I wanted from the company and it was unlikely it would be detected for weeks or even months. Unfortunately, I lacked the keypad code, so it was a moot point.

I had few options. I was sealed in a locked room.

I went back to observing how the equipment worked to see if there was a way I could use any of it. There was a freight elevator that had a door on this floor, but the call buttons had the same keypad lock on them that the doors had. Apparently, all raw materials came up in that elevator and all finished letters went down in it. There were no apparent robotics for moving the boxes of finished mail that were stacked on palettes as they came off the conveyor belt. That meant that workers had to enter the room at some point to load the material in the elevator and actually do the shipping at the post office. The palettes were nearly full, so I began to wonder what time the night shipping crew arrived.

I looked for all the usual ways to get out of a room. The heating ducts and air vents were twenty feet overhead. The few places where the ceiling was only one story high were behind locked doors like the computer room. I sat in a corner near the door and pulled out my tablet, connecting remotely to my company laptop in the office. From there I began searching for access codes in the manufacturing center. Wherever they were located, they were well-guarded. It looked like I'd found the one truly secure place in the company.

If I were a thief, I'd want this room, I thought. It surprised me. Wouldn't a thief try to spot the least secure access to what they wanted? The most secure part of a system could become the weakest simply because of its impregnability. With access to this room, I could have access to any credit card being created on the system, and I got in pretty easily. If I waited until the cards were packaged and ready for mailing, I could have cards, cardholder addresses, and security information. Technically, it was a postal offense since the last machine in the line stamped postage on the sealed envelopes. If I was stealing credit cards, I don't think I'd hesitate at robbing the postal system.

But there were other options as well. I could launch an attack on an entire range of cards, in fact, essentially make cards that appeared valid, by just taking one good card off the conveyor belt. It was called a BIN attack. The Bank Identification Number is contained in the first 12 digits of a credit card. With one card, especially a newly released card, I could simply change the last four digits of the card, keep the same expiry date, and advance the CCV code. Five sequential cards would show me any variance the system had put in place to keep customer codes and CCV codes from advancing at the same pace. I could sit at a computer and order cash advances on each of my dummy cards for an hour, close my accounts and strip my computer of all records, then fly to South America with the cash.

I'd always held that if I was in the same room as a computer, I could own all the data on the computer. This was a step up. Being in the same room with the manufacturing equipment for bank cards, I could own a slice of the banking world.

Back on the tablet, I changed my search parameters to find who went through the security doors into this room. I assumed that it was limited to the technicians who did maintenance on the equipment and the shipping clerks who moved the raw materials and finished products in and out of the room. But there was always a chance that someone else was helping themselves to untraceable credit card information. I concluded my search parameters by having the results emailed to me at one of my Internet mail accounts and erased the search spiders from the network. I didn't want to leave evidence on the company laptop.

Before I got results back from the search, I heard the electronic lock on the door next to me click. I flattened myself back behind the frame where I was partially sheltered from a direct sightline. Two technicians in white lab suits opened the door and headed straight for the shipping area. Before the door snapped closed, I squeezed out through it and was in the hall. I scraped my miniature RFID reader off the bottom of the card reader and got out of Dodge.

◼◗▐▞▚▗▞ ▜◀▞▞◿▞◿◢▞◿◤▞◣◿◥

I DIDN'T STAY around to see if the cameras had picked me up. As long as I hadn't tripped any alarms, the video would never be looked at. I went to the main lobby, switched elevators and flashed my ID at the after-hours card reader to head to my twenty-third-floor office. It should look like I had just come back to the office to pick something up. Tomorrow was my day to work remotely, so I needed my equipment.

I closed things up, took the laptop and headed up the hill. On the way I called Andi.

"'Lo?" Her voice sounded groggy and I glanced at my phone. *Damn!* It was nearly midnight. She'd been asleep.

"Sorry, Sweetheart. I didn't mean to wake you."

"Dag? Are you okay?"

"Yes. Just wanted to let you know I got out and am on my way home."

"Okay. Stop by before you go up."

"You don't need to get up. You can just go back to sleep."

"No. I really want to see you. Don't knock. I'll watch for you at the door."

"Okay. I'll see you in fifteen minutes."

It was the longest fifteen minutes of my life. By comparison, my time in the manufacturing room had flown by. I was panting up a storm by the time I'd walked up across the freeway on Olive and turned onto Summit to get home. I passed the giant sequoia in front of my building and practically ran up Andi's steps. I was huffing and puffing like crazy after the fast walk uphill. It was almost as bad as climbing the stairs to the thirteenth floor.

True to her word, Andi opened the door as soon as I stepped up on the porch. She was wearing a plush bathrobe and fuzzy slippers, but it looked like she'd just brushed out her hair.

"You really didn't have to wait up for me," I said as she came into my arms.

"Shhh. I don't think Cali's asleep. I didn't wait up. I was asleep. But I wanted to see you."

"Not that I object, but why so urgent?"

"Because I said something on the phone that I shouldn't have." My heart fell. There was only one thing she'd said that I could think she might regret. I braced myself for the worst. She looked me straight in the eyes and I nearly fell into them. "The first time you tell a man you love him, it should be face to face, not on the phone. I love you, Dag Hamar." With that, she closed the distance between us and pressed her lips against mine. I was lost in her kiss. When we parted, I caught my breath for a moment then started to speak.

"Andi..." She pushed her finger against my lips.

"Shhh. I don't want any 'Me, toos.' When you tell me, I want it to be first." With that she kissed me again and pushed me toward the door. "Sweet dreams, Dag," she said, brushing my ear with her lips. I stumbled across the lawn to my own back steps and looked back in time to see the porch light go out.

Sweet dreams, indeed.

{18}
A Hurting Heart

I DIDN'T GO IN to EFC on Wednesday because it was my day to work in my own office. I did, however, intend to investigate what my search spiders had found overnight. Unfortunately, Andi was unable to get together for more than a pleasant good morning kiss before she left for class. She said she was scheduled to go back to the University for interviews in the afternoon and that she had a committee meeting this evening. She'd be bringing Cali home about ten if I wanted to stop by for a cup of tea before we said goodnight. I told her I wouldn't miss it.

"Unless you are locked up someplace," she sighed.

"Locked in."

"Mmmhmm."

That left me with a day to work in my office on 15th and to begin putting together the pieces that were left by the police. Yesterday, they'd finished gathering the evidence I'd left them and the tape was removed from my door. With my new toys, I had more computers lying around than would fit on my desk. I closed up my old laptop and plugged in the new one to recharge. It was powerful, but it ate batteries.

I immediately logged in to the computer in the EFC office by remote access on my tablet. The first search I wrote gave me limited results. It showed that I was online in the office but none of the other people I wanted to find. The second search result was more productive. I had a log of employee numbers of everyone who had entered the manufacturing facility in the past forty-eight hours. I matched names with employee numbers from the Human Resources database and waited for my list to be downloaded.

In the meantime, I started my gaming machine and called up the entire record of the game I'd run Monday night. I wanted to know who was playing and where they were physically located. While that was running, I flipped on my desktop unit to take a look at what the police had left me. Surprisingly, that was the first computer that gave me results to look at as all three struggled to access the cloud through my wired connection at the same time. The picture on the screen that greeted me was chilling.

The mutilated body of a child flooded my largest monitor. A message flashed across the screen that read "A worthy opponent? Two can play this game. Who do you love, baby?" The screen blanked and then images started flashing across the screen with a timer bar that told me there were two million files waiting to download.

I jerked the network cables out of the wall for all three computers as I noticed images starting to download on the laptop as well. This was not good. A quick scan of the files that were downloading told me my computer had been hit with a motherload of porn, much of which was still downloading. I pulled the power out of the desktop and the laptop, then pulled the battery from the laptop as well.

Damn!

I called Jordan and had to leave a message. Things were heating up. I knew Patterson was a predator, but I didn't expect to be the prey. Then a thought struck me. I dialed into the office and asked for Don. The call was routed to Darlene.

"Darlene, I need to talk to Don immediately."

"He's in conference with Mr. Dennis."

"Put me through to both of them, then. This is an emergency." There was only a moment's lag before I heard the phone connect.

"What's going on, Dag?" Arnie asked.

"Is Don with you?"

"I'm here," Don's voice answered.

"Here's the situation. I was logged in remotely a few minutes ago when I was hit with a massive attack on my office network. It blasted past my firewalls, virus detectors, and several other bells and whistles I've got running in my office. It's nasty stuff. There is a chance the worm got through to my laptop in the office. If so, it could propagate through the network. You've got to isolate my computer from the rest of the company." I could hear a door slam, but the only other sound for a few seconds was the clacking of keys. "Are you guys there?"

"I'm here," Arnie said. "Don is in your office. How long ago did this attack take place?"

"Less than five minutes ago. I disconnected my computers, called the police, and then called you."

"You called the police?"

"I've been doing some consulting for them on tracking down an online predator. This looks like it's related."

"That's bad news for you, Dag. Very bad. If you've infected our network…"

"I haven't infected anything," I said hotly. "If the corporate firewalls are working the way they should be, nothing should be able to get through the connection."

"Still, I can't afford to have risky behavior in my department. We're under scrutiny as it is."

"Well, with luck that will all be taken care of soon, too."

"You've got a solution to our little problem?"

"I'm closing in on one. I should be able to tell you more by the end of the week."

"Good. That's good, Dag. We'll mop up here. You take care of your equipment. See you tomorrow."

What was that all about? Arnie went from being threatening to exceedingly calm in a heartbeat. Just telling him I was onto a lead shouldn't have changed him that much. Maybe he was just regretting having snapped at me in the first place. No matter. I needed to clean up the mess of my electronics. I started by pulling the hard drive in my tower. I sealed it in an anti-static bag and pulled a spare out of my locked file cabinet. Something told me I was going to need to expand my inventory of spare parts if I kept going in this business. I installed a clean system on the machine. I loaded it up with all the anti-virus software I had and connected an old modem to my landline. My T1 was obviously compromised as a route out. When it came time to get back online, I would have to use the old-fashioned way.

I grabbed my tablet and logged on to the cellular network. I wasn't going to identify myself any further on the Internet than I had, but I needed to check my mail accounts. I knew exactly who had launched this attack, and he wouldn't have done it without leaving me messages. Patterson was the kind of guy who loved to talk.

Sure enough, my email had been bombarded with messages, some ranting about Internet spies, some flaming me directly, and all of them containing an invitation to click on a message that I could see would lead to another virus. The last mail message, however, was one I hadn't expected this time. It read simply "Unit purged with no harm. IGotUrBak." What was this? Could it be that Don was the one working to back me up and watching to see what I would do? He certainly had the skills and access to everything in the company.

<hr>

MY PHONE BUZZED.

"Hamar."

"What happened?" Jordan was speaking.

"Booted the computer this morning and an attack message showed up on screen. Started downloading porn and unpacking it to everything on the network. And I'm not talking legal porn. This stuff is sick. I disconnected everything and bagged the hard drive. This was complete with a threat, Jordan."

"I'm on my way there now. I've got a tech with me that will verify. See you in twenty minutes."

<hr>

TWENTY MINUTES GAVE me just time enough to check the laptop. By disconnecting everything as quickly as I did, I'd aborted the download to the new laptop, which was a relief to say the least. I wanted to know more than ever now who was accessing that room. I looked at the results I'd received from my match. What I saw was not what I expected and not what I wanted to see.

I pulled my ID badge out of my pocket and looked at it carefully. The log showed that every time I'd walked by that room the past week, I'd been logged as entering it. I checked the times. There was video footage that showed me approaching that door twice last week and twice again this week. And there was an access log that showed me entering it!

What was it Jen had said? "We may not have been brought to do the job our bosses described." I was beginning to look like pigeon. *Damn!*

Before Jordan got to my office, I stashed my laptop in a bag by the front door so it wasn't in my office. I was going to need a computer later tonight.

THE INTERNET IS a dangerous place. The fact that I called the police and that my entire interaction with Patterson had been recorded by a court-assigned witness as a tech tore apart my computer kept me out of trouble. The hard drive that was now filled with a self-replicating virus that kept unpacking level after level of highly illegal porn was confiscated as evidence not against me, but against the scum who attacked me.

The problem was the cops had yet to make a hard ID on the guy that would stand up in court. We all knew it was Patterson. None of us wanted to believe it. But the evidence so far was all just one step away from being enough to make an arrest.

What bothered me most were the words that had scrolled across the screen with that first horrid image. "Who do you love, baby?" It reversed an old television catch-line and turned it from a comfort to a threat.

Patterson was launching attacks against me, possibly to damage my credibility with the police and possibly to take out a sick revenge. Someone at EFC was setting me up to take the fall for a crime I didn't know for sure was even being committed.

I needed to think. And for this thinking, I needed to drive. There was a game being played, and just as when I shifted positions in the physical world when I ran a game, I felt safer being on the move. I packed my uninfected tablet and chargers and got out of Dodge.

I sent a text to Andi. "Called out of town. Not back until tomorrow. Sorry."

Half an hour later, I was cruising south on I-5 in the Mustang, feeling the horses in the muscle car whine with power. As soon as I was south of Tacoma, I opened it up and let it roar at eighty-five, slowing down just enough at Olympia, Centralia and Chehalis to not draw attention. Then I put the pedal to the metal and spent forty-five minutes over ninety. That car moves like a demon, but it drinks gas. I refueled near the Cascade locks on I-84 and swung back onto the Interstate until I hit Route 82 headed north. I'd been driving nine hours with hardly a break when I reached Ellensburg, going around in circles. It was nearly midnight and both the car and I needed fuel.

I thought about the paper trail I was leaving and what it could mean if there were stolen credit cards that just happened to land in the places I was visiting this night. I was seeing a threat in everyone I knew. *There can't be a connection between EFC and Patterson, can there?* I was plain spooked, but I didn't have much cash on me, so I ran the card through the pump and went to sit in an all-night truckstop for food.

Had someone at EFC been lifting credit cards? Did he or she print an untraceable batch of 'gift cards?' Download customer data files?

Or were they waiting for the next time they could verify I was in the building? It was best that I stay away, but I was going to have to go back tomorrow. There was only one person who could answer the ultimate question. I had to come up with a plan for asking it.

In the café, I ordered tomato soup and a grilled cheese sandwich. It came with chips and a pickle on the side. I wolfed it down with a cup of trucker coffee while my computer was booting up. The truck stop had free WiFi, so I logged in and accepted the terms on the browser screen. It was time to get into the office and see what was going on. I was far enough away that I couldn't be there making off with cash while searching the corporate data for a traitor. Right now I had no less than seven suspects at EFC—everyone on my team—and they had kept me so occupied that I couldn't even begin to guess who else might be involved. I still thought the key would be in finding out who was on the corporate network during my game Monday night. I opened the email account to which I'd sent the search results and started comparing them with known markers on the network log from that night. Five out of seven suspects had logged in between one and three a.m. But none had visited sites associated with my game.

That didn't mean they weren't there. I showed up as logged in as well, but none of my game activity was logged. I was pretty sure that I could identify who was online. I already knew that Jen was following me around the city until close to one, so it was unlikely she had been online. But I had no evidence that she was following me—just her word. I was getting stuck. Everyone was still a suspect.

I decided to come back to the problem later when my computer chimed. I'd set up an alert system earlier to let me know when anyone used my ID to open a door at the company. I scanned down the list of doors and saw that somehow, I'd just opened the door on the twelfth floor into the manufacturing facility. I quickly paid for my snack, using a credit card and checking the receipt for the timestamp. I spotted a security camera at the gas pumps and made sure I got right in front of it as if examining it. With physics operating the way it does, I couldn't be there and here at the same time.

⸎

WHEN I GET stumped by a puzzle, I sometimes change projects just so my brain will disconnect from the logic of the problem. Often, while I'm working on this new problem the answer to the previous one will simply come to mind. That's one of the reasons I work on Sudoku puzzles and why I take multiple clients. So I decided to shift my focus to a client that seemed simple by comparison. I'd do some of the research that Cali had asked me to do. I already knew I wasn't going to betray Andi, no matter what I uncovered, but I did need to show Cali there was nothing to worry about. I ordered a BLT and a bowl of chili with more coffee and started searching for Andi.

It was completely possible in my mind that the yearbook staff had screwed up the pictures and had put someone else in Andi's place. That was my operating assumption. So I started searching for Anne D. Sullivan in Florida.

I wasn't happy about what I found. The Sullivan family in Sarasota, Florida had a daughter named Anne. Photos posted online showed that the family was, indeed black. A further search revealed an obituary dated two weeks after graduation. Anne D. Sullivan was dead.

I should have known.

Somehow, I was going to have to prove that the woman I loved hadn't taken the identity of a dead woman. But until then, I had to draw the same conclusion that Cali had over a year ago. Andi Marx was not Anne Doreen Sullivan. For some reason, that made my heart hurt.

{19}
Hero

I WAS CAUGHT IN morning traffic coming into Seattle. I'd sat in the café running searches through the night until I finally ran down the batteries of both the tablet and the laptop. I drove back to Seattle with less pressure on the gas pedal. I still didn't have a great answer. In fact, I didn't have an acceptable answer. Andi simply was not who she said she was. I'd even run a search designed to find a news story about a death with a smile, a martini, and a pregnant wife. I was amazed at how many of those there were.

And really—what could I say about it anyway? I couldn't just open a conversation and say, "By the way, now that I've told you I love you, who are you?" Occam's Razor demanded a simple explanation. Most I could think of meant she was on the run from someone who wanted to hurt her—witness protection program, cops, bad domestic situation, mob, you name it. I wasn't about to blow her cover.

Now it was Thursday morning. I wasn't sure what I was going to do. I was walking downtown toward the office with my computer in a backpack, but I hadn't determined whether or not to go in. I showered and shaved when I got home, dressed in a gray suit, and then got online at EFC from home to see if anyone was missing me. I didn't care if I got there on time and wasn't sure if I was going back at all. Still, here I was walking up Third toward the office. There were a lot of people on the street for eleven in the morning. Experience told me most people in the financial district at this hour were in offices. The rigid schedule of the financial community meant everyone would flood out onto the streets at exactly noon and the street would be empty again at one. It was always a curiosity to me as to why no one ever changed their lunch schedule, but maybe today was the day.

I hadn't slept in thirty hours and the world around me was a kaleidoscope of invading sights and sounds. A woman walked toward me looking like she had just come from Capitol Hill herself. She wore a plaid lumberjack shirt with a knit cap. Her motorcycle boots were pulled up over faded khaki denims. Her nose was pierced with a hoop through it. There were several rings in her ears and a tattoo was visible under her left ear. I didn't really want to imagine where else she had things stuck through her body.

A couple walking behind me argued about something that sounded trivial to me—the time they were supposed to meet a friend—but what is trivial to one person could be the most important thing in life to another. False identity could be trivial or vital.

Two men in black suits and white shirts walked past me. If I lived in the suburbs, I'd automatically assume they were missionaries wanting to tell me about this religion or that. Two-by-two. Another war waiting. Worlds collide. Maybe that was what I was arguing with myself about. This time I couldn't see either a right way *or* a possible way. I'd been set up and I didn't know who on my team I could trust. I'd started my tenure distrusting everyone, and now I had to find a way to expose the right person while exonerating myself.

I STILL DON'T know what alerted me—a scuffle, a gasp, a shout, a scream. It seemed they all happened at once, directly behind me. I spun in my tracks.

I've heard people describe events like this with words like 'everything went into slow motion,' and then they describe in great detail everything they saw. I can't honestly say I saw anything that my brain could process quickly enough to comprehend. But my body seemed to act without me. Even after the fact, all I could put together was that a woman was falling into the street, a bus was coming, and as I grabbed her and spun her out of the path of the bus she screamed, "He pushed me." Then there was a sharp pain in the back of my head and everything went black.

I WAS BEING lifted into an ambulance on a gurney when I opened my eyes. I was strapped down securely and could see a blue uniformed police officer standing over me on one side while a med-tech pulled an oxygen mask off my face. My pack was lying on the seat to my right. The EMT was asking if I could see his fingers while I heard the officer rambling on about my rights. "You have the right to remain silent. Anything you say or do can and will be held against you in a court of law…"

"Can you raise your finger? Do you feel your toes?"

"You have the right to speak to an attorney. If you cannot afford an attorney, one will be appointed for you…"

"Is there any pain when I press on your stomach?"

"Do you understand these rights as they have been read to you?"

I couldn't speak and I couldn't move my head. My mouth wagged open and closed a couple of times.

"Is there anyone we should contact for you?"

"Why did you push her?"

It was too much. The overload blacked me out again.

I CERTAINLY WASN'T expecting Jen there when they wheeled me into a room after x-rays. I'd been summarily stripped of my clothes—an expensive gray suit cut to shreds—while they examined my body for additional damage. Apparently, the twelve stitches the doctor had put in my scalp and a mild concussion from where the bus mirror hit me in the back of the head were all the damage they could find. I felt like I'd been run over. I looked around for the policeman.

"Jen? What are you doing here?" I asked.

"Arnie and Phil were coming back from a morning coffee just in time to see the commotion. When Arnie recognized you, he caught a cab up to the hospital and Phil alerted the rest of the team. I came down because I knew Arnie had a budget meeting this afternoon. Phil came over with me, but both he and Arnie left as soon as we heard you were going to be okay."

"Police?"

"Big mix-up. One rode here with you and another came with the gal you rescued. Apparently she'd claimed you pushed her, but when asked to identify you, she screamed that it wasn't you, it was her boyfriend. A woman

across the street said she saw you save the girl. As soon as they realized they
got the wrong message, one of them got on his radio and called in an arrest
bulletin for the boyfriend.

"Why did you stay?"

"I thought I might be easier for you to look at when you woke up than
police and doctors." She smiled and I realized she was joking. Still, she was
pretty easy to look at. She was dressed in a dark suit with three buttons up
the front and apparently no more than a black camisole under it. Under
other circumstances I'd have been salivating. Under current conditions,
however, she was still a suspect.

And my affections, even though tested by what I'd learned in the past
twenty-four hours, lay elsewhere. All through the painful flashes and con-
fusion after the accident, the only thing that kept me in the real world was
thinking of Andi and that we'd just begun. I knew for a fact that it would
make no difference to me why she had changed her identity. I had fully
thrown my lot in with her. I had no reservations.

"I need to call Andi."

"The girlfriend? You can use my cell phone. I think Darlene already
called, though."

"What time is it?" I had no idea how long it had been since the accident
and I hadn't called Andi last night in the turmoil of my net search.

"Two o'clock. Darlene called Lars and he suggested she call Andi."

"Which I did, and she's on her way," Darlene said coming into the
room. "I'm sorry we didn't call her sooner, but she wasn't on your contact
list. Your mother is on her way as well. She's the emergency contact in your
personnel file." *Poor Mom.*

"Thank you, Darlene," I still grasped Jen's phone, dialing in Andi's
number. Even if she was on her way… Darlene fussed about straightening
the room and arranged a big bunch of flowers in a vase next to the bed.
They looked a little wilted.

"Sorry I didn't have time to go to a florist for you. These are left over from
Admin Day last Friday." I laughed a little, but my head was beginning to throb.

"I hope I'm out of here before they lose all their petals," I said. I pushed
the connect button to dial Andi. A second later I heard a phone ring outside
the door and Andi in stereo saying "I'm here." I heard her through the phone
and from the door as she came into the room.

I dropped the phone on the bed in time to catch Andi in my arms as she practically threw herself on me.

"You said it wasn't dangerous! You said you'd be okay! We just got started, don't get yourself killed yet!" She was laughing and crying and smothering my face with kisses between words. Beyond her, I saw Jen reach to the bed beside me to pick up her phone. The next time I looked, she was gone.

"I guess none of us is needed here," Darlene said as she, too, edged away.

"Wait," I said. "Andi, this is Darlene, the Admin in our department at EFC. She's the one who called."

"I don't know how you knew to call me, but thank you," Andi said extending a hand to Darlene. She still kept one hand clutching me.

"If it hadn't been for his boss seeing the accident, none of us would have known he was in the hospital at all," Darlene said. "I'm sorry it took so long to reach you."

"I appreciate all you did, Darlene," I said. "Please thank the guys at the office for me."

"You're a lucky man, Dag," she said looking at both Andi and me. "I hope your luck holds." With that, she nodded goodbye and left Andi and me alone.

DURING THE REMAINDER of the afternoon, my mother, Lars, and Jordan all showed up. The doctors told me they wanted to keep me for observation overnight to be sure there were no lasting effects from the concussion. They also seemed to think I was a lucky man.

I was pretty exhausted from the effect of the accident, the drugs, and having been awake most of the previous night. I drifted in and out of sleep as people milled about. My mother was suitably impressed with Andi when I introduced her as my girlfriend. Andi outright giggled at the pronouncement. Before Mom left, she looked at me sternly and said, "Keep this one."

Once she was satisfied that I was not in danger of dying on her and that I was really a hero and not a target, Andi reluctantly left to take Cali to final dress rehearsal. I asked her to stop by my apartment and pick up some clothes for me. She waved away my offered keys and said she'd ask Jared to go get some for me. She seemed hesitant to enter my private living space without me.

When it was just Lars and Jordan and me, things got serious.

"**We can't get** a positive ID on the bastard," Jordan said. "Somehow we've got to flush him out in the open. If we walk in there with less than an open-and-shut case, the courts will eat our lunch. Even the attack on your systems yesterday came by such a circuitous route that it looked like a dozen different sites were downloading to your computer at once. It's nasty."

"He's a gamer," I said. "We've got to think of him that way. To him it is just another game." John Patterson was one of the few entrepreneurs who emerged from the dot com bust with both his reputation and his fortune intact. He'd been investigated for insider trading, but no evidence ever emerged on that either. He built a billion-dollar fortune in a matter of three years and then surprised the world by signing most of it over to a charitable foundation. At that point the investigations stopped. He was chairman of Patterson Trust, but drew no salary, living what was deemed an exemplary life within the means of the small fortune he had retained for himself. Only in our small group was he suspected of being an online predator and brutal murderer. And only I knew that his trust controlled the vast charitable network I'd dubbed Philanthropolis. I'd found enough evidence to make him a person of interest, but even with the threat I'd received we couldn't positively make a link between the online harassment and the series of unsolved kidnappings I'd uncovered.

I told my colleagues what I suspected was happening at EFC as well. Lars was appalled, but he said that the accident in front of the building might have bought me enough time to sort it out. He was not happy that I was contemplating walking back into the building.

"Stay out of there until you get the evidence," he said flatly. "Use your recovery time as an excuse. If nothing else, that might force them to change their timeline and tactics. If they have to move in a different way, they could expose themselves." We were using the term they, not knowing yet how many of the employees at EFC were involved in this scheme. I was content to stay out of the building for now.

I was relieved when visiting hours were over. I needed rest. My brain was still whirling, though, so just before Lars left I asked him to hand me my backpack. I figured I could at least check my mail. I said goodbye and for the first time during the day I was alone.

I DOZED OFF with the backpack still clutched in my arms. When I jerked awake the digital clock across the room read 10:17. There were no sounds and no movement anywhere near. I'd been told to ring if I needed a pain reliever. There was no longer an I.V. drip or monitoring device connected to me. The scene from the morning flashed through my brain and I found myself sweating. I didn't know what instinct had caused me to dive in front of that bus, or how I'd escaped being killed. It just happened.

I unzipped the backpack and pulled out the big laptop, intending to take a look at my other search results to see if I could make sense of them. When the computer came out of the bag, it caught on the zipper and the bag slipped sideways. An envelope fell out of the bag onto the bed.

I stared at it in disbelief. We'd just said they would have to adjust their schedule, but I hadn't prepared for this. I reached for a paper towel on the bedside table and used it to pick up the envelope. I'd seen several identical envelopes just two nights ago when I was trapped in the robotics room. I could feel the card through the envelope addressed to someone I didn't know in Kansas.

I upended the bag and a dozen more credit card mailers fell onto the bed.

{20}
Elegant Lines of Code

THE HALL WAS empty when I poked my head out the door. I'm sure I could have talked my way out of confinement if I needed to, but there was something about walking around with my butt hanging out of a hospital gown that affected my confidence. I wasn't connected to any beeping machinery or medicine bags so at least I could walk quietly to the stairway and make my way to the lobby. No one uses the stairs in a hospital at night when the elevators are no longer in high demand.

I looked out the lobby door and saw the reception desk almost out of sight of the elevators. Unfortunately, the mailbox was directly across from me. I clutched the dozen credit card envelopes in my latex gloved hand. One thing about hospital rooms—there's never a shortage of latex gloves. I straightened my back and walked straight across the lobby to the mail slot and I dropped the envelopes in. I turned on my heel and went back to the stairwell and inside. A young couple slept in the lobby leaning against each other. The guy opened an eye, but he shook his head and went back to sleep. I didn't think the night watchman had noticed.

Before I slipped back into my room, I dropped the gloves in a hazardous waste bin. When I was safely tucked back in bed, I buzzed the night nurse. She arrived a few minutes later.

"I was just wondering if I could have something for my headache," I asked politely. She looked at my chart, took my pulse and nodded.

"I'll be right back." True to her word, she was back with two pills and a glass of water in just a few minutes. It was ten-forty-five when I rolled over and coaxed myself back to sleep.

I was down to four suspects. The only EFC employees who had come to my room were Jen, Darlene, Phil, and Arnie. That bastard.

THERE WAS A bit of a scuffle and a quick "Hush. This is a hospital. You have no right to interfere with a patient's rest."

"Ma'am, unless you can tell me the patient is at risk, we have a warrant and service is timely."

"Just don't wake anyone else," I heard her concede as the light in my room came on. I rolled over and squinted through my eyes. There were two uniformed officers in the room and just behind them I could see Arnie.

"What's up officer?" I asked groggily. "I gave a couple of statements this afternoon when they thought I pushed the girl. Is there something new you want?"

"This doesn't have to do with that matter," the first officer said. "I'm Officer Rick Newton and I have a warrant to search your personal effects for stolen property."

"Stolen property? I don't have much here. They cut my clothes off of me this afternoon and I'm not sure where they went. They brought me a bag with my personal items in it. It's in the drawer. My backpack is here. I don't have much else."

"I warned you, Dag," Arnie said, stepping around the officers. "I warned you that you would be watched. But you had to prove how clever you could be."

"Excuse us, sir," the second officer said looking at the plastic bag that contained my wallet, handkerchief, pen knife, change, cell phone, and car keys. Both policemen wore gloves as they pawed through my possessions. "You'll need to stand back." Thing One had pulled the few items that I carry in my backpack out. Laptop, power cord, tablet, writable disks, and a few assorted cables. Thing Two had moved to the closet and was rifling through my shredded suit. Man, the pain pill that nurse gave me was having some interesting side effects.

"We'll have to search your person as well," officer Newton said after shoving my laptop back in the backpack. I pulled off the covers and slid out of bed to stand on the floor. He patted me down while the other officer ran his hands through the bedclothes, under the mattress, and into the pillow.

"This gown doesn't even conceal me, officer," I said. "I'm afraid I can't hide much of anything else in it. Do you mind telling me what you are looking for?"

"Can you tell us your whereabouts last night at one o'clock a.m.?" Newton asked.

"Ellensburg, Washington," I answered. Arnie's eyes popped open in surprise.

"Do you have proof of that?"

"In my wallet, you'll find several credit card receipts." I answered. "I'm pretty sure I saw a security camera at the truck stop I was at. My attorneys will subpoena it."

"What were you doing in Ellensburg?"

"A lot of things were happening in my life on Wednesday. Detective Jordan Grant in cybercrimes can fill in any details you'd like. I decided I needed to go for a drive to clear my head. I got carried away. When I finally got to Ellensburg, I just sat in a truckstop and did Internet searches until five. Then I made a couple of phone calls and drove back to town. I'd just come down to go to the office at eleven this morning when I was caught in an accident. By the way, you know that your failure to read me my rights means you can't use anything I've said in a court of law?"

"That's not possible," Arnie said. "We clearly have him on video surveillance entering the manufacturing facility at one o' clock and leaving fifteen minutes later."

"My ID card doesn't open that door, Arnie. You made sure of that."

"Building security showed me the footage," Arnie hemmed. "They can't just make that stuff up."

"Sure you can. You asked me to find out who was dipping in the till. Now I know." I said it with bravado, knowing that Arnie was on the line. With me unconscious, it was an ideal time to plant the evidence. He just shook his head.

"There are no envelopes in this room," said Thing One. "The search is a failure."

"I'd like your names and badge numbers, officers," I said. I motioned to a pad of paper on my night stand. The officer nodded. Legally, he was obligated to leave me the information. Jordan was going to be pissed.

"Sorry, Dag," Arnie said. "Things have been so tense in the office the past two weeks that I'm jumping at everything. Just get well and nail her." He looked apologetic and defeated as he walked out the door with the two police officers. I didn't believe him for a minute.

THE DAY HAD been long and exhausting and I still hadn't managed much sleep. After the cops left with Arnie, I called Lars. As much as my ass was on the line, EFC had hired Lars's agency to work undercover. It wasn't long after that when I got a call from Jordan. I predicted rightly. He'd gone after the patrol that was called on the credit card theft. There was no way uniforms should have made the investigation. Even if the theft had technically not been a cybercrime, in this day financial crimes were so closely related that they all sat in the same department. He was on the warpath.

I hadn't really slept long when the doctor came in and summarily released me. That created a problem because I had no clothes that I could put on, but a nurse came in and told me Jared had dropped off a sack of clothes on his way to work at five. I was more than thankful just to be back in my jeans and t-shirt. I packed up my meager belongings and caught a cab outside the hospital.

I was still in the cab when my phone rang and Andi asked if she could come and pick me up. I laughed.

"That's a great idea," I said. "Why don't you come out to the curb and open the taxi door for me?"

The cab pulled up two minutes later and Andi was in my arms.

"I'm going to call in sick and cancel my classes today so I can take care of you," she said helping me up the steps to her house. Cali came rushing out the door and grabbed me from the other side.

"Oh my god, that was you! Mom told me all about the accident." Somehow the two sentences didn't connect in my mind. I shook it off as being a result of my fuzzy-headedness.

"Wait, wait," I said as we entered the house.

"I can't stay here and cause you to miss work. And you have to go to school. I'm not going to do anything all day long today but sleep, so there isn't a thing either of you can do."

"But Dag…"

"No. Just seeing you both here this morning is more than any guy could hope for, but the doctor gave me some great pills. I'm going up to my room and take one, then sleep until faculty lounge this evening."

"You can't seriously think that you are going out tonight!" Andi was shocked.

"I have a date with a really sweet woman tonight, whom I've stood up twice. I am not about to miss another," I said. Andi launched herself at my lips and scored a direct hit. She clung there for a minute and I savored her taste.

We'd probably have kept kissing if we hadn't heard Cali's "Aww." We broke our kiss and I'm sure the color of my face matched the blush on Andi's cheeks. "You guys are so cute. I'm going to school now. Glad you're okay, Dag." With that she was off and I was being led across the lawn to my stairs.

"Are you sure you don't just want to stay with me?" Andi asked softly.

"I want to have all my faculties when I stay with you, sweetheart," I said softly. "Right now I need to sleep and my own bed is the best place for it." She walked with me up the steps, but didn't come inside the apartment building.

"I'll see you tonight, then," she said, placing her lips softly against mine once more. It wasn't passionate, but it was infinitely sweet. I was ready to fall asleep wrapped in her love.

◼◼◼◼◼◼◼◼◼◼◼◼◼◼◼

I CHOSE JEANS, a plain white t-shirt, and my cashmere sweater for the evening. It was still pretty cool out, but I didn't want to take a jacket to the club later. I came out of the apartment building, and looked up the hill toward Broadway. I sat down on the steps, pulled out my cell phone and called a cab. Twenty minutes later, longer than it would normally have taken me to walk to the Blue Bastion, a cab pulled up and took me up the hill. I'd slept all afternoon, but I just didn't have the energy to walk anyplace.

Lars and Jordan showed up at the lounge as well. Neither talked about the accident, but simply came to enjoy the collegial atmosphere. I felt like they were checking up on me. I was given to understand that Lars had stormed Arnie's office this morning and raised holy hell regarding the midnight raid on my hospital room.

"I'm one step away from putting the screws on him," I said. "He knows. I haven't figured out how he's doing it yet, but it's coming together. The whole stolen cards thing was a red herring. It had all the signs of being an impromptu scheme thought up after I'd shown interest in manufacturing."

"As soon as you get something concrete, I'll have a team ready to move in and mop it up, Dag. I'm getting a little frustrated having big collars one step away from positive ID." Jordan was obviously not in a good humor. His techs still hadn't closed the loop on Patterson and the longer it took, the more likely Patterson would be to find shelter in a faraway land. We weren't even sure he was in Seattle now.

After everyone had gathered, Jan turned to Andi and me. "You two look very happy tonight. Have something planned?"

"We're going to see Two Man Flash at SoDo tonight," I answered.

"What's the occasion?" Sara asked.

"No special occasion. We just happened to have tickets," I smiled.

"Actually, there is kind of a special occasion," Andi broke in. I looked at her expectantly. This was new. "You see, while you were sleeping today, I got a phone call. I got a job offer from the University!" *Wow!* The news put us in a celebratory mood. "I'll be teaching one section of Intro to Literature and one of Reading Fiction. It's a part time gig, so I'll still be able to teach at the community college." We all congratulated Andi. She'd wanted to get into the U for as long as I'd known her, and even if she was only teaching two classes, she had her foot in the door.

We relaxed and sat there eating and talking until much later in the evening than usual. Andi and I didn't need to be at the club until nine, so we were in no hurry. Other members of the Lounge were in various stages of spring fever. We just sat and enjoyed each other's company until Andi and I had to leave for the concert. We laughed when we realized we'd sent identical text messages to Cali: Break a Leg!

The concert was fun, though by eleven I was already feeling a little weak and the heat, noise, and press of people in the club were getting to me. At eleven-thirty, I asked Andi if we could go now, even though the band had another set to play. She quickly agreed and we caught a cab in front of the club.

Frankly, I'm not all that comfortable in Pioneer Square at night these days—even as far south as SoDo. There's a pocket of light around each of the popular nightspots with huge voids of darkness in between and enough booze flowing in the gutters to make the seagulls sick. The shadows hid all manner of danger and I was glad we had a cab right in front of the club and could send him directly out of the neighborhood and up to Capitol Hill.

On the ride, we barely broke our kiss to breathe. Our hearts were still beating in time with the music we'd been listening to and there was no way we were ready for the night to end, even if we wanted a change of venue—to someplace, maybe, softer and quieter.

I tipped the driver and we stumbled into Andi's house. We were so wrapped up in each other that it took us a moment before we realized we weren't alone. We heard the sniffles first and then Andi turned on a light and we saw Cali lying on the sofa crying.

Andi turned from passionate girlfriend and near-lover to concerned parent in an instant and I was left staring with my mouth open.

"Cali, baby. What's wrong, honey?" Andi asked as she scooped her daughter up in her arms. "Was the show that bad?"

"The show... was... fine," Cali sobbed. "But Mel didn't come."

"She's never missed one of your openings. What happened."

"I... I... called after the show. Her mom... said... said... she'd run away from home. And then she said it was my fault. She said she never should have let her little girl run around with an undisciplined brat like me with my liberal upbringing and no rules. She said it was my fault that Mel ran away. Mommy, why did she do that?"

I couldn't honestly tell whether Cali was asking about Mel or Mel's mother. I guess it didn't matter.

"I can't believe she ran away and she didn't even tell me. What am I going to do without Mel?" Cali was wailing and Andi was rocking her baby in her arms. I went into the kitchen to find the one remedy that every parent I've known has used. I boiled water and made tea. I found chamomile tea in the cabinet and made two steaming mugs. As Andi rocked Cali on the sofa, I held the warm cups for them and tried desperately to think of a nice fatherly gesture to make. Apparently the tea was it. Cali looked up at me.

"Thank you Dag. I'm sorry I ruined your night for you."

"Tweety Bird, nothing is more important when you are hurting," I said. Her smile flickered at the sound of that old nickname. "Do you want me to try to find Mel?"

"Can you?"

"I don't know, but I'll look. It's hard for a girl who is so used to being connected to just drop out of sight."

"Thank you Da… Dag." My heart skipped a beat. For a moment, I thought she was going to call me Dad. Andi kissed her daughter on the forehead and told her to go take a shower and she'd cuddle her in bed. Cali took another sip of tea then left the room.

"That was so sweet of you, Dag."

"I don't know if I can find anything, but I'll try."

"Maybe you aren't such bad parent material after all."

"I love you, Andi. Cali comes with that." I'd said it without realizing it. It wasn't the way I'd imagined saying it. It wasn't how I'd planned. But with all my intentions aside, it seemed the right thing to say. Andi's arms went around my neck and she lifted herself off the floor getting to my lips. The kiss was a more effective painkiller than anything the doctor could have prescribed. My head, while not exactly clear, was suddenly pain free.

"Good night, darling," she said. "I'll see you tomorrow."

I climbed to my room in the apartment building next door. I felt light and free. It was the kind of feeling that makes a man want to write poetry.

Only I don't write poetry. I write code.

Short, beautiful, elegant lines of code.

{21}
That Scottish Play

I HADN'T SLEPT YET when Andi called and asked if I was interested in a cup at the Analog. I glanced at the clock on my screen and realized it was after eight in the morning. After I said yes, I looked at the results of all my research during the night. What I had to report wasn't good, but neither did it explain why Melissa would suddenly up and run away without even telling her best friend. I met Andi at the foot of the back stairs in the alley and we walked down to the Analog Café. We'd done this dozens of times in the past, though usually not quite so early in the morning. And never before with her hand in mine as we walked.

It was a beautiful clear day, though the streets were still wet from last night's rain. The Space Needle punctuated the view down Thomas with Puget Sound glistening in the distance and an amazingly clear and crisp view of the Olympic Mountains. I had the feeling this was going to be a good day after all the stress of the week past. One thing for sure was that I had no intentions of going back to EFC this weekend, and probably not Monday either. While searching the Internet for signs of Mel during the night, my brain was processing the clues to the credit card fraud in the background.

I was down to four suspects based on who had access to my backpack after the accident. I'd been at EFC two weeks. Phil had been on vacation half that time. We'd had very little interaction. Darlene had been nothing but helpful to me since I started there. She was sweet, loyal to her boss, efficient at what she was doing, and great at covering for me when needed.

I'd looked into Jen's eyes and seen a degree of raw lust there—maybe even a challenge—but no outright malice. She had the same kind of dogged determination to get to the bottom of a puzzle that I had. Then there was Arnie. Position of power. Access to everything in the company. Technically adept. And when it came down to it, I really disliked executives. I was pretty sure I had my villain. I just needed proof.

I was so wrapped up in the pleasant sensations of walking hand in hand with my newfound love that I scarcely noticed the sights that were so commonplace in our neighborhood. I saw people I recognized—like the very cute brunette dressed, like so many people on Capitol Hill, all in black. She wore a brightly colored scarf around her neck and cowboy boots. She was hard to miss when she bent to fasten the leash of her pug to a chair leg outside while she ran in to get a coffee. I didn't even notice. Yeah.

"How's Cali this morning?" I asked Andi.

"Better, I think. She's still asleep. I popped my head into her room to see if she wanted to come along this morning, but she pulled the covers up over her head. Between the show and her best friend running off, she was pretty exhausted. I cuddled her until she finally fell asleep last night. Afterward, I was wishing someone would cuddle me." She smiled up at me and I placed a light kiss on her lips just before we ordered our coffees.

"You could have called me."

"Mmm. I glanced up, but your room was dark. I assumed you were asleep."

"Not yet," I said.

"Young love," Lonnie the barista commented while he waited for us to place our orders. "I wondered when you two would finally get together. What a difference a week makes." We grinned at him. He was already pulling our shots.

"Do you know everything about everyone in this neighborhood?" I asked.

"Pretty much," he replied. "It's our own little soap opera. Do you know how many hearts you've broken by finally choosing Andi? There've been more tears than coffee on this counter this week."

"You've got to be kidding," I said. "How could anyone even know?"

"Well, I certainly don't gossip about anything, but I do hear things." Andi was blushing almost scarlet. I looked around the café. Did I just imagine that people's eyes were turning away from us just as I glanced their way?

"There isn't even another girl in the same generation in this neighborhood," I joked casually.

"Who was talking about the girls?" Lonnie said, sighing. This time I blushed—I could feel it. We left and took our drinks outside to enjoy the sunny morning. As soon as we were out of the coffee shop, Andi started giggling.

"What?" I asked.

"Pheromones. Now I'm sure of you," she said cryptically. I raised an eyebrow. I had no idea what she was talking about. "As soon as a man falls in love, he starts exuding an aura that attracts other potential mates. It's the perceived last chance before the boat sails."

"Hey," I said. "This boat has already left the harbor."

"Hmm. This boat hasn't even entered the harbor yet." That shut me up, but good! We strolled south and ended up watching an early morning soccer game at Cal Anderson Park.

"What did you find out about Mel?"

"It doesn't look good," I said softly. This was going to be hard. "I'm suspecting she had assistance."

"You mean she met someone?"

"Actually, I hope that's all. She might have just put herself in danger."

"Kidnapped? But the police…"

"If you have an eleven-year-old who disappears, the police will immediately assume kidnapping and put out an Amber Alert. But if the child is over fifteen, the first assumption is that she's a runaway unless you can provide specific evidence that it wasn't voluntary. The police have a bulletin out on her, but there is no active search or alert. But Mel…"

"I can't believe that Olivia accused Cali!" Real anger flared in Andi all at once. I knew she was concerned for Mel, but the fact that her own daughter had been verbally attacked brought out the momma bear in her. I clutched her to me tightly.

"Whatever happened, Cali is not to blame for it," I reassured her. "You are the best mom in the world and Cali is a great kid. She didn't lead Mel astray. But the truth is that Mel was acting dangerously online. It's going to be almost impossible to get her parents to see that. She was very good at keeping an image of perfection at home."

"What was she doing?"

"I ran various searches and comparisons all night long. I still have some running. The social network account where she and Cali are friends is only one of her accounts. It's public, and I'm sure her parents monitor it. They are both friends on her profile. Her posts are sweet and controlled. In fact, too controlled. Even Cali has slipped up and posted an occasional profanity on her updates. But Mel never expresses profanity in the way we know she uses it. Her posts are always upbeat and rah-rah. It got me thinking that this wasn't her real profile. It took a long time to verify, but I found an account that was marked 'members only.' That's a dangerous sign, but I joined it. She has over 3,000 followers on that account and they are nearly all male."

"How do you know it is her account?"

"The photographs."

"Oh God, no! She's not doing pornography is she?"

"Not openly, if at all. There were enough face shots that I could recognize her clearly. The rest of the pictures were not explicit, but were suggestive. Alluring. Some were even provocative. But none of them likely to get a person thrown into jail for possessing child pornography. She's been doing this for at least two years." Revealing this information to Andi was hard. She was the parent of a seventeen-year-old girl. Hearing what her daughter's best friend was doing was not going down well.

"Cali… Cali isn't involved in… Please tell me no, Dag."

"No. Believe me, once I found out what Mel was into, I did just as extensive a search on Cali. Nothing came up."

"Thank God! What do we do now?"

"I don't know. I still don't have any kind of evidence that suggests that she was kidnapped—nothing I can turn over to the police. What I need to do is get access to her private email on this forum. I'm doing a search on everything I can come up with as a potential password."

"How? How can you find a person's password?"

"I'm using a hackerazzi technique. You've read about stars whose cell phones and Twitter accounts were hacked—pictures stolen, personal information given out? Essentially, most people use a password that is easy to remember. It's usually something that has meaning to them. It could be the name of an old boyfriend, a dog, a favorite movie, an old address, even a private nickname or name of a sibling. Mother's maiden name is popular. Now that I've got several different accounts where Mel has posted social updates, I'm downloading everything she's said online into a database. I'm searching for specific types of information. I'll do a word map to see what she's said most frequently. Sometimes a password is simply a favorite word or phrase, and that shows up in the word map."

"Cali's name?"

"Too short. Passwords on most of these accounts have to be at least seven characters. And I already tried California."

"You knew?"

"Cali's full name? Yes. Was it a secret? How did you ever come up with that?"

"Charles used to say he was the King of Florida. I'd say, today Florida, tomorrow the world. He'd answer, no, tomorrow California." There was a twinge in my chest. I had to wonder how well rehearsed that story was.

I knew there had been no Charles Marx.

FOR ALL MY efforts, my research between naps the rest of Saturday came up with nothing that worked. Granted, I was pretty tired and suffered periodic headaches, but it irritated me that I couldn't find an answer yet. I met Andi at 6:00 and we got a bite to eat before going to Cali's closing performance of *Macbeth*.

Cali got involved with Rainier Youth Theater when she was in grade school. According to Andi, she had been a shy, insecure child with no friends. Apparently, Andi grew up much the same way and thought acting would help bring Cali out of her shell. Cali had blossomed and soon had acting, dance, and singing classes at the theater. She was cast in her first musical as a munchkin in *The Wizard of Oz*. She was hooked and had grown into what theater folks called a triple threat. She could sing, dance, and act.

Mostly, I'd admired her singing voice over the years. I remembered her first impromptu performance for the faculty lounge about five years ago when she sang a very campy "Wash That Man Right Out of My Hair," with Mel clowning as a man caught in her hair. The singing was a little hesitant, but the clowning the two did had all of us in the restaurant laughing our heads off. Whenever Cali convinced Mel to join her in one of her performances, Mel was a silent clown. Her own bent was toward sports and she was a very physical girl.

The last time I'd heard Cali sing in a musical, she'd nearly broken my heart as Johanna Barker in *Sweeney Todd*. Her voice was like crystal and filled the auditorium. She planned to study theater in college.

Based on what she'd said last week, she had me braced for a truly awful, amateurish rendering of *Macbeth*. What we got was nothing short of stunning. The director made two choices that freed the actors from stilted performances. First, rather than try to get his teen actors to master the English and Scottish dialects, he focused them on cadence and pronunciation. As a result, we could hear the music in Shakespeare's language and could understand every word that was spoken. Second, with the exception of a couple of seriously older characters—notably the assassinated king and his advisor Ross—the director had interpreted the cast as adolescents who were thrust into their roles without adult supervision. They were ruled by their passions, impulses, and superstitions. They automatically believed everything that everyone said, and as a result stood by while their friend and gang leader turned into a ruthless bully. Setting Macbeth on the streets of the city in a gang war environment, complete with allusions to drug abuse among the cast, was a reminiscent of *West Side Story*. At the same time, it made complete sense to see Macbeth hallucinating a vision of dancing kings when he was sitting in a dark room stoned out of his mind.

And Cali. I don't know if it was the pain of losing her best friend or if she is truly a gifted actress. The transition from confident, scheming, adolescent wife of Macbeth to the shell-shocked waif that wandered the battlements crying, "Out damn'd spot!" was poignant. Andi clutched my hand and both of us had tears in our eyes.

Rainier Youth Theater had a ritual of letting the cast meet parents, friends, and well-wishers in the theater lobby after the show. It wasn't Cali who reached us first, though. It was a bouncing redhead wearing black-rimmed geek glasses with silver filigree running the length of the bows. She was in jeans, a black production t-shirt that said 'That Scottish Play' on the back, and a floppy straw hat. She was still wiping some kind of adhesive off her face and I recognized her as the actor who played Siward in the last act. She rushed straight to Andi.

"Hi, Mrs. Marx," she said.

"Hi, Alex. Good show!"

"Thank you. Before Cali comes out, I was wondering if it would be okay with you for her to come to my house tonight after the strike party. I'm having some girls over and…" She paused and reconsidered what she was about to say. "We all love Cali and she's really hurting over Mel running away. We don't want her to go off alone tonight like she did last night. She belongs with us."

"Alex, that is so sweet of you. Of course, if she wants to come to your house for the night it's fine. In fact…" Andi seemed to consider something for a moment and caught her breath slightly. "In fact, I agree that it's a good idea for her to be with friends tonight."

"Yeah. Things just aren't right without CaliMel." *What was that?*

"CaliMel?" I asked, breaking in to the conversation. "Did you call her CaliMel?" The teen turned toward me as if wondering who I was to be breaking into her conversation.

"Oh, Alex," Andi came to the rescue. "You've never met my friend, Dag Hamar." There was an instant look of recognition in Alex's face. She was a good foot shorter than I was, but I swear that when she turned her attention on me she looked me straight in the eye.

"Oh! You're the computer geek!"

"Alex!"

"I'm sorry!"

"It's okay," I said, laughing. "I can't honestly think of a better way to describe me."

"I don't think it's a bad thing," Alex rushed on. "I'm a geek, too!" She held up a hoodie sweatshirt she was carrying and turned the back to face me. Across the shoulders were written the words "Talk nerdy to me." I laughed.

"Cali said you're trying to find Mel."

"I'm doing some searches. Which brings me back to my original question, for which I'm sorry I interrupted you. Do you always call her CaliMel?"

"Them. A lot of us do. You never see one without the other unless it's on stage or on a sports field. We used to joke that when Cali was in a show, Mel took the curtain call and if Mel hit a homer, Cali signed the ball. It's just not right for them not to be together."

"Thank you. I don't know if I'll be able to do anything about it, but I am trying. You don't have any ideas about where Mel might have gone do you?"

"No. I really only know Mel through Cali. Now if my robot were as smart as I'm making him out to be, I could just let him solve the problem."

"Robot?"

"It's my senior project. I'm writing a one-act, one-woman show in which I carry on a dialog with my artificial intelligence robot. See? I told you I was a geek." We laughed and I saw Cali approaching.

"I'll look forward to seeing that," I said.

"Say, do you know anything about artificial intelligence? Could I use you as a resource?"

"I'm not an authority, but if you have any questions, please feel free to give me a call." I handed her one of my business cards and she spun around into the arms of a very tall, blonde guy with a ponytail and a voice much deeper than a teenager's should be. They had a quick hug and were off to visit other parents and friends in the crowded lobby.

Cali was already wrapped in a big hug by her mother. I had to ask myself, whatever happened to teens who kept their chins against their chests and mumbled when they were around adults? These kids walked with their heads held high and a sense of confidence and accomplishment that just oozed out of them. They looked adults in the eye and spoke clearly and comfortably. They carried on actual, intelligent conversations. I just don't get kids.

It was my turn to hug Cali and I was a little surprised by the ferocity of her grip. She didn't let go when she stopped hugging, but wrapped one arm around her mother and pulled all three of us together in her hug. She looked up at the two of us and asked a little fearfully, "Was it okay?"

"Oh, sweetie, it was magnificent. I'm so proud of you," Andi answered immediately. Cali's eyes shifted to mine as if she was waiting for my assessment before she could relax.

"You lied to me," I said softly. Her eyes got big. "You told me it was awful and would be a big flop. You told me you didn't understand Lady Macbeth. You told me it was no big deal." By this time, she was grinning shyly. "I brought earplugs so I wouldn't have to listen to the butchering of the bard," I continued. "You didn't prepare me to be wowed. You didn't tell me you were such a professional that you could pull off one of Shakespeare's hardest roles and make it look so natural. The show was great and you were spectacular." I was rewarded with another death-grip hug that brought the three of us together. The show was great, but I really loved this.

After saying our goodbyes and affirming that Cali had everything she needed to spend the night at Alex's house, Andi and I left the theater.

{22}
Make Love to Me

ANDI DROVE FROM the theater to her house in silence. I was afraid to break it. My arm resting on the seatback let me softly touch her shoulder as she drove. Once at a stoplight, she pulled my fingers to her lips and kissed them, then put my hand securely back on her shoulder. Much though I wanted to, I didn't dare put my hand on her leg beside the console. I didn't want to seem pushy—or to cause an accident. I hadn't felt this nervous since high school.

She pulled the van into the spot behind her duplex and as soon as we were both out of the car she grabbed my hand tightly as she went to the back door and unlocked it. She didn't bother to ask whether I wanted to come in.

As soon as the door shut behind us, Andi's lips were pressed against mine and we both moaned as we found each other's warm, receptive mouth. I held her... no... I clutched her against me, willing her to simply know how much I loved her.

When Eric's three-legged cats finally decided they liked me a few years ago—or at least that I was a fact in the building and wouldn't suddenly disappear—they attached themselves to me at every opportunity. If I sat on the back steps to drink wine with Eric, or if a group of us gathered around a hibachi to grill steaks on the outside landing, they would twist around my ankles, rubbing and purring. If I failed to pet them in the right spot, they rubbed against me until they had satisfied themselves. Once, when I was juggling two bags of groceries that I'd carried down the hill from QFC, they slipped past me into my apartment. When I sat in my recliner they were suddenly both in my lap kneading my leg with their one front paw each and pushing every part of their bodies against me with purrs that shook the picture on my wall.

I swear that Andi was purring against my chest as she molded her body into mine.

Nor was I idle in petting her.

Whenever I took a breath to say something, she captured my mouth in another kiss. We were lost in each other. When Andi pushed me away firmly, I thought we were ready to return to cautious reality.

"Dag, Cali is spending the night at Alex's house. Will you stay with me tonight? Please."

"Andi…" It was what I wanted more than anything, and still I was so afraid that our relationship wasn't ready. "Andi, are you sure? Once we do this we can't go back. I love you desperately, but I don't want to lose what we have."

"Dag, my darling. We don't have to sacrifice what we have for what we want. You're a good man. I know you might break my heart one day, but I also know you would never be cruel or hurt me if you could avoid it. Now come with me." She turned and headed toward her bedroom. I started to follow but stopped abruptly.

"Andi, wait." She turned and I saw a moment of doubt and worry on her face. "I'm not prepared. I didn't bring anything…" *Damn the age of safe sex!*

"Take one from the cookie jar," she said, laughing at me. Then she stepped back into the kitchen and looked me straight in the eye. "Grab a handful."

<hr/>

ONCE WE WERE in Andi's bedroom, everything slowed down. It wasn't that we didn't both desperately want to consummate our love, but neither of us wanted to miss anything about the experience. I looked around. In seven years of friendship I'd never seen Andi's bedroom. Her bed was actually bigger than mine, no matter that I was nine inches taller. There simply wasn't room in my apartment for a big bed and so I slept diagonally on a standard double.

The décor in Andi's room was feminine, but not girlish. She had match-ing sheets, duvet cover, dust ruffle, and pillows. The patterns told me the simple dressing chair upholstery and drapes complemented the ensemble, though my lack of color acuity told me nothing. There was nothing ornate. A simple throw rug in a darker hue was in front of the bed, and a couple of very nice pieces of artwork—which on closer examination proved to be quite erotic—hung on the wall. The rest of the room was decorated in pictures of Cali at all stages of her life. There was Cali in school pictures and Cali in plays. I was a little nervous about undressing in front of so many pictures of the girl.

Andi took that decision away from me. We gently helped each other out of each item of clothing, showering kisses on each other as we removed each piece. We let our hands touch each other and our lips taste each other. Both of us wanted to remember this moment for the rest of our lives and neither of us wanted it to be a blur of frantic passion.

But the passion was there. As we settled our naked bodies between the sheets, we kissed and even laughed at each other's reactions. She softly kissed my head near my wound and asked if it was okay. We surprised each other with impromptu discoveries of erogenous zones that neither of us knew we had. When I dragged a finger lightly from the hollow beneath her collar bone across her breast and down to the valley of her navel, Andi shuddered in my arms. Then she giggled like a teenager and quietly said, "Do you want to... now?" I smiled at her wickedly.

"No. I was thinking we'd just tease each other tonight." Her eyes got big and then a fit of giggles took us both over. Her hand caressed my ribcage and I could feel an electric tingle all up and down my spine. I pulled her to me and kissed her eyelids. "Oh, Andi, I love you so much."

"Then make love to me, Dag."

We slid together and, with a minimal amount of fumbling, I entered her as I looked into her eyes. Not for the first time, I felt I could lose myself there. I pressed my cheek against hers and sank slowly into her. She caught her breath, her whole body shaking. I felt moisture against my cheek and looked again at her face. Tears streamed from her eyes, clenched shut. I panicked slightly. I don't know what possessed me.

"Andi... I... Are you okay? Were...?" I couldn't finish the sentence. She panted shallowly.

"I have... a... seventeen-year-old daughter. I don't think it grows back." There was something determined about the way she said it. She opened her eyes, filled with tears and a smile broke across her face that filled my heart.

"Andi...?"

"Just make love to me, Dag. I've waited forever for you."

{23}
Runaway

TWO MOUNTAIN RANGES, back to back across a continent with a vast high desert between—a desolate wasteland or a fertile playground? When I awoke on Sunday morning facing a wall, I glanced over my shoulder and on the other side of the bed saw Andi, still asleep with her back toward me. I felt a pang of… regret? No. Guilt. I'd betrayed our friendship. I'd turned my best friend into my lover. My love. And now we each hugged opposite edges of the same bed with a cold chasm between. I could feel a sob welling up in my throat.

Then she turned toward me, her eyes opening a slit and then her smile causing them to crinkle up as she looked fully at me and I rolled toward the center of her bed. We met in the middle with arms wrapping around each other and a kiss that welcomed more than bodies together.

"Hello, lover," she whispered.

"Good morning, my love," I answered softly.

"I'm not used to sleeping with someone else in my bed. Cali and I haven't done it for so long, I've forgotten how."

"Shhh," I said. "I think it's something we'll learn. I felt so alone when I woke up and wasn't touching you."

"Oh, darling. Please let us never be alone like that again."

Romance stories would have us immediately falling together in passionate sex—again—but they never seem to take into account basic needs of the body when it wakes up in the morning. I waited my turn and then used the bathroom after her, seeing the various cleansing products, hair products, and feminine products for the first time with my eyes fully open. I hadn't seen a sight like that in a long time. When I returned, I was relieved to see that Andi hadn't dressed and left the room. She sat in bed with a sheet pulled up to her chin, but when she saw me, she let it fall away from her. She took my breath away. The blood drained from the upper half of my body. Half faint, I stumbled back to the bed where she welcomed me into her arms and her body.

❦

As we lay together in the afterglow we whispered softly.

"I could get used to this, you know?" Andi murmured.

"To sex in the morning?"

"That. And to seeing your face when I wake up. To smelling your scent on my pillow. To seeing you come out of the bathroom. To you."

"I'd like to get used to that. Andi, you know I've been married. You know I've had a live-in girlfriend. You know I've had little trysts. So tell me—why have I never felt this way before? Why have I never woken up in the morning thinking this is where I belong for the rest of my life? Darling, why has it taken me so long to find you?"

"I love you."

"Oh, and I do love you."

There was a crash in the kitchen and a cupboard door slammed closed. Andi sat straight up in bed and my heart skipped several beats.

"Oh shit! Cali's home," Andi whispered. Before I could respond she pushed a finger against my lips and whispered "Stay!" She jumped out of bed, grabbed the plush robe and fuzzy slippers I saw her in only a few nights ago, and left the room. I didn't try to listen in, but it was a small house and I couldn't help but hear the conversation as I got up and quietly pulled on my clothes.

"Honey! I didn't expect you home so early. Did you have a nice sleepover?" Andi asked. I could imagine her going over to hug her daughter.

"Where did you stash our computer geek? Or did you push him out a window when you heard me?"

"Cali! What do you mean?"

"Mom, it's okay. I know Dag was here all night."

"And how would you know that, miss know-it-all?"

"All my life there's never been a time when you didn't hear me come in at night and say hi," she answered. "Not in all my life have you not been up waiting when I came home."

"Cali, I thought you spent the night at Alex's house."

"I couldn't, Mom. It was really super-nice of Alex. I mean, they really wanted me to come, but I just couldn't do it. I mean… I'm just not ready. After the strike party we all went to Denny's and I asked her to drop me off before they went home."

"But that would have been at…"

"About 1:00."

"Oh dear."

"Don't worry, Mom. You were quiet. I went right to sleep." I'd finished dressing and was debating whether to try to sneak past or just boldly go out and face the music with Andi. I could tell that I needed a shave.

"Honey… Please, Cali. Understand this. No matter what my relationship is with Dag, you are my daughter and I love you. First. Foremost. And forever."

"I know, Mom. I was going to make coffee for you, but I dropped the can."

"We could all go to the Analog if it isn't too early," Andi said.

I decided that I could safely walk in now, but I stopped in the doorway as I saw them both on the floor sweeping up spilled coffee grounds.

"Mom, this is real isn't it? I mean you aren't just trying to prove something, are you?"

"Prove something? Like what?"

"Like, oh, that you aren't gay." I almost choked on my own tongue. I remembered my conversation in the car with Cali a week ago.

"What?!"

"Um, never mind." Cali saw me in the doorway with a smirk on my face shaking my head. I didn't expect her to rush on with the next thing she said. "It's just that you've never had a boyfriend before, Mom."

"Well, it's a little early to call him a boyfriend." Cali looked straight at me.

"It's a little late to deny it." Andi followed her gaze and jumped half out of her robe when she saw me.

"Agh! Don't sneak up on me like that!"

"I didn't sneak," I laughed.

"I turned around and you were just there."

"I walked in from the next room." I avoided saying the word bedroom.

"You didn't make any noise," Andi said, now giggling as she came to me and gave me a morning hug in front of her daughter.

"You want me to wear a bell?" I asked. All three of us started laughing. I don't understand how a hundred-and-ten-pound girl or her almost-as-petite mother can make so much noise walking in bare feet on carpet. I'm sure there were times I could feel the floor shake in my apartment on the third floor next door.

I caught Cali up in our hug as well and suggested we go have coffee at the Analog since there didn't seem to be any to brew here. Andi went to change and Cali reached up to kiss my cheek.

"Don't you ever, ever hurt her," Cali whispered in my ear fiercely. I kissed the top of her head and she slipped out of my arms and followed her mother to the bedroom. She didn't really whisper when she joined her mother, so I couldn't help but overhear, even though I couldn't see what transpired. In fact, I think Cali was speaking loudly enough for me to hear on purpose."

"Mom. I think I owe you this," she said.

"What is that for?"

"Well, he paid me back for the tickets you bought."

"I guess you made a little spending money in the deal then, didn't you?" They giggled.

The tickets? Andi paid for... Two devious women! I didn't stand a chance!

I SAT IN my room with the drapes open—something I rarely did. Sunlight filtered through the needles of the giant sequoia outside my window. We'd had coffee as if we were one big happy family, but when we walked back it was obvious that Andi and I were not going to spend a lazy Sunday in bed reading the comics and making love. Cali was still hurting over the disappearance of Mel and that meant that I still had work to do.

I opened the log-on screen for Mel's erotic forum account and entered CaliMel in the password box. A welcome message flashed on the screen with the announcement that she had 273 email messages. I read two and decided I didn't want to read any others. It still wasn't obvious she was supplying any of these perverts with the things they were requesting, but what they were sending her was sickening.

I downloaded all her email and private messages to a database and then started sorting the results. Most frequent contacts. Most frequent phrase used. Most recent outgoing messages. Any clues that I could pull together. I needed to know first if Mel went willingly or if she was coerced, and then I could worry about where she was.

By two o'clock, I'd pulled the drapes closed. It was the last day of April and it was going out like a lion as the wind picked up and the morning sunshine turned to a threat of rain. But more than that, even living on the third floor I had a sense that I didn't want anyone able to look over my shoulder through the window. The crap on my computer was leaving me sick to my stomach and my bruised and stitched-up head was throbbing.

I'd found nothing that overtly suggested a rendezvous or enticement away from home, but there were dozens that suggested where they would be if she happened to find herself in the vicinity. There were also her own updates that suggested her locations. They called them 'check-ins.' "MaybeLegal just checked in at Jaqui's Lingerie Boutique." "MaybeLegal just checked in at The Rack." I had news for these two or three thousand guys who followed her. MaybeLegal wasn't. A person is guilty of sexual exploitation of a minor (under age eighteen) if the person aids, invites, employs, authorizes, or causes a minor to engage in sexually explicit conduct, knowing that such conduct will be photographed or part of a live performance. It's a class B felony. Jordan was going to have a field day when I turned this over to him.

I was dealing with a huge volume of information. The simple fact that every name on her site was an alias meant that identifying the voyeurs would be a project for more computing power than I could muster. But I wanted to find out who could possibly be an influence on her. It struck me that I was looking for Mel because she was missing. She wasn't the only girl ever to go missing in Seattle. Unfortunately, less than half the missing persons in the country are actually reported because they are either not missed or family and friends assume they have left of their own accord. Of those who are reported, there is no coordinated effort to recover them unless foul play is suspected or the person is considered to be 'vulnerable,' as in developmentally handicapped or a child. The assumption of vulnerability, however, is that the older the child is, the less vulnerable, so a seventeen-year-old runaway is not as high a priority as a twelve-year-old missing person. Digging through the Internet for records of missing persons over the past five years was a painfully slow process and the results were limited.

It was part of a long shot plan, though. I wanted to cross-check the names of all these girls against the list of Mel's followers. I had no expectation of getting results, but I was running out of options.

Her last check-in had been at a Gelato shop on Third Avenue Thursday morning. As far as I could tell, that was the last record of her whereabouts. I could find no more recent posts, messages, or updates on any of her accounts.

While my search and compare software ran, I decided I'd have to try the inevitable. I called Mel's parents. I'd met Olivia and James at a play a couple of years ago. It was one of Cali's first leading lady roles and the entire faculty lounge had come to support her. We'd done the same kind of field trips to hear Sara and Sandy in concert, to watch Jan and Donna's son in his college football debut, for an art showing, and at other times. My meeting with Mel's parents was brief and I felt they were a little standoffish, but even that did not prepare me for my conversation with Olivia.

"I heard about Melissa's disappearance," I said, "and I'm calling to offer my assistance if you need anything. Have there been any developments?"

"What kind of developments would there be," Olivia snapped. "She left. She walked right out on everything we've done for her. She's done irreparable damage."

"You don't think there was anything suspicious about her disappearance? She wasn't having any difficulties at school was she?"

"The school, where we all send our children thinking they will be watched over, told us that her attendance record showed she was there for her first two classes and didn't show up for third period. They saw no reason to let us know about that until the police interviewed them. The police say she ran away. Well, if that's all she cares about her family, then so be it."

"Olivia, this must be very hard on you. Has she made any calls or sent any messages on her cell phone since she left?"

"We disconnected her phone. If she thinks she can just walk out and that we'll continue to pay her expenses, she has another think coming. We cancelled her credit card and put a stop on her bank account. She's still a minor and without access to our money she can't get far. She'll come back when she finds out she can't make it on her own, and when she comes home she'll be grounded until she's thirty. We never should have given her so much freedom."

I couldn't help but think that maybe if they had given her a little freedom, she wouldn't have felt such a pressing need to rebel or to get free. It certainly sounded like Olivia and James believed she'd run away and they weren't about to offer any other suggestions. I made one last attempt at expressing my sympathy and then disconnected. I thought about the difference between Olivia and Andi and the differences between their daughters who had become best friends. It just didn't add up. I could see Mel running away from home, but I couldn't see her running away from Cali. Runaways often seek shelter with trusted friends. Only in cases where there is no friend or there has been a big fight do they just disappear.

Or, as I suspected when Cali came home in tears, when someone makes them disappear.

{24}
Secrets in the Dark

BY A QUARTER till five I was wrung out. My software chimed and I looked to see that it found more than 4,000 correlations. I groaned. I was too tired to face it now. I saved the results, shut down the computer, and lay down in my bed. I was asleep instantly.

And just as quickly awakened.

I glanced at my phone and saw that it was seven. It hadn't felt like I'd been asleep for a minute. Then I realized there was a light knocking on my door. I groaned, but got up and went to answer it.

"I, uh… well… um… I missed you," Andi said as soon as I opened the door. Oh yes! I wrapped her in my arms and planted a kiss on her that told her how much I'd missed her as well. Noting that we were still in the doorway, I pulled her into the apartment with my lips still locked to hers. When the door shut behind us and she heard it click she pulled away from me and looked into my eyes, then, as if just becoming aware of her surroundings, she stared around her. "It's black!"

Andi had never seen the inside of my apartment. Well, very few people had. Even when I had girlfriends, I never brought them here. I didn't mind sharing it with Andi, though. My apartment is always clean. That's not a problem. I only have 350 square feet and if I didn't keep up with cleaning, before long I wouldn't be able to move. It's not like I have a lot of stuff to clutter the place up. I just never started buying stuff after I moved in here. I tried to imagine what it looked like through Andi's eyes.

"They let you do this? The apartment management, I mean?"

"I had to pay an extra month's damage deposit and promise to restore it to pristine white before I leave," I said. "Eric helped me choose the materials."

She moved around the little room, touching my desk, my bed, my chair. Each time she reached out her hand, I felt like she was exploring another part of my body. It wasn't like everything was black. The kitchen, closet, and bathroom were still white. But I had heavy black drapes hung over the closet door, the kitchen archway, and both windows. With the bathroom door closed, you couldn't see the white room. A shower curtain that Eric picked out for me had demure nudes in black against the white curtain. The drapes across the kitchen and closet doorways kept any light leaks from those rooms and the drapes over the two windows were floor to ceiling, so no ambient light leaked in from the street lights below.

"Do you mind that I came over?"

"Not at all. I was napping, but I'm suddenly wide awake. I kind of like showing you my room."

"Would you like to see me naked in it?" she asked. I almost swallowed my tongue, but it was hers that was suddenly in my mouth. Our lovemaking was more relaxed than it had been the night before. We laughed more as we explored each other's bodies. She traced a scar on my back I got when I fell into a dumpster as a kid. I simply marveled at her pristine, beautiful body as I took each piece of clothing from it. We were joyful and playful in our lovemaking and I wanted to please her in every way possible.

Nearly two hours later, we hugged each other in my bed, our sweaty bodies practically glued to each other. I was spooned behind her, still teasingly nibbling on her ear and whispering to her about how happy I was.

"Is it completely dark when you turn out the lights?" she asked. I'd left two lamps on low while we made love—each of us wanting to see the other.

"It can be."

"Show me." I flicked off the power strip under my desk and my equipment, stereo, and desk lamp all went out. I made sure the bathroom door was closed and all the drapes were sealed before I flicked out the lamp over the painting on my wall. I slipped back into the bed from the end and crawled up her body until we were spooned together once again. Then I pulled a black sheet up over us. Not only did the room get dark, but with all my electronics turned off, it was silent as well.

Even after our eyes had time to adjust to the darkness, we really couldn't see anything. I could hear our breathing, synchronizing together so that we inhaled and exhaled at the same time.

"I can hear your heart," she said softly. "It's like being in a womb."

"I was in a womb not long ago," I laughed softly.

"Mmm. Just the foyer. Now we're both tucked inside and we can't see a thing. We can only feel each other's presence and hear each other's heartbeat for company."

"Yes, but I smell the fresh citrus scent of your hair," I whispered. "I feel your soft silky skin beneath my fingers."

"I feel you poking me in the butt," she giggled. She rolled in my embrace and after bumping foreheads and smashing our noses together we managed to find each other's mouth. I would never tire of kissing her. It erased everything else from my mind. She snuggled close to my chest and spoke so softly that even in the darkened room I almost missed what she said.

"Do you have any secrets, Dag?"

"Yes. I have things I don't talk about. I deal with confidential information that I don't share with anyone."

"No. I mean things about you that you can't tell anyone. Not someone else's secret you won't divulge."

"Maybe. I'm not always as upstanding as I like to believe I should be. Sometimes, I do things that I think better of after the fact, but have no way to correct. I sometimes tell clients what I think they should hear rather than what they ask. I struggle with the ethics of confidential information, especially since I have an almost insatiable desire to find out everything about everything. I stick my nose into other people's business and then regret knowing what I do. Sometimes maybe I stretch the boundaries of what is legal when I investigate." We were quiet for a few minutes, almost dozing as we listened to the silence around us—relishing in the fact that our only sensory input was from one another.

Her face was buried against my chest and I could feel the area heating up. I was aware of the moisture between us and I wiped her tears away in the darkness.

"I have a secret," she said. "A secret I've never told anyone." I kept very still. This was not the time to ask questions. It was only a time to love unconditionally. "You know, don't you? I knew that you would know one day. When I decided to let myself fall in love with you, I decided I would tell you, and I can't go any longer without." She was whispering to me as I stroked her hair and kissed the top of her head. I had figured out she wasn't Andi Marx, but I didn't care.

"You don't have to tell me."

"Yes, I do. I planned to tell Cali when she turns eighteen, but I know she suspects something and I can't keep it from her." I wasn't prepared for what came next. Nothing could possibly have prepared me.

"Cali isn't my daughter. She's my sister."

ONCE ANDI STARTED telling the story, a floodgate opened and more than seventeen years of living a secret life spilled forth.

"Our mother was stupid only in her choice of men. My father was a mean man who only showed up once every few months and never more than for a week or two at a time. From the time I can clearly remember, Mom would keep me hidden when he was there. I had a special room I went to with lots of books. She home schooled me, not because of any religious ideas, but because she didn't trust anyone. I think she felt the authorities would try to take me away from her if they knew what a violent person my father was.

"When I was fifteen, nearly sixteen, Mom got pregnant again. Only it wasn't my father's child. He threw a fit the next time he came home, beat her up, and then swore he'd kill us both the next time he came home.

"I'll never understand why she didn't just take us and leave. She certainly knew how to do it. She knew where the shelters were and even how to change her identity. But instead, she took me away and we hid until the baby was born. She convinced me I knew more than any other girl my age, so I could be six years older and have my college diploma right now. She said I'd have to change my name, but one day she would come for Cali and me and we'd be safe again. She took Cali and me to a shelter for abused women and told them that my husband was dead, I'd just given birth, and I wasn't safe from my father. She gave me a packet of documents that included birth certificates for Anne Doreen Sullivan and California Celeste Marx, a marriage certificate to Charles Marx, his death certificate, and an insurance policy. It also included my college diploma. I made up the whole story about Charles Marx and how he died after my college graduation. I read a story about it somewhere and just adopted it as my own. I don't know where Mom got the name California, but Celeste was her name. I stayed in the shelter until I could find a job and then they helped me get day care for Cali while I worked and picked up more education credits to fill in the blanks of a college education that I'd never had.

"It was only a couple of months after I went to the shelter that my father killed Mom and then shot himself. Since they'd moved again recently, no one knew about me or Cali. I stayed away. It was almost a year later that I remembered the insurance policy in my packet of papers and called the agency. They said the funds were payable to a trust and they would be happy to have it signed over to me. It was for half a million dollars. I checked the policy and it was for $250,000, but since she was murdered, it paid a double indemnity.

"Once the paperwork was finished, Cali and I moved to Washington. You see, I'd never made it out of Michigan before. I've never even been to Florida where my diploma says I graduated. I did get my teaching certificate once I got here and I was surprised at how easy it was for me get a job teaching high school kids who were the same age I was. While my students started college, I got my Master's in Literature and Education and then got a big break when I got a job at the Community College and could lighten my schedule. With careful investing I was able to buy the duplex and pay most of the mortgage out of the rent. Cali and I have had a comfortable life for a single parent except…"

It seemed like her story had run its course and I was so dumbfound that I couldn't speak. I just held my precious girl in my arms and smothered her with kisses and love. Eventually she rubbed her cheek against mine.

"Except I'd never let myself get close to a man because I was so afraid he'd find out and they would take Cali away from me. Until you."

"I love you, Andi. I will never betray your secret. It's really nobody's business. You are the only mother Cali has ever known and she loves you."

"I knew you would find out. It's who you are. But I know I can trust you. I've been alone so long." She was sobbing against my chest. Tears were flowing freely from my own eyes. My poor, precious girl. We rocked each other in our arms and maybe we even fell asleep for a bit when the weeping subsided. I would never let her go.

"What's your real name, Andi?" I asked softly, not really sure if she was awake.

"Rachel Evans. And don't worry. I did the math. I pass the half plus seven test."

We laughed. Our laughter turned to more kissing and the kissing to more loving. There in the dark womb of my room we couldn't tell where one left off and the other began. We shared one body and we came as one person.

{25}
The Light of My Life

ABOUT ELEVEN-THIRTY, ANDI slipped out of bed and started feeling around for her clothes. I turned on a bedside light and just watched her beautiful body as she gathered her things together, apparently in no big hurry to dress. She turned and smiled at me as I watched her.

"Do you have to leave?"

"Curfew," she said. "What's fair for the daughter is fair for the..."

"The mom," I finished. "In every sense of the word except biological you are her mother and always will be."

"Yes. But I'll have to tell her now. Soon." I slid out of bed and stood with her in the tiny pool of light. I helped her on with her clothes. It was a lot more difficult than helping her off with them. I finally gave up as we laughed over tangled underwear and then began pulling my own clothes on. "You don't need to get up."

"What would your daughter think if your boyfriend didn't even walk you home after a hot date? Besides, it gives me five more minutes with you." We left my apartment and went down the back stairs across the alley from her door. She unlocked her door and turned to kiss me goodnight when the hall lights came on.

"Well, you're finally home," Cali said from inside. She came down the hall wearing Andi's plush robe and fuzzy slippers with her hair in curlers. "I guess I can go to bed now that I know you're safe." It took us a moment and then all three of us broke up.

"You don't really wait up for her like that, do you?" I asked Andi.

"Not like that! What would her date think if he saw her mother looking like that?"

"Well, maybe I overdid it with the curlers," Cali laughed. "Anyway, I'm going to bed now so you two can kiss goodnight. Just don't stand out there on the porch where all the neighbors can see you."

"Night, Cali."

"Night. Love you, Mom. Love you, Dag." She kissed each of us on the cheek and went back down the hall. I stepped in far enough that I wasn't on the porch, but we kept the door open.

"See? That was much more effective than if you had come home alone. She'd have been so disappointed."

"I think she likes you."

"I'm glad. I intend to be around for a long time."

"I love you, Dag." We kissed.

"You are my heart's desire, Andi." I looked at her for a long moment and then retraced my steps back to my apartment.

FIVE HOURS EARLIER, I'd been so exhausted I couldn't keep my eyes open. After an evening spent in the arms of my lover, I was so energized I could scarcely sit. I had work to do. My little girl's friend was missing. I needed to find Mel.

There were 4,173 correlations that my search and compare algorithms had revealed. That sounded like a lot, but when compared to the fifteen million results a standard Google search yields, it seemed manageable. I plunged into the life of a rebellious teen and was sucked into the slimy dregs of America.

It was a neighborhood—if you could call it that—in which bright neon lit up a thousand doorways with promises that paled against the reality inside. Crossing any threshold could result in loss of money, reputation, or civil liberty. I could defend myself against the threats of these commercial venues. It wasn't that I could walk with impunity anywhere I chose, but I was well-protected. It took more than a casual touch to cripple me.

More dangerous were the darkened alleys between various strip shows, sex shops, and offers to get laid tonight by imaginary bored housewives.

Drugs, guns, sex in every variety were offered by people with no front door presence. Unwilling organ donors wailed in the distance as their bloody body parts were offered to the highest bidder. And as ineffectual as policing the district was, any alley could hide a cop waiting to arrest patrons for the least suggestion of solicitation.

I had new leads to follow up now that I was in Nowhere Land. I started by entering a reverse phone booth and feeding the list of numbers into the device. In minutes it started feeding back a list of names, addresses, marital status, spouses, children, and even a history of where each man had lived for the past thirty years. There were a few people smart enough to use an Internet phone service that yielded less ready information, but the vast majority had solicited favors from a fifteen-to-seventeen-year-old girl using their personal cell phones. The world was filled with the illusion of privacy.

I focused on the numbers in the same area code and when I had addresses, I narrowed my search to those who were within the residential and business community of downtown Seattle. I walked through their neighborhoods tacking up posters where their friends and neighbors could see them with a picture of Mel and the message, "This seventeen-year-old girl is missing. Reward for information." I used my own Internet phone number connected to a message collection service that I book for a month at a time. I included an email address routed through one of the adult services websites. I didn't expect any of the men on my list to respond. As soon as they realized the woman they'd solicited was a minor, they'd flee the sites where they met her. But it was always possible that someone else in their more respectable neighborhood might have spotted her, especially if she'd been seen with one of their neighbors.

I put up posters around her school community and the various sports groups she participated in. It was always possible that her disappearance had nothing to do with her activities on the adult forums and I didn't want to leave anything to chance. I even posted at her church. Somehow, I didn't think her parents were the type who would alert their critical-thinking religious community about their wayward daughter. They'd be surprised, but there really wasn't anything they could do about it.

And finally, I contacted her cellular system. Her parents had disconnected her cell phone. I wanted to know the instant it was reconnected or reassigned. That took some tricky hacking as the big cell systems don't freely give out that information. I had to settle for attaching a flag to her phone number so that it would notify me if a call was made in or out.

In the old days, detectives did this footwork literally on foot. By sunrise, I'd covered more virtual territory than Sam Spade could have imagined existed. I'd posted notices on the message boards of every 'friend' Mel had on the Internet as far as I could tell. There was no question in my mind that she could run away and hide if she truly wanted to, but if she had been taken, she would become a hot property quickly.

My email started lighting up at about seven o'clock with messages. Most were innocuous ping-backs, testing my spam filters. Nothing related directly to Mel's disappearance. I started seeing one message appear from several directions at once. At first I thought it was one of those phishing schemes that start off, "I couldn't believe it was you in this video. ROFLMAO." Usually those were followed by a link to a porn video that demanded an account password in order to view the footage. But this link kept appearing with a caption that began trending on some of the popular sites. "Unsung super-hero rescues woman. You won't believe this guy!" The link led to a legitimate video sharing site and when I finally decided to follow it, I was stunned.

The video clip of less than thirty seconds showed an oncoming bus, a woman being pushed into the street, and a guy jumping out to catch her and swing her to safety before the bus mirror hit him in the head. It showed *me* on Thursday morning.

I WAS STILL in my jeans and sweater with a Gore-Tex jacket and a baseball cap protecting my eyes from the morning rain as I swung off the bus at Third and Union. I'd watched the video a dozen times—maybe twenty. I still couldn't figure out how I'd moved the way I did or what had alerted me to the fact that there was a danger just behind me. Granted the video compression had certainly dropped some frames from real time, but even slowing it down, most of the action was blurred.

But one thing was clear: There was a fourth person involved in the incident.

I hadn't been following the case closely. I knew that if it came to trial, I'd be called as a witness. I would be unable to provide any details because the action of pushing her off the sidewalk occurred behind me. She had accused her boyfriend and he had been arrested and was out on bail with a restraining order against being within fifty feet of her. The video showed that it clearly wasn't the boyfriend who pushed her, but it didn't show a clear image of the person who had.

I forwarded the link to the police detective in charge of the case, pointing out that the video cleared both the boyfriend and me. It was clear that the squabbling couple had turned their heads away from each other—her toward the street and he toward the sidewalk—when a person directly behind the couple pushed her. The boyfriend was too far away and facing away from his girlfriend to have been the one doing the pushing. He turned as I moved and the culprit had slid past on the right. The video ended before the perp had come fully into view, though. I needed to find the rest of that footage and in order to do that, I needed to know where the camera was that took it so I could request the rest of the sequence.

I was only half a block from the EFC office when I stopped to measure out where the accident had happened. As best I could tell, I was in the right place. I waited there, just listening and trying to put myself back in that space. I turned to see an approaching bus.

Damn! They move like hell down that street until they screech to a stop at the shelter in front of the office. It's a wonder I wasn't killed! I looked at the tail of the bus as it stopped to pick up passengers. That gave me a reference point. I pulled out my tablet and replayed the video, trying to reverse the perspective and look up at where the camera was. Yes. The perspective was from several feet above the sidewalk which confirmed my suspicion that it was not caught on a cell phone by someone at street level.

A few years ago when I was complaining to my cell phone carrier that I kept losing calls, I started observing where I had good service and where I didn't. A little research showed me what a cellular tower looked like. I started looking around me when I had good service and gradually became aware of cell towers within my line of sight. They weren't always towers. They were stuck to the sides of buildings downtown, on rooftops in the suburbs. Huge towers were located every few miles along the freeway. I suddenly started seeing cell towers everywhere. And when my service started to improve, I could almost always identify a new tower within sight.

The same was true now. As I looked up I spotted a black glass globe hanging from what would otherwise look like a street light. I recognized it for no other reason than the ceiling of a casino is peppered with the things. Each one contains a camera—some static and focused on a single table or game, some panning from side to side like the cameras inside EFC. This black globe hung off the wall of the EFC office building. As I looked down the block, I saw four more exterior cameras. I turned around in place. Jutting up off the nearest traffic signal was a white bar with a camera on top. In front of the bank, there was another series of cameras. At the entrance to a parking garage across the street, a camera was pointed at incoming autos. Even under the awnings of Benaroya Hall, there were security cameras. A camera across the street and fairly high on the building looked like it was pointed at the bus stop. A matching camera was positioned opposite.

I wasn't sure there was *anyplace* I could walk downtown and not be caught on a security camera.

The one I wanted access to, though, was one I could actually get to. It was part of the EFC security system.

⌐◻╘╤╧◻▒◥◈◙◢◣◤◥▒◣◤◢◻

MY PHONE BUZZED as I was walking up the street holding my tablet in front of me recording the locations of the various cameras I saw on the built-in video recorder. The unique chime I set up told me it was Andi.

"Hello, darling."

"Ooo. I like hearing that."

"I like saying it. Did you sleep well?"

"I've slept alone all my life. Why does it suddenly seem so lonely in my bed?"

"Mmm. I'd love to take up residence in part of it."

"You'd want to be in the same part as me, though."

"That's true enough."

"Where are you?"

"I'm downtown at the office. I've got something really remarkable to show you."

"Really? Sounds like a big break-through. Why don't you come for lunch?"

"Lunch? Aren't you teaching?"

"I completely forgot that today the college is closed for a symposium that's occupying every corner of the campus. I have the day off, and Cali gets off school early today. Come on. How does lunch with your two favorite girls sound?"

"Absolutely wonderful! I can be there by eleven-thirty. Is that okay?"

"Make it noon. Cali needs some supplies for a project she's working on. We're going out as soon as she gets home."

"Great. I'll see you at noon."

"Oh Dag…"

"What is it, Andi?"

"I love you."

"You're the light of my life, Andi."

{26}
Hard Evidence

I SAT IN A food court a block away from the office drinking black coffee and setting up my plan of attack. Someone with access to the company security cameras had set me up by editing footage from security cameras so it looked as though I was making a midnight raid on the manufacturing facility. Someone had also posted footage from my incident in front of the building on a video sharing site. I suspected I was being taunted. If I could triangulate on the two events and the missing ten seconds of network logs, I was pretty sure I would find out who was playing games inside EFC. I set up my laptop with a cellular connection and logged onto the company network.

◨▷⌸⚡⚞⚟✶⚒⚶⚵✖⚒⚤⚆✦⚘⚙⚶

THE PATH LED me through a dusty attic in the EFC archives. The camera system was an early model that came out nearly twenty years ago. The company had made minor additions and modifications to the system over the years, updating to higher resolution cameras, improving their archiving system, and transferring data to the cloud. Occasionally, they replaced or added cameras but it was essentially the same system they started with. In fact, I discovered many of the company's systems were outdated. The network technology, managed by Don Abrams and Allen Yarborough, was state of the art. On the other hand, accounting systems that were set up when the company was founded were essentially unchanged, the biggest advances being updates to current software versions.

My usual method is to scan through huge amounts of data very quickly, looking for anomalies and inconsistencies as much in the form of the data as in the actual numbers and names. But as I strolled through this dusty archive with neatly labeled boxes stacked in rows that no one would ever touch, I was struck by a uniform feature rather than an anomaly. One name kept appearing on the records of every significant development and installation in the company for decades. An employee number that was mostly zeroes.

The company leaked like a sieve. But it wasn't leaking money—not in the normal sense. How clever to send me into the system looking for an embezzler. EFC was losing money because every promotion, system, update, and account had been sold to the highest bidder in the biggest corporate espionage case I'd ever heard of.

"JEN, THIS IS Dag."

"Good morning. How are you feeling?"

"My head hurts, but it doesn't look like there'll be any long-term damage."

"That's good to hear. When can we expect to see you in the office?"

"Jen, how long have you been with the company?" As far as I was concerned I wasn't planning to come into the office again, but she didn't need to know that yet.

"Eighteen months. Why?"

"When did you put together the team?"

"That was my assignment when I was hired."

"Always the same team members?"

"We've had a little change in the past year, but pretty stable—only the best and brightest."

"What is the most significant project the team had executed before I came on board?" There was silence at the other end. For a minute, I thought Jen had just disconnected instead of answering me, but I waited.

"You know, don't you?" There was another pause as she tried to outwait me. I'd figured it out, but I needed to hear it. So far I was just making assumptions. I heard a door close and then Jen spoke lowly and rapidly. "I'm so sick of this crap. The team was put together to assess and expand the company's ability to respond to a cyberattack. It was to focus on rapidly identifying and neutralizing a new threat. You were invited onto the team to provide a target. You'd be let loose inside the firewall and the team would track and neutralize any attempt you made to access data. Whatever Arnie hired you to do undercover was just a ploy to get you to search through every possible sensitive point in the system. You were to be the threat and we were to stop your investigation. It turned out you were slipperier than we anticipated and the team's efficiency has risen thirty percent since you arrived. I'm sorry, Dag. It wasn't personal. No one knew who you were. It was just a lucky draw that Arnie hired you instead of some other hacker."

That hurt. But it hadn't been random. Arnie had known the work I'd done on the Henderson case. He knew if he waved the red flag of stealing corporate funds, I'd charge at it. He wasn't expecting I'd actually find something.

"You've been played, Jen. I'm only here to distract you," I said. "Tell the team you don't think I'm out of the game yet. In fact, I'm sending you a file that suggests that I'm still in the system even though I'm not in the office. They should stay alert for what I do next." I sent her the login information for six smartcards that I'd received from my bug on the manufacturing facility. That would expand their target awareness and give them more to look out for, even though I had no intention of using any of them again.

There is a longstanding principle regarding the control of mass behavior, explored in social studies, politics, and philosophy. The best way to hide a real internal threat is to focus on or create an imaginary external threat. Hitler managed it brilliantly. Bush managed it somewhat less successfully, but well enough to send the country to war for more than a decade. Countless other politicians and business leaders had managed it. Launch the rumor of a takeover bid from a rival company and watch the deflated stock value rise long enough to cover a cash shortfall that can't be explained. Fabricate an external threat to rally the troops around and you will get them to ignore a very real internal danger. It's what Lars was teaching us in our Navy intelligence drill. You could even avoid—or start—a revolution. EFC was focusing its top talent in the company on stopping an imaginary external threat. None of them knew there was a very real problem inside.

And the one person who was on every team that implemented a system, who had a top level engineering degree, who had been feeding me material as a cover for my activities, sat a few doors down from my office masquerading as an administrative assistant.

I needed just a few more bits of data to tie it all together—an actual trace of information leaving the company. I began writing a routine that would help me tag and identify the controller. I would need to lure the team back into an engagement, but I already knew who the target was.

◼◻▨▧▨▧▨▧▨▧▨▧▨◻◼

I PACKED UP my computer and headed back to Capitol Hill just before noon. I'd transferred my virus into the system where it would lie dormant until one of several key phrases appeared on the network. When that key phrase appeared, the virus would activate and bundle the user's ID and every file they touched and ship it to me. I'd set up a game tonight and tomorrow it would all be over.

I arrived at Andi's house right at noon and was greeted like she hadn't seen me in weeks. I smelled something delicious as I went into the house.

"What is that wonderful aroma?" I said.

"Homemade bread," Andi responded. She placed a long sensuous kiss on my lips and then whispered in my ear. "Before we go in, please take this." She handed me a thick brown envelope. "It's all the material I'm going to give to Cali. I'd like you to look it over and help me make sure it… well, that it won't hurt her. Now that I've decided to tell her, I'm nervous. I don't want her to think any of this was her fault." I took the envelope and slid it into my backpack. I kissed her again.

"I'll look at the stuff, but when it comes down to it, it's because Cali loves you and you love her that it will all work out. Don't worry, darling."

We walked into the kitchen in time to see Cali stuff a piece of bread that was mostly butter into her mouth.

"Mmmgh!" she choked out as she drank a huge glass of milk. "It's so good!"

"Don't eat it all before the soup is on the table," Andi laughed.

"You guys were out there snogging so long that I couldn't help myself," Cali teased, licking her fingers.

Andi handed me a slice of the still-warm bread and I smeared it with butter. I took a big bite.

"Oh, this is good! Why do we need soup?"

"You'll like this, I promise." We sat at the kitchen table and Andi put a big bowl of incredible chicken soup on the table in front of each of us.

I took a taste of the soup and realized this was not the kind of soup that comes from a can. I also realized how long it had been since I last ate. "Wow! The soup is great. I haven't had homemade food this good in as long as I can remember."

"Oh, it's just leftovers."

"Leftovers? You eat like this all the time?"

"No. I cooked a big batch of soup and fresh bread a few nights ago when I thought I was going to have company. When he didn't show, I just put the soup in the refrigerator." She looked at me and smiled sweetly. It dawned on me what she was saying. This was the meal I missed while I was locked in the manufacturing room. I hung my head sheepishly.

"*Mea culpa*," I moaned.

"Going out for a week and he stands her up the first opportunity he has," Cali smirked.

"It was unavoidable," I tried to explain.

"Yeah, you were all tied up. How are you going to make it up?"

I thought for a minute and came up with an idea.

"How about some entertainment?" I asked, grabbing my backpack.

"You sing, dance, or act?" Cali asked.

"No. You're the triple threat. I'm just superman," I laughed. "This is all over the Internet. You've got to see it, but don't tell anyone you know who it is. Secret identity and all that." I opened my laptop and loaded the video clip I'd saved. Then I turned it toward Andi and Cali. "Just watch this." The video played.

"That's unbelievable," Andi said. "Play it again. It goes so fast!" I ran the clip again. "Again," Andi said. I glanced up as the video played my thirty seconds of glory for a third time. Cali was staring, open-mouthed at the screen and was scooting her chair back away from the table. Tears were springing to her eyes. She started gasping and I thought at first she was choking on something. I backed my chair away from the table.

"Cali!" Her chair toppled back behind her as her hands came to her face and a long mournful wail escaped from her lips. Andi turned to her daughter and reached for her but I caught her as she fainted away at the table. Andi grabbed a glass of water as I carried the child to Andi's bedroom and laid her on the bed. In a moment, Cali had her eyes open and was spluttering on the water. Her eyes were still filled with tears and she was hyperventilating.

"I'm sorry, Mel! I'm so sorry! Oh my God! I'm so sorry. What have I done? I didn't mean to." Andi wrapped her arms around her daughter and rocked her back and forth as she sobbed and repeated over and over again how sorry she was. This couldn't have been about knocking the chair over. Cali was sweating and her hair was hanging in clumps, stuck to her face by the sweat and tears. Heart-rending sobs broke from her lungs.

"It's okay, Cali," Andi soothed. "It's okay, sweetie. Tell Mommy what it's all about." I stood next to the bed with my hand resting lightly on Andi's shoulder, unable to understand anything that was going on. Was life with a teenaged daughter always like this?

"Mel! I'm sorry! Mel! Mel!" Cali wailed.

"What is it, Cali?" Andi asked in exasperation.

Cali started to thrash around on the bed and we soon realized she was trying to get up. She couldn't express herself verbally through the continuing sobs. In seconds she had led us back to the kitchen table and started the video playing again. She pointed at the video but instead of the action that had captivated me when I'd first seen the movie and that Andi had asked to have replayed repeatedly, Cali was pointing to action happening in the background, nearly half a block away from the accident. It went by too quickly for me to see the first time and I replayed it at a slower speed while Cali continued to point and moaned "Mel!"

Andi and I saw what she was pointing at simultaneously and both of us gasped. There, half a block from where I was being a superhero, Mel was walking up the street. Like everyone else, when the action happened in the foreground, Mel started to run forward, but just before the clip ended, Mel peeled off away into the entrance to the bus tunnel. She was not alone.

A man had wrapped an arm around Mel's shoulders and was guiding her away.

"He took her!" Cali screamed.

WHILE ANDI CALMED and comforted Cali, I went back to the computer. I'd already forwarded the link to the police as part of the bus accident investigation, but then I'd broken into security at EFC and downloaded the full length of the video including several minutes before and after the thirty seconds that were posted. I opened the file and began examining it frame-by-frame. When I looked at the full video earlier, I was focused entirely on the foreground, following my own progress up the street. I'd seen the man step out from behind a pillar directly behind his victim and just when the couple turned their heads away from each other, push the young woman into the street. I was sure the police would be able to subpoena the full clip and have legal evidence to find and convict the man. But I hadn't paid attention to what was happening in the background.

I saw Mel emerge from a shop up the street. The timestamp of her last known location told me she had just come out of the Gelato shop. The camera's focal length is not the greatest for items in the distance, but after Cali identified Mel, I could pick her out easily. The timing was incredible. Just as the man in the foreground stepped out from behind a pillar, a man also stepped out of a doorway behind Mel. Even though there was no sound track, I could tell exactly when the bus brakes squealed. The attention of everyone on the street shifted to the accident. People started to run toward the bus, including Mel. But she only moved one step when the man behind her swung his hand across her mouth, moved her into the bus tunnel entrance and disappeared.

Before the scene had played out, I was on the phone to Jordan.

"You're keeping me busy, Dag. What is it?" he answered the phone.

"We've got a kidnapping that was reported as a runaway and I have hard evidence that it involves Patterson." I sent the full video to Jordan as we talked. He had another phone at his ear calling in the Seattle kidnapping task force. They would have video experts on it in no time to enhance the images. There was no question in my mind. The man behind Mel had clapped his hand over her mouth and maneuvered her out of the street while the accident was being staged. It was a coordinated effort. But what caught my attention, now as I was focused on the background, was where Mel's kidnapper had emerged.

All along Third there are a mix of old and new structures. Many of the old ones have businesses at street level—a deli, a brokerage, a travel agent—and offices above. The door from which the kidnapper emerged was the building that housed the Patterson Foundation.

{27}
Eyes on Seattle

As soon as I was satisfied Andi and Cali were okay, I headed to my apartment. I was on a mission. I knew now that Mel had been snatched from the street by someone who knew where she would be and when. I knew that there was more than one person involved. And I knew that Mel's time could be up already.

I launched all computers and dove directly into my previous searches. One of these bastards had to be Patterson or involved with him. Whom had Mel told she would be downtown on Thursday morning. Who was waiting for her? And where had she been taken? I received an Amber Alert notice on my cell phone as I was just diving in. Mel's disappearance had been officially reclassified as a kidnapping. Jordan's timing was perfect.

I started scanning the neighborhoods where I'd posted notices and the email that had come in as a result. Each notice I'd posted had been vandalized. A big stamp reading "Canceled" defaced each bulletin. I ran through the 250-some email responses I'd received since posting the notices and finally came to the one I feared.

"Too bad. Such a filthy slut. I want a nice girl."

I called Andi but got no response. I'd been digging for over two hours since I left her and Cali. She must have turned the phones off so they could have peace while they slept and recovered. I left a message and went back to work. I didn't want Cali out of Andi's sight.

With the number of cameras in downtown Seattle, the obvious next step was to try to track where they had gone after the bus tunnel; and bus tunnels had twenty-four-hour camera surveillance. I tapped into the Metro site and started worming my way inside. Metro was a county agency and as a result I had to fight my way through a whole different set of protocols than those for the city government. I ended up using a crude hack to get to the video feed from KC Metro. From there, I had to search back through archives to find the date and time of the kidnapping. It was tedious work and I was already wishing I had more coffee. I couldn't remember the last time I'd slept, but my eyes kept closing on me.

When I finally found recordings of the right tunnel and the right time, I kept replaying them and rechecking the time.

There was nothing on the tape that showed Mel entering the bus tunnel.

MY OPTIONS WERE running low. I opened my curtains and saw that it was dark outside. How long had I been at this, vacillating between intense concentration and sleep? I needed more coffee, and I needed more information. Why was Mel downtown when she should have been in school?

I slid my tablet into my belt-bag and crossed the alley to see Andi and Cali. I knocked lightly on the door, realizing it was already past ten o'clock and they could be sound asleep. A few seconds later, the porch light came on and Andi opened the door. She looked drowsy and fell into my arms as she pulled me through the open door.

"What a day," she sighed. "I fell asleep in front of the TV."

"How's Cali?"

"She slept most of the day. I haven't heard her stirring yet. I should get her some food."

"The poor kid."

"She thinks it's her fault because she wasn't with Mel. She said Mel wanted her to cut school and come downtown with her. Then with Olivia blaming her for Mel running away, she's just been a wreck."

"What did Mel want Cali downtown for?"

"Something about the prom. Mel kept telling Cali she had a surprise for her. Everyone was so dead sure Mel ran away that Cali believed it, too. What a mess."

"Did anyone contact Olivia and James?"

"I called them right away, but while I was on the phone, the police arrived and they kind of freaked out and hung up."

"I'd like to ask Cali some questions if you think she can handle it. The police are moving, but they don't have all they need yet."

"I'll go see if she can wake up enough to talk and eat something. She didn't even finish lunch." Andi went down the hall and I stepped into the kitchen. It wasn't like Andi to have left the food and dishes from the meal on the table, but there they were. I started cleaning up the mess we'd left and wrapped the remaining bread—already turning crusty—in a plastic bag. I heard Andi moving from place to place down the hall and then she burst back into the kitchen looking panicked. "She's gone!"

<hr />

"JORDAN, WE NEED help. It looks like Cali has gone to try to find Mel. Andi had her cell phone off so they could sleep this afternoon, but when she turned it back on there was a text from Cali that said, 'Got a text. Going to help Mel.' I don't think Mel sent any text messages. Her parents cancelled her cell phone the day she went missing and it hasn't been reactivated."

"I'll subpoena the phone records," Jordan said, "but I can't get into town to help you. I'll put out an APB and an Amber Alert. As soon as I've got a search coordinator, I'll forward the name and number to you. We're getting ready to board Patterson's yacht out in the Sound. I'm half a mile off-shore."

"I'm going after her. I think I know where to start, at least. The correlation of the other missing kids over the past five years have all been going downtown sometime close to the last time they were seen. We're starting at University Street Station."

"There will be uniforms in the area. I'll let them know to watch for you. Keep your phone live so we can reach you and let me know what you see. Don't try to make a capture. Let the police do their job."

"It's not a job to me, Jordan. It's Cali."

I disconnected and grabbed Andi by the hand. She already had her jacket on and we went to her car. While Andi drove, I tapped into the gaming community. This wasn't the game I intended to play tonight, but it was much more important than tracking down a credit card thief. Still, the EFC team could be useful. I sent the message via my office email. Even though I wasn't using a tapped keyboard, I was sure my email would be monitored. Just to make doubly sure, I cc'd everyone on my team.

"Eyes on Seattle. Find the Kidnapper. Starting Now! *It's not a game.* Big reward!" I attached the video of the original kidnapping, a photo of Cali, and estimated time she went missing. She had an hour's head start.

I desperately hoped we weren't too late already.

ANDI DROVE DOWN Third as we scanned the area hoping we'd see Cali on a street corner. You can't get in or out of some of the garages down here after eleven, so we didn't try to park. By the time we stopped at Madison, forty players had registered and were receiving data files from me for tapping into the city's many cameras. I just didn't have time to waste on bastards who weren't playing my game, so I heightened my online defenses. I was here to find Cali and I needed every single one of my fellow geeks to help me do it. I started keying instructions into the tablet calling for maps of the city and camera angles on the bus tunnel entrance.

My cell phone chimed a text message and I read "Amber Alert: Cali is missing. We need help searching downtown."

"Did you just text me?" I asked Andi.

"I sent a message to the faculty lounge list."

"Good thinking. I've got online help, but we need feet on the street. We can use all the help we can get." I heard Andi's phone start buzzing with incoming messages as one by one our friends told her they were on the way. "No word from Cali yet?"

"No answer on her phone and no response to the text messages," Andi said. Tears were running down her cheeks. She shook her head and turned the car onto Columbia and then raced up First to Pike and looped around on Second. My gamers started reporting in with images from cameras located in every conceivable place—garage entrances, bus stops, traffic cameras, banks. The number of feeds was overwhelming, and the fact that I was controlling four online computers in my home and office remotely didn't help. The first images, of course, came from the EFC external camera recording from the past hour. It began running at 4X speed, streaming images of a mostly empty street. I had a thought and contacted a gamer I knew from experience to be a good strategic thinker.

"I think the kidnapper operates from these coordinates," I said in my message. I fed him a package of data that included the IP address of Philanthropolis and the path I'd used to track him down. "He's egotistical enough to think he could be online while we do an IRL search. Here are some known aliases. See if you can track him." I got a grin in response and saw a team of players peel off into Philanthropolis.

Then I got an alert that chilled me. In the images playing on my screen I could clearly see Cali standing outside the bus tunnel entrance. The time-stamp showed 9:50 p.m. Three minutes later, a man emerged directly behind her and dragged her back toward the tunnel with his hand over her mouth. This time the image was clear.

I immediately forwarded the clip to Jordan and got confirmation a minute later that an update to the Amber Alert had been issued, sealing off ferry and train traffic. The image had been forwarded to bus drivers, taxi drivers, and local media. "I need eyes in the tunnel at all stops starting at 9:50. Move outward from the tunnel in one block increments. I want every live camera in Seattle raided."

A gamer message flashed on my screen. "Is that John Patterson in the video?" I replied in the affirmative and received a skull and crossbones emoticon. The gamers were pissed.

❖◗▸▰▚▚▞◖▞▚◆◖▚▞▰◖◗◉◖▞▞▨

JAN AND DONNA Garrick rolled up beside us and asked where we wanted them to check. We sent them to cruise up and down the waterfront. That was where Seattle was most vulnerable and was the furthest out that I could imagine Patterson and Cali could have gone by now. Jordan had said Patterson's yacht was anchored out in the Sound, so the Marina was a logical place for him to head. Sara Gates and Sandy Halstead were then sent south. Of all our friends, the two musicians would be most familiar and comfortable with Pioneer Square. Andi took over coordinating our friends as I started reviewing images flashing on my screen from various cameras.

He'd done it again. He disappeared into the tunnel entrance, but never showed up on the security cameras once inside. Andi turned up University and I jumped out of the car and headed for the tunnel entrance. Watching a live feed of the University Street tunnel and the EFC security camera on my tablet, I entered and headed to the escalator. I saw myself disappear from the EFC feed just after I left the street. I watched the tunnel cameras as I emerged into the tunnel at the bottom of the escalator. I didn't come on camera until I was ten feet into the tunnel. In that ten feet, there was an access door to the maintenance shafts. I felt my stomach tie in knots as I tested the locked door. I sent a message to the police ground team and was joined in the tunnel five minutes later by two uniformed officers and a Metro maintenance worker. I was ordered to stay out of the tunnel as they unlocked the door and went in. I ran back up the escalator. All busses and trains were being stopped and the tunnel stations searched.

Andi brought the van around on Third to the entrance and was anxiously waiting for me when I came out. I slid into the seat next to her and gave her a hug. "We'll find her," I said with more confidence than I felt. "I swear we'll find her." She nodded. I could see her jaw clenching. Her hands both gripped the steering wheel so tightly her knuckles were blue.

I looked at the game status. Eighty more players had joined in the past ten minutes. Word had gone out that we were chasing down John Patterson. Once they saw the video of the kidnapping, the gaming community went out for blood. When one of their own became a pariah, there was no mercy. Everyone felt betrayed. But, predictably, nearly a dozen had joined forces with Patterson thinking it was just an exciting new game.

Damn!

I scanned the video feeds that were continuing to come in from around the city. It was just too much data for my tiny screen. I reached for my cell phone and dialed Jen.

"This isn't what I intended to spring on you tonight."

"I didn't think so, but you never know."

"Look, I've got too much information flowing in to handle it all. I need a filter."

"You want us to watch first and feed you what we think is pertinent."

"Is the whole team there?"

"Yes. Even Arnie and Darlene are set up."

"I'll transfer all the video feeds into the company and you can sort them out. I'm betting he headed north, but it wasn't on a bus. There could be an access to his fricking office down there or a garage or a tunnel all the way to the Marina. But his yacht is anchored off Shilshole Bay. I'm betting he's headed that way."

"Route the feed to Supurnurd," she said. "That's Ford. He'll distribute to the rest of the team." I thanked her and hit the switch to distribute my info feed to Ford. I recognized the name. He was one of my six pursuers in the game a few nights ago. Well, if they were that good, then I definitely wanted them on my team. I could imagine the feed suddenly lighting up the eight-foot-wide screens in the various conference rooms around our office where a dozen windows could be opened onscreen and observed at the same time. I contemplated the maps of Seattle that now took over my screen.

Paula and Dick Wagner pulled up beside the van and handed coffee through the window to us. They had loaded their vehicle with mammoth urns and were handing out cups to everyone engaged in the search. Their coffee shop was in Pioneer Square and the name played off the most popular tourist attraction in the area: Under Grounds. I stared at the cup, thinking.

After the Great Seattle Fire of 1897 when more than thirty blocks of wooden buildings in downtown Seattle were destroyed, the city started rebuilding according to a new code—all buildings had to be made of stone, steel, and masonry. The new buildings went up almost as fast as they'd burned down. But in order to stabilize the constantly sinking and flooded streets, the city built retaining walls on either side of First Avenue that were ten to thirty feet high. They filled the street with sand and gravel and then repaved it. The new shops and buildings found they needed entrances on the second and third floors in order to let people in from the street and new sidewalks bridged the gap above the underground city.

A civic activist in the middle of the 20th century—known for his wit and for founding the popular Seattle Underground tourist attraction—once quipped that he could walk from King Street Station to Pike Place Market and never see the light of day. People joked that he would make the trip at night. But gazing into the pit that begins any reconstruction project in Seattle will quickly show that as much of a building on the western slope of the city will be underground as above ground. I was wondering if Patterson would ever emerge from beneath the City of Seattle.

My computer flashed with new video feeds and a message on the game boards. There was video of a couple emerging from the east side of First Avenue and crossing to enter an abandoned building on the west side near the Art Museum. Just fifteen minutes ago. I motioned Andi into action as she drove down the hill to First and began to circle the block. That's an impossible thing to do. First rises away from the water as it approaches the market and for eight blocks there are no streets that connect to Western and the Waterfront.

"Where are eyes on that area?" I demanded, even as I was routing the new images to the police. From the Harbor Steps to the Market, no one had brought a camera online on the West side of First Avenue.

"Everything in that quadrant has gone dark," Ford responded. "We're working on a solution."

The gameboard chimed and I dove into the alternate reality that my players were experiencing.

"We're under attack! Every time a player moves, he's knocked off the board. Patterson's gathering players to his side and they're pulling the plug on every camera in the area as fast as we can bring them online."

"Philanthropolis is chaos. Defense systems are activating across every street. We're digging tunnels to get from one area to another."

"Wherever he is, he's got more computer power in his hands than we have combined."

The reports from the game board showed people pulling out, reporting viral attacks, and crashes. I sent out a general bulletin to all the game boards people were accessing, repeating my first statement and adding a warning.

"Eyes on Seattle. It's not a game! Anyone aiding and abetting Patterson online will be prosecuted IRL."

I saw a few people pull out of the game, but there was still a lot of resistance. Patterson knew we were searching in both physical space and cyberspace and he was hiding in both. But if he was launching attacks in cyberspace, I had to believe he was capable of launching them in the real world as well.

"We need to cordon off the waterfront so he can't move west of Alaskan Way. If he gets out into the Sound, we won't have a chance of finding him," I told Andi. She pulled off Spring onto Western and stopped to send text messages to the Faculty. They had called in friends as well and by now there were at least thirty cars prowling the area. Police were at the doors of the building on First and were going in.

My cell phone rang and Jen barked at me.

"We're going mobile," she said. "You'll get the first live video feeds within two minutes. I'm at the south end of the Market looking over the back toward the Waterfront. Ford is managing the feeds from the office. We grabbed infrared security cameras." By the time she finished speaking, my computer was lighting up with feeds as my team lined up on foot down the Harbor Steps and along Western. Andi and I continued to move north on Western as I scanned the screen and she scanned the street.

My tablet and my phone alerted me at the same time. I flipped open the phone as I scanned the new images I was receiving from the video feed.

"Hamar."

"Dag, it's not good," Jordan answered. "Coast Guard has just taken charge of the yacht and our police boat is headed in. The guy's a maniac. The girl is dead. So is all his crew. He's way off the deep end."

"We've got a reading of body signatures going into a warehouse between Western and Alaskan Way. I'm following. We've got to stop him before he hurts Cali."

"What do you mean, body signatures?"

"Part of my team is filling holes in the video with infrared."

"Someday you'll have to tell me how you get access to so many toys. I'm on my way."

I looked at the message at the bottom of the video feed coming in to me with the infrared images. *IGotUrBak.*

"And I've got your ass," I whispered. "But that's for tomorrow."

▭▶▤▦▰▨▞▒▰▦▞▨▞▰▨▤▞▨▤

I TRIED TO get Andi to wait with the car, but there was grim determination in her face as we moved toward the warehouse. Her only words were a whispered, "She's my baby." I shoved the tablet in its pouch as feeds continued to come in and Andi clutched my hand as we found the entrance and went in. I could hear sirens wailing in from the south, but they'd been going on and off all night. The security chain on the door had been broken and we pushed the door open. There was no light, but I used the LED on my keychain to cast a ghostly blue light out ahead of us—just enough not to stumble and fall over anything in our path.

At this part of Western, the street was higher than Alaskan Way, so we were two stories above the back of the building with another two above us. I bet on his moving down toward the back with a planned escape out toward the Marina. I signaled everyone to close in on the west side of the building. He was being surrounded. I got a triumphant cheer from the gamers as the entire area lit up with video feeds again. They'd neutralized him in cyberspace. In my mind, that doubled the danger in real life.

Seattle building codes require masonry and steel construction, but once inside the warehouse, huge wooden pillars supported wooden floors on which were stacked crates and palettes of unknown merchandise for an import/export company. We made our way down a stairway flashing the weak beam left and right and listening intently. I was surprised to find that once we'd reached the ground floor on the west side of the building, the stairs continued downward. This building was built below sea level. We'd seen and heard nothing since entering the building and both of us were sweating, our palms slippery where we held each other.

The scream from below us almost knocked us off our feet. We hit the last flight of stairs running and slid to a halt, faced with a sudden wall of fire. Across the warehouse floor, Cali was tied to one of the massive wooden pillars. I automatically hit 911 on my cell as we skirted the flames and ran to her.

Her face was bruised and her hands and ankles were duct taped to the pillar. I pulled out my pen knife and began sawing through the sticky mess while Andi comforted her daughter and checked for other injuries. Cali was in shock, staring fixedly at the fire as it progressed toward us while I stripped tape off her arms leaving huge red welts where it had stuck to her. The smoke was getting dense and I could barely see the stairs across the warehouse. When she was finally free of the pillar, she slumped to the floor.

The fire was spreading fast through the dry wooden crates and packing material that acted like kindling. Boxes were exploding from the inside as the heat outside increased. There was no time to waste. I scooped her into a fireman's carry as we ran for the stairs. We were only two flights up to the lower ground level and we rushed across the floor, already feeling the wood heating up beneath our feet. We were running through a tinderbox. But the doors on this side of the building were all chained shut.

Damn! There had to be an emergency exit. But every access we found was padlocked and chained. We had no tools to break them. We sprinted to the stairs again, seeing flames shooting up the freight elevator next to them. Something exploded to our right and suddenly this floor was engulfed in flame. Andi pushed me from behind as I gasped for breath, carrying Cali up the stairs. We'd made the first landing and I turned to launch myself up the next flight when another explosion ripped the stairs from beneath my feet. As I fell forward, I pushed—no—threw Cali to the landing in front of me as the stairs gave way. I heard a scream behind me and dragged my body up with my hands. I turned to see Andi, still on the landing—trapped against the wall, the steps between us all but gone.

We locked eyes for a terrified moment. I reached out to her, but the gap was just too wide to touch. I had only the wagging stair railing to hang on to as I leaned over the inferno. Then she screamed at me.

"Save my baby! Please, Dag. Save Cali!"

I was choking on the smoke and my own tears as I mouthed to her "I love you." I saw her return the motion as I threw Cali over my shoulder and charged up the remaining two flights to the Western Avenue floor and crashed through the doors.

A fire truck had just pulled up and I stumbled to a firefighter in full gear and dropped Cali into his arms. Before he could react, I grabbed his axe, turned, and dove back into the burning building.

{28}
We'll Survive

"**W**HAT'S YOUR SUPERPOWER?"

    "I can tie a knot in a cherry stem with my tongue." A fat lot of good that power was going to do me. I needed to be superman.

"What's your superpower?"

"I can hold my breath for two minutes." I couldn't even catch mine. *Hold on, Andi. Hold on.*

It couldn't have taken me more than thirty seconds to dump Cali outside the building and run back in. I grabbed the railing as I rounded the last landing, burning my hand on the hot metal. I would hold out the axe to her and pull her out.

But neither Andi nor the landing she clung to was there.

☐▷╫╌╪╌╲╎╱╗╬╱╬╌╎╲╎╱╬╪◁╣

I WALKED OUT of the hospital at four o'clock in the morning without bothering to tell them I was leaving. I walked every painful step to my apartment with my lungs still aching from the exertion and smoke inhalation. I used the front entrance so I wouldn't have to pass Andi's empty house.

I left the lights off in my darkened room and woke up my computer. Only the glow of the screen lit my face. I started pulling together the evidence against a thief.

She'd made a career of being invisible but indispensable. How had she put it? "My job is to make sure that there is nothing standing in the way of Mr. Dennis doing his job." The more the picture evolved, the more it looked like her job was making Mr. Dennis *appear* to be doing his. Arnie hadn't originated the research reports that Darlene provided me, she had. Her signing authority on expenses was higher than Jen's. Her access to information was unlimited, simply because she was the administrative coordinator of every huge technical and security project the company had done in the past twenty-five years. I suspected Arnie didn't even know he was little more than a front for his administrative assistant—and when he found out, he wouldn't be happy.

The virus I'd let loose in the company network attached itself to every outgoing message. When it discovered a key word at the destination, it worked its way back. When I'd set the trap that fateful afternoon, I expected it would lead back to Arnie. I wanted it to lead to Arnie. I *wanted* to nail another executive. *God damn it!* The chickens aren't supposed to raid the hen house.

The thing is, if she hadn't been so focused on helping me find Cali, she could have easily spiked my virus and stayed free.

JEN MET ME at the front desk and we walked together to Arnie's office. Darlene was sitting opposite his desk taking notes. We didn't knock. We just walked in.

"Dag! I didn't expect you to be out of the hospital so soon. Please accept my sympathies," Arnie said. He stood and offered his hand, expressing surprise when I slapped my security badge into it, my burned and bandaged hand stinging with the impact.

"We were just talking about setting up a fund for the little girl," Darlene said. "I'm so sorry for your loss, Dag." I stared daggers at her.

"You don't even count anymore," I rasped. I had almost no voice left. Smoke inhalation. Screaming. Sobbing. "It's over."

"What's this about?" Arnie asked. "Why are you here, Jen?"

"I needed a witness," I said. I threw a thumb drive onto the desk on top of my badge. I handed Jen an identical one. "You wanted—or said you wanted—an embezzler. There never was an increase in losses that you were worried about. They've always been high. Instead of an embezzler, I found a corporate spy. She's been selling information on the black market for twenty-five years. You're a patsy, Arnie. You don't even manage your own team."

"Yes, sir," Jen said. I noticed she was wearing her Bluetooth earbud. "Arnold Dennis and Darlene Alexander, I've been given authority by Mr. Davenport to dismiss you from employment effective immediately. Security is on its way to escort you from the building. Do not attempt to gather up any personal belongings from your work areas. Anything deemed nonessential to the security of EFC and its customers will be boxed and delivered to you. Please lay your smartcards on the desk."

I saw two security guards arrive at the door.

Arnie was near apoplexy, unable to get a coherent word out of his mouth. Darlene sat calmly with a little smile on her lips.

"Nice work, Dag. Think you've got the big fish now?" she asked.

"Thank you for your help last night," I responded, ignoring her challenge. "I'd have lost both of them without it."

"Some thanks."

"I hear there's nice beachfront property available in Costa Rica," I whispered.

"Visit me sometime."

I knew that if Darlene wasn't under arrest when she walked out the front doors of the building, she'd never be heard from again. She was ready to retire. Jen knew it, too. It was Mr. Davenport's decision.

I WENT HOME. The black walls of my apartment were suddenly oppressive. I stumbled back against the curtained doorway, grabbing the fabric as I fell to my knees. The rod pulled away from the wall and fell next to me. That was all it took. I screamed at the top of what voice I had left and began stripping the paper from the walls and the drapes from the windows.

When the room was bare, I fell into the bed with my bandaged hands bleeding and clutched to my chest. I could still smell Andi's and my love-making in the sheets.

I wept.

THERE WAS A memorial service at the college the next week. I went in my remaining gray suit, white shirt, and the tie she'd picked out for me. I saw Cali across the room. She was surrounded by friends from school and the theater. I wanted to rush up to her and hold her, but the one time our eyes met, she dropped her head and turned away from me. Child Protective Services had arranged temporary housing and care for her. When she was eighteen, she would be allowed to return home alone—possibly sooner if she applied to become an emancipated minor. There was no question that she was sole heir to Andi's estate, but I didn't know how they took care of property and mortgages and such in the interim. I was worried about her.

I didn't go to Melissa's memorial. I saw Olivia and James at Andi's service. I'm sure they were in shock over their daughter's murder. James came up to me and started to speak, but couldn't. As he started back to his wife he turned back to me and croaked out, "They told us she'd run away. We'd never have…" He left the rest unsaid and escorted his wife out of the auditorium. They'd always assumed the worst about their daughter. I wasn't about to confirm any of it. Pain was all any of us knew anymore.

I went home.

THE DOCTOR HAD given me some pretty kickass drugs to combat the pain of my burned hands and various other injuries I didn't know I'd received. A hospital counselor added a brochure on the seven stages of grief. Shock, denial, anger, bargaining, depression, testing, acceptance. I couldn't find anything in the damn brochure about bitterness and regret. If I had known it would all end so soon… *Oh god!* I'd have started so much earlier.

I didn't remember anything about getting out of the burning warehouse. I was carried out, I was told, and woke up in the hospital. All I remembered was the ache in my lungs as I struggled back to where I'd left Andi. The exhaustion from carrying Cali up the stairs. The smoke and blindness that overwhelmed me when I found she wasn't there.

Jordan came by. He told me that when the firemen got to me I was smashing my tablet with the axe and screaming "Escape! Escape! Escape!" Maybe the screams had saved my life. I was keeling over when they dragged my sorry ass out of there.

My throat was sore. The doctor said it was an effect of the smoke inhalation and the screaming I'd done.

I knew it was from the constant weeping.

I WAS LOUSY company when I took my mother to brunch on Mothers' Day. I didn't have much appetite and she never ate much. We both sat next to the window looking out at the fishing boats. She dreamed, I suppose, of my father getting off one of them and coming to meet her. I dreamed of getting on one and sailing away into oblivion. We held each other's hands as we looked out at the blue sky and tears fell from our eyes.

Oh, damn! How long does this go on?

I HAD TO start pulling myself together, even though I knew I had nothing to do in the office. Monday morning, I showered, shaved, and dressed in my suit and tie. Somehow, the suit made me feel close to Andi. She and Cali had done my makeover. I wanted them to be proud. I stopped at the Analog for a coffee to go and then walked over to Olive before I headed uphill so I wouldn't have to pass the place we'd first made love. It was bad enough that Lonnie's mournful look and silence had nearly crippled me. The sun was shining and I broke a bit of a sweat by the time I got up to 15th Ave. The folks in the other offices must have heard me come in as Cora soon poked her head around my doorframe.

"Just wanted to make sure it was you," she said when I nodded at her. "How are you doing?" I started to say something, but I knew she wouldn't accept "fine" as an answer. I just shook my head. She didn't know the entire story, but she was aware that the guy they arrested was the same one who was stalking her client Daniel. "Look, if you need to talk, I've got a pretty open calendar today. Just stop upstairs."

"Thank you, Cora. I don't know what to say yet. I can't say it." I'd wept, I'd shouted, I'd even gone to a bar, but the first swallow of the straight vodka I ordered came spewing out my nose as I choked on it. I hadn't been able to simply say, "She's dead."

"Well, I'm putting a fresh pot of coffee on. Help yourself." She turned toward the kitchen but turned back before she'd taken a step away. "And Dag. Don't blame yourself. God only knows how many children you saved."

I wanted to scream at her. I couldn't save the most important person! But maybe I had. I'd saved Cali. That was Andi's last desperate plea to me.

I CAN'T SAY I accomplished anything. I was in the office for several hours, but couldn't name one productive thing I did. Stupid computer maintenance—defragging the drive. Installing software. Throwing out most of the mail that had piled up in the past two weeks. EFC paid me two weeks' sick leave and company insurance was covering all my hospital bills. I didn't know how that worked. I only vaguely remembered signing the necessary forms, but apparently the coverage was effective on the first of the month. Just in time. Nonetheless, Lars was still arguing with them about what the company owed the agency for my work. Without Arnie or Darlene approving checks, no one was willing to agree.

That left just one thing. The brown envelope on my desk. I was still contemplating what I would do with it when I heard the outer door open and steps approach my office. I looked up in time to see Cali round the corner and step through my door.

I don't think she expected to see me there. She caught her breath and stood staring at me.

"Cali?" The sound of my voice seemed to startle her even more and I was afraid she was simply going to bolt from the room. She wore blue jeans and a sleeveless shirt and carried her school bag and jacket. She exhaled slowly, trying to calm herself, but each time she inhaled it was like a gasp for air. She cautiously moved around my desk to take the seat facing me. She had a folded paper in her hand but she made no move to give it to me. I was afraid that if I said anything she would fly away like the frightened bird she appeared to be. So we sat in silence, staring at each other.

"You're fired!" she suddenly blurted out. "I want my money back." She threw the paper across the desk. "I wrote cancelled on the contract." I laid the manila envelope in front of her with my bandaged hand and heard a mewling sound as she curled herself up in the chair. "I'm sorry."

"It's okay, Cali. Your mom did all the work. It's here."

"I don't want to know! I want to remember her like she always was. I don't want to know what she did or who she was. Take it away!" I pulled the envelope and cancelled contract back and slipped them into my desk drawer.

"Cali," I said softly.

"I hate you!" There was a fierce storm building in her eyes and her ragged breathing now was coming in deep sobs. "I thought you were a superhero.

I thought you'd make everything better. But you couldn't save Mel. You couldn't even save Mommy and you loved her. I know you did! You loved her and I thought someday you'd be my daddy. And now I hate you and I hate myself."

Please don't do this Cali! I hate myself. And for just an instant I regretted not leaving her to the flames and saving her mother. I'm not a superhero. I'm not even a good person!

I had only a moment for the tears to flood my eyes when Cali moved and launched herself at me. She was hanging from my neck with her face buried in my chest wailing and all I could do was hold her and cry out all the pain and horror that we both experienced.

She kept sobbing, intermittently gasping, "My Mommy. My Daddy." I knew in that instant that she was my baby girl as much as if Andi and I had married. I could never have left her in that building, even if it had been my life that was forfeited. I wondered if I could adopt her.

I saw a movement a caught a glimpse of Cora at the door to see if everything was okay. She disappeared and I heard the sound of cups rattling in the kitchen. Gradually, Cali's sobs let up and for a few minutes I thought she was asleep while I held her. During that time, I saw Cora again. This time she slid a tray with two cups of tea onto my desk quietly, nodded reassuringly to me and left. Cali stirred and pushed away from me. She looked at the cups of tea suspiciously, but took one as she sat back in the chair on the other side of the desk.

"It's like that all the time," she said, finally. "One minute I'm fine and the next I'm a wreck. I hope I didn't ruin your suit." I looked at the tear stained front of my jacket and just shrugged.

"It wouldn't make a difference if you did, Cali. I would hold you forever."

"I know you did your best, Dag. I know you tried to save her—both of them. I don't blame you. But I get so angry. And they didn't even put him in jail!"

That wasn't quite true. He'd been jailed without bail, but then moved to a secure hospital. Jordan told me it looked like he wasn't mentally competent to stand trial. He still kept muttering over and over, "It's just a game." John Patterson had tipped over the edge—no longer able to tell the difference between cyberspace and reality. It was a condition I was dangerously close to myself.

"There is so much evidence against him that he will never be free again. He'll either be in a hospital for the rest of his life or in prison for the rest of his life."

"But he won't hang!" The venom in Cali's voice was frightening, even if understood. I've always been opposed to capital punishment, but I confess that if I could get my hands on him I'd kill him myself.

"Where are you living?" I asked, trying to shift the conversation away from our anger.

"Can you believe they put me clear out in Bellevue! Thank God there are only a few more weeks of school left. The bus ride is like an hour long. And so much for theater. This is going to kill my career. They say I can transfer my Running Start to Bellevue College, but it's like being sentenced to Siberia."

"Cali, do you want me to…" I wasn't sure how to broach the subject of adoption with her. It probably was too soon, but if she wanted me to advocate for her I'd step in.

"I already asked them. CPS said there is no way they'd allow me to live with a middle-aged man, no matter what your relationship to my mother was."

"Middle-aged?" She looked at me and finally we both laughed. It wasn't much, but it was the first time either of us had laughed since that night.

"You need a new dye job. Your roots are showing." Well, it had been a month since Andi and Cali touched them up in their kitchen. There was a halo of blond surrounding my head and mustache.

"I'm going to let it grow out," I said. "I can't maintain coloring it every week. I'm going to keep it all trimmed and short, though. Your mom liked it like that."

"I see you dressed in a suit to come to the office, too."

"I'll need to buy a couple more or this one will be worn out." We were chitchatting about nothing, trying desperately to live in a moment when everything was normal. We both knew it wouldn't last.

"Dag, what did Mom say?" I reached back into my drawer for the brown envelope. "No! I don't want to know. I just want to know… It wasn't something terrible that she did, was it?"

"No, Cali. Something wonderful. She was so brave. And she loved you. She loved you so much she gave her life for you. Twice." Her lip quivered and for a moment I thought we would both return to tears.

"Can you keep that for me? Someday, I'll come back and get it. When

I'm ready. Right now, I just want to remember Mom the way I always knew her. I just want to love her like she loved me."

"It will be here." Cali rose from her chair and put the tea mug on the tray. This time I stood and walked with her to the door. She stopped and looked up at me before she left.

"We'll be okay, won't we? Someday?" she asked.

"We'll be okay. I know I have a client I made a promise to. I have to be okay. And you have school to finish and a big career on stage and screen waiting for you. You can't disappoint your public."

"I'll invite you to all my openings," she said. She hugged me again and I kissed the top of her head. She smiled up at me sadly and then headed off to catch her bus back to Bellevue.

Somehow, we would survive.

www.ingramcontent.com/pod-product-compliance
Lightning Source LLC
Chambersburg PA
CBHW051243250626
47155CB00009B/3148